Melv

Melvyn Bragg is a writer and broadcaster whose first novel, *For Want of a Nail*, was published in 1965. His novels since include *The Maid of Buttermere*, *The Soldier's Return*, *Credo* and *Now is the Time*, which won the Parliamentary Book Award for fiction in 2016. His books have also been awarded the Time/Life Silver Pen Award, the John Llewellyn Rhys Prize and the WHSmith Literary Award, and have been longlisted twice for the Man Booker Prize. He has also written several works of non-fiction, including *The Adventure of English* and *The Book of Books* about the King James Bible. He lives in London and Cumbria.

'The 12th-Century love story of the brilliant scholar Heloise and radical philosopher Peter Abelard has long endured, and here Bragg recreates their tragic tale for a modern audience. It's an atmospheric, thought-provoking retelling.'
Simon Humphreys, *Mail on Sunday*

'What is distinctive about Bragg's approach is his emphasis on the intellectual content of the learned lovers' affair. In Pope's poem, Eloisa makes just one reference to Abelard's "adored ideas". Here they are central, and so are hers.'
David Grylls, *Sunday Times*

'[Arthur's and Julia's] reflection on Heloise and Abelard's vividly drawn, complex relationship deepens how we understand its importance. As Arthur says at one stage, the goal is to rescue history from being "just another story". In *Love Without End* we gain access to politics and religion in another time, but also to human passions that influence us all.'
Will Smith, *Cumbria Life*

'Bragg succeeds in showing how important philosophical debates about the true meaning of the Bible were in this century, and how the rivalries between philosophers became ferociously competitive.'
Shirley Whiteside, *Herald* (Glasgow)

'Melvyn Bragg has shed fresh light on a poignant, obsessive, and magnificent love affair that has been an enduring fascination for readers throughout the centuries. It is Romeo and Juliet before Romeo and Juliet, but it's real, and the passion has such cerebral and emotional depth that it is all encompassing and beyond time. His novel is keenly observed, and the dual timeline brings modern analysis and perception to the story of these medieval lovers, making it new and fresh for a contemporary audience.'
Elizabeth Chadwick

'The historical and philosophical research in it will be noticed and admired by those in the know, but most readers will scarcely be aware of it because they will be dazzled by how beautifully he handles the tale itself and its central relationships . . . I have never read such true and compellingly depicted accounts of sexual desire and encounter.'
A.C. Grayling

Melvyn Bragg

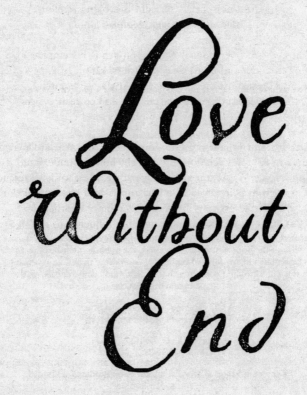

Love Without End

SCEPTRE

First published in Great Britain in 2019 by Sceptre
An Imprint of Hodder & Stoughton
An Hachette UK company

This paperback edition published in 2020

I

A CIP catalogue record for this title is
available from the British Library

Paperback ISBN 9781473690943
eBook ISBN 9781473690950

Typeset in Sabon MT by Palimpsest Book Production Limited,
Falkirk, Stirlingshire

Printed and bound in Great Britain by Clays Ltd, Elcograf S.p.A.

Hodder & Stoughton policy is to use papers that are natural, renewable and
recyclable products and made from wood grown in sustainable forests. The logging
and manufacturing processes are expected to conform to the environmental
regulations of the country of origin.

Hodder & Stoughton Ltd
Carmelite House
50 Victoria Embankment
London EC4Y 0DZ

www.sceptrebooks.co.uk

'The heart has its reasons that reason does not know'

Pascal

To Gabriel
with love

Part One

Chapter One

Her hopes of Paris had vanished and only she could restore them.

'I must have a real teacher.' She was vehement. After months of confinement, her frustration had finally erupted and overcome her strong sense of obedience. 'I want somebody who can tell me what I don't already know. Look outside this house, to the Cloisters – look at the hundreds of young men who have come to Paris to hear great masters and philosophers. They travel here from Hungary and Italy, from Spain and Portugal, from all over France, from the German states and England: why can I not learn what they learn? They have teachers and they have Master Peter Abelard. All these young men can hear him – why not I?' She was not to be interrupted. 'I need walk only a hundred paces from this house to be with them in the Cathedral School. But that is forbidden. And what do you give me instead? An ignorant Bible-babbling clerk, who comes to this house and tells me what I knew as a child. He knows nothing about the pagan authors. His Latin is disgraceful. He misquotes St Jerome. Did you bring me to Paris to kill my mind, Uncle?'

Fulbert looked at his daughter with pride. What greatness was in her! His Heloise, the cleverest woman in all of France, they said. Her classical Latin was perfect. She contained a library of knowledge. She corresponded on matters of biblical scholarship with bishops. She was known to the king for her music and poetry – and she was *his*.

Niece, she thought she was, and he had never told her the truth. For an ambitious churchman like Canon Fulbert, taking in a niece was an act of praiseworthy charity. It was too dangerous to confess to a daughter in a period when the Catholic hierarchy was exerting an increasingly menacing pressure to enforce the chastity and obedience of its clergy.

Gone were the cheerful days of bishops with their concubines, daughters and sons, who inherited their fathers' ecclesiastical estates. Heloise's parentage was a secret well kept. But now, as this tall, pale, powerful young woman, her dark hair loose and free, stood across the table from him, alive with anger, in the study of his house in the Cloisters of Notre-Dame, he wished he could trumpet his paternity to the world. The frisson of her challenge excited him. Her skin glowed. Anger transformed her normally severe, abstracted expression. Yet again he looked for similarities between himself and her. There were the grey eyes, the broad shoulders, but Fulbert's wine-raw face, with its lantern nose, and his ripe paunch were unrecognisable in the austere, commanding Heloise. Yet who on earth was like his Heloise? Only her mother, who had died soon after her birth.

'I brought you here from Argenteuil because the abbess told me they could teach you nothing more,' he said. He left unsaid that she had added Heloise was too restless and fierce to be a teacher, and would not stay to become a nun. 'Everything was open to you there,' he said. Had she taken vows she would certainly have become a powerful abbess. But, as she had repeatedly told him and her abbess, she had no vocation. She had kept to herself the increasing sense of suffocation she had felt among the ceaselessly chanting women, who accepted all the practices and commands of their order without question.

Since she had entered the convent at the age of ten, Fulbert had visited her regularly. Argenteuil was an aristocratic and richly endowed convent. It was less than two hours from Paris. Such pleasant outings. Such cherished anticipation. But over the last year she had first begged, then demanded to come to live with him. 'Paris is the centre of the whole world,' she had said, with the certainty that always left him helpless. 'All the great scholars and all the great debates are there. You must bring me to Paris. What prevents you?'

Fulbert had surrendered and reassured himself that he was not being forced to do this because Heloise was right. She should live in Paris. Fulbert was proud of his city and would boast of it at every opportunity. He cherished its greatness and, as a canon of the cathedral, felt himself part of it. It was the biggest and noblest of cities, he claimed, and how elegantly it fitted so much onto an island, the Île de la Cité, in the middle of the river Seine. At one end sat the magnificent Royal Palace of the kings of France, with its celebrated gardens, and at the other the schools, which made his city, he claimed, the world centre of learning, and the several times rebuilt Cathedral of Saint-Étienne, next to the Cloisters of Notre-Dame. Here Fulbert lived, in no modest style, in one of the finer houses reserved for the canons. It was built on three substantial floors, a place of fine rooms, dark corridors and ample servants' quarters, with gardens down to the Seine.

And which other city had the variety found in Paris? There was the synagogue in a thriving Jewish quarter, the Bishop's Palace, two bridges swarming with merchants, who came along the river from all parts of France and whose quarters towered high on the bridges like castle walls. There were

5

the Italian money-changers, traders from remote lands, and all the famed crafts that France could deliver. The crowded population, including the constant flow of students, who lived in the riddling riot of alleys and streets amid unceasing chattering, songs and calls for custom. Fulbert and his friends would occasionally stroll out to enliven their evenings. The noise and moods of the place! And, by the grace of God, Fulbert believed, it was blessedly without trace of plague. God favoured Paris. All this was his gift to his daughter.

Each morning, just before dawn, a horn was blown to start the new day and the bells would ring. Heloise would wake, as alert as a hare, grateful for another morning in this paradise of the mind. Fulbert saw her happiness and felt he had served her well. He benefited from her presence, too. His status grew as he showed her off. 'This is my niece, Heloise,' he would say, to the curious who came to see this rare woman with a fine mind. 'There are those,' he would fight to appear modest, 'who say she is the cleverest woman in France . . . or anywhere else!'

Heloise's education at the convent of Argenteuil had also taught her patience and silence. She drew on those resources to endure the intolerable prying of inwardly mocking churchmen, who asked her questions she thought any simpleton could answer. They applauded when she delivered the correct response, which she thought even more insulting. But it was worth it, she reasoned, to be in Paris. A price, it seemed, had to be paid.

But the few months of residence with her uncle had begun to unnerve her. He was more inclined to touch her arm affectionately or kiss her cheek than he had ever been on his visits to Argenteuil. She sensed a desire for greater familiarity and a degree of intimacy that made her uncomfortable. It was as if he owned her.

With one of Fulbert's servants, Marguerite, she escaped as often as her fussy uncle agreed that the weather was suitable. She liked to walk across the island, from the Grand Pont to the Petit Pont, from one channel of the Seine to the other, the two like a safe cordon around the royal island. The steady run of water set off the heady and, to Heloise, seductive vivacity of the crowded streets, the vigour of the students, the beckoning coin dealers, the pleading hawkers, the finely clothed, high-horsed aristocrats and those crippled by war or punishment. The sprawl of life! Who did not long to come to Paris?

But now how could she have what the horde of young clerics, who swarmed into the lectures, took as their right? Her chaperoned walks always took her back past the school to her home in the Cloisters, which were now becoming as confining as the convent. The Cathedral School was so close but so far away, unattainable, yet how strongly the rumours of the new philosophy festered in her mind. Sometimes she heard the laughter of the young men inside the lecture room of the school's master, Peter Abelard, and would stand outside with Marguerite, praying that God would open the doors and let her in.

Early on, Heloise had found a way to slip out on her own. Fulbert's movements were not hard to predict, given his canonical duties, while Marguerite had to spend time in the kitchen or supervising the laundry. Heloise could lock her door, to signal study or sleep to the servants. There was a small door at the back of the house that led into a little copse at the head of the common garden, and from there, as drably dressed as she could manage, she would escape.

Walking around the city with Marguerite could be entertaining enough; with Fulbert and his fellow canons it could be instructive. But once she had acquired the taste for solitary meandering, it was as if she had shed a skin and she felt herself become . . . What? There lay the difficulty.

Become . . . ? Certainly more physically liberated than had ever been permitted at Argenteuil. This was another world, she concluded. Perhaps it was a fallen world, outside the convent's walls and away from the prayers that were claimed to sustain the real world.

And there was freedom! She could walk towards the synagogue, turn left or right, and take herself on an adventure, without harm to her soul or danger to her scholarship. She was on a quest to observe, to see. What had the classical authors taught her of the twilight women, the begging amputees, the glittering pageant of the king's court, who moved aside those on foot as they wended their lofty way to the palace? She studied the city to find meaning.

Heloise was stirred by the shock of life. Back in her room she would lie down to calm the stir of images, phrases, actions, the sounds of laughter and threat that had infiltrated her thoughts, like hornets. Later, with the self-discipline driven into her from early childhood, she would return to her Latin masters, substitute the tales of Ovid for the freedom of the streets, wonder restlessly how she could grasp the new life Paris promised but from which she seemed barred.

Chapter Two

Arthur drew a line under the chapter he had corrected but let the image of Heloise linger. He continued to think about her. She was an orphan, incarcerated in childhood, yet found herself opposed to the vocational life. That might have been a negative. Yet she had been favoured by it, discovering the mind maps of ancient classical scholars and Christian sages and embracing their thoughts: a positive. Her life had grown through their books, which had become her closest companions.

Now that she had wrenched herself from that cocoon, how would she face up to the melee, the unscholastic confusions of this world outside books? She could hold on to her learning, and she would, but the move to Paris had brought her independence. It was a way of living she had had to deal with, far removed from the narrow focus of her convent.

Arthur walked through the side-streets of Paris with the swing and pleasure he had experienced on his first visit nearly forty years earlier. As a young man from a sluggish English province, he had, he could admit, fallen in love with the city. Nothing had blemished that. He could still be thrilled by walking the same pavements as the Impressionists and Existentialists, his feelings coloured by that first visit – a *coup de foudre* – when Paris had seemed to combine glamour, boldness, freedom, ideas, and a coherence of classical beauty and warm democratic pavement culture that had, once and for all, snared him. He had never tired of it but kept it, like a long friendship, in constant repair. Even now, the terror attacks and the fear of further ones had failed to dent his loyalty.

His daughter, Julia, seemed unperturbed by the possibility of more violence. Or was that just bravado?

She was three years out of university, 'between jobs' and, Arthur guessed, feeling rather alone in the world. Otherwise why would she have had the time and been in the mood to accept his invitation to join him for two or three weeks in Paris while he was working on his novel? It had been a rather casual, routine act of generosity, to which he had been expecting the usual evasive reply, but instead, here she was.

There was plenty of room in the flat that belonged to his brother, Matthew, and was close to the boulevard Saint-Germain and l'Odéon-Théâtre de l'Europe. Matthew's assignments could take him abroad for long spells – he would be away for two months in India – and he had been happy to offer the place to Arthur, who was taking advantage of the summer vacation from his university to push on with the novel about Heloise and Abelard, which he had been writing for the past three years.

He had arranged to meet Julia at his favourite bistro and strode out to ensure that he was punctual. Punctuality had become a fetish in his single life. Besides, though she was in her early twenties, Arthur still had what she would consider the ridiculous notion that it might be unsafe or unsavoury for her to sit alone in a foreign bistro.

Yet there was a fragility about her. The previous evening

he had taken her to a Messiaen concert in Saint-Sulpice and afterwards picked up her air of sadness. It had struck him as a rather dark mood that did not want to speak its cause, and had prompted guilt in him, which he suppressed. Julia, the younger of his two children, had suffered most when he and his wife had separated seven years previously. Her older brother was already out in the world, with a job, a fiancée, and sailing every weekend.

She had left the flat earlier, to leave him time to write. It had been a considerate gesture, for he knew she needed to be with him, especially on the first couple of days after her arrival. In fact, he had spent most of the morning thinking about how they could spend more of her visit together. Now he was eager to meet her with his plan. He arrived ten minutes early.

They had given him his usual corner table. Au Sauvignon was a small bistro a few hundred yards north of Saint-Germain, on a busy corner. As far as he could judge he was the only foreigner. He liked that. Unpretentious, it attracted a clientele across the generations and was invariably full for lunch and supper. The menu was limited and inexpensive, which suited him. Dogs were allowed and he liked that too. The inside was covered with saucy cartoons and photographs while the ceiling sported innocent cherubic erotica; the tables were small, with checked cloths, and the waiters – male and female – quick, professionally polite but just the acceptable side of brusque. He read *Le Monde* and drank water while he waited.

When Julia came in he felt the rush of emotions she always set off in him. How like her mother she was – the opulent dark hair, the marble skin and an attractiveness that could not be accounted for by her fine features alone. Something in the way she walked? Something in her presence? Part confidence, part shyness, something hurt, something brave. Guilt welled in him again, as did his love for her, and his unextinguished love for her mother.

She smiled: a smile that instantly triggered his. It was so good to see her – so long since they had had more than a snatched encounter.

When they had ordered and each had a glass of Chablis in hand, he raised his to her. 'Welcome to Paris.'

She looked around. 'This is perfect, isn't it?' She was tentative, fearing either to offend or flatter.

'It is,' he said, and sipped the wine. 'Do you have plans? While you're here?'

'Well . . .' Julia hesitated.

'In that case—'

'You do!' She laughed. 'I knew you would. And I bet it's all worked out. Mum said your "rules of engagement" got on her nerves.'

'Ah, well.' There was still pain. 'They're my safety net.'

'Safe from what?'

He shook his head and plunged in. 'There's a friend of mine in London,' he said. 'She worked in the same place as I did in the early years. She's probably my best friend.'

'Irene.'

'Yes. When I'm at this stage with a book, I usually send chapters to her for comments.'

'Would you let me do that?' He saw she had anticipated him and felt the joy of relief that he had found a way to help them be together, work together. Her instinct was faultless. No need for an awkward paternal request. 'It could be work experience.' Julia pulled out of her bag a paperback copy of *The Letters of Abelard and Heloise*. 'I got it this morning at that bookshop you told me about.'

'Shakespeare and Co.'

'It's an amazing place, isn't it?'

'It is. I could give you chapters as I go along and, if you felt like it, we could talk now and then. If not – not.'

'What could I say?'

'Anything that came into your mind. That's the point. I guess you know little about the twelfth century or the monopoly of religion. After all, I was out of my depth a few years ago. The English department doesn't burden itself with French history and medieval religion. But you'll know enough of what's really going on – at the heart of it, the things that don't change. Does "work experience" cover that?'

She nodded, then raised her glass. 'Here's to Abelard and Heloise! Thank you for this.' There was a catch in her voice.

Arthur was moved. What else could he give her that would matter as much to her? And perhaps she could breathe the present into this once-so-famous medieval story of passion and philosophy, of friendship and God.

'Do you really trust me, Dad?'

'Completely.'

She looked as if she couldn't have been more pleased, and took a gulp of wine.

Chapter Three

Peter Abelard was the talk and, for the young, the toast of Paris. He revelled in it. He was spoken of, by himself as well as others, as 'the greatest philosopher in the world', that 'world' being, largely, twelfth-century France and some of Christendom. His lectures attracted far more students than those of any other master. He was renowned in the Cloisters for his learning, in the streets for his chastity and sentimental songs. He was merciless in open debate and fearless in pursuing his mission, which was to challenge the sacred books of the Bible and the influential Commentaries written by the Church Fathers through the centuries. He saw them as books of wisdom to be disputed, not merely obeyed, to be analysed, not merely accepted. He was bent on changing the thinking of his time.

His passion for the newly discovered Greek logic gave him a weapon that sliced through centuries of enforced obedience. Those in authority felt undermined by every wave of laughter that came through the open doors of his lecture hall when a long, dust-encrusted passage of venerable Commentary was satirised. For the Roman Catholic Church, increasingly ferocious in its determination to control human life on earth and into Heaven, the scriptural Commentaries, written by defenders of every word in the Bible, were its fortress. Abelard, tolerated only because of his genius, his success and his high connections, was the enemy at the gate. He stood almost alone in Christendom, by far the most effective and arrogant of the sacred Church's critics.

The number of those who envied and feared him was growing and slowly gathering strength. But the dazzle of his intelligence was devastating. His fame as a teacher was so widespread that rich young students were coming to Paris in droves, and the energy, income and influence they brought to the city and the Church were not to be jeopardised. There was already talk of using Abelard's magnetism to found a university on the Left Bank of the Seine, on Montagne Sainte-Geneviève. That would be a substantial gain for France.

And then there was the man's cunning. He never openly doubted the authority of the Church or the Holy Trinity. He argued that he was helping it with the clarifications he offered. He was so hard to fault. And he lived as chastely as a monk, yet he acted like an aristocrat.

Which he was. When Heloise was allowed to sit against the wall in her uncle's parlour and listen to Fulbert and his eminent friends discussing the day, Abelard's activities often played a leading role in their talk. After they had sighed over his success and spoken with envy about the impact of his lectures and books, she had noticed that one of the company would always say, 'But we must remember he is of good family.'

'A Breton. Not a Frenchman.'

'He seems proud of it.'

'But undoubtedly he is an aristocrat and well connected.'

'That makes it very difficult to unseat him.'

'Why should we want to?' Fulbert always made the same intervention. It was one of the few things that made Heloise warm to him. 'Why should we, my friends? He brings us honour. He brings us riches. Some say he is the new Aristotle.'

'Aristotle was a pagan.'

'But very clever, I'm told, nonetheless.'

And Peter Abelard is a philosopher, Heloise wanted to cry. What can be more glorious than that? But she knew her place among the church elders and held her tongue. However much they liked her to perform – especially to demonstrate how easily and elegantly she could turn common phrases into classical Latin – her opinions were never sought.

That a man compared to Aristotle was alive and in the same city as herself moved Heloise to awe. That she should be living in such a time and place! That this philosopher should be teaching in the schools a few score steps from where she lived. It was as if a part of the wisest ancient learning had broken away from its historical context and drifted through the centuries to lodge in Paris.

She made it her business to find out as much as she could. Abelard was the eldest son of a noble Breton family. At a remarkably early age he had given up all rights to the titles and benefits of the first son to devote himself to philosophy. His younger brother would inherit the estate. As a youth he had declared – so it was rumoured – that he preferred Minerva, the goddess of learning, to Mars, the god of war. Heloise had absorbed that statement and would often return to it. But the knightly quest and temperament had never wholly left him.

He had found public debates to be like jousts. On his quest for fame he had sought them in schools outside the capital until he had arrived in Paris as master of the Cathedral School of Notre-Dame. Then there had been a mysterious and lengthy disappearance. Heloise had discovered only that he had gone to Brittany to be with his ailing parents.

The students had greeted with joy his return to Paris after a few years on the Breton estates. The city's streets had also missed their troubadour. Other teachers braced themselves – the more so when they saw him reappear in such style: clothes of noble cut, a handsome stallion, a servant, and money enough to rent lodgings on Montagne Saint-Geneviève since the Cloisters had no house to offer him.

Heloise saw him for the first time on one of her walks with Marguerite. It was the older woman who stopped suddenly in the street, as if stricken, which she was: a tall, well-built aristocrat was mounted on his stallion, pacing through the streets towards the schools.

'Master Abelard,' Marguerite breathed rather heavily. She did not turn to Heloise, clearly reluctant to lose a moment of his presence. 'I know every one of his songs,' she whispered. 'By heart.' She stood stock still, her country face bright as the full moon.

Heloise tried to memorise everything about him. His hair was hay-coloured, long, boisterous. She liked that: it gave him the aspect of boldness. His face – if only his horse would move more slowly! – was . . . beautiful. It was the only word that began to do it justice. A strong nose, eyes – what colour? Blue? They must be blue – seeming, she thought, to scan everyone and see everything. Did they settle on her for a moment or two? Or did they retain the privacy and intense internal life she imagined was defined by the full, firm mouth, the strong jaw and his confidence? It was more than confidence, she decided later. It was an aura. He held the reins with his right hand, and on one of the fingers she saw a heavy ring, which must have had a seal on it. He looked, she thought, as if he could move the world. This, Heloise was certain, was how all the truly great philosophers had looked. Seneca and Cicero had been rich men, as Abelard appeared to be. But that was not what the discerning glance observed. It saw pure thought, a mind dedicated to philosophy.

After Abelard had passed by and Marguerite had watched until he turned a corner and the murmur of admiration from bystanders had subsided, she turned to Heloise and said, with pride in her voice, 'I'll teach you his songs.'

Heloise was silent as they walked back to the Cloisters. She had seen a philosopher.

When Abelard looked back at the time when he had begun to pursue Heloise, he wrote:

> Success always puffs up fools with pride and worldly security, weakens the spirit's resolution and easily destroys it through carnal temptation. I began to think myself the only philosopher in the world with nothing to fear from anyone and so I yielded to the lusts of the flesh. Hitherto I had been entirely continent.
>
> There was in Paris at that time a girl named Heloise, the niece of Fulbert, one of the canons. In looks she did not rank lowest, while in the extent of her learning she stood supreme. I considered all the usual attractions for a lover and decided she was the one to brighten my bed, confident that I should have an easy success for at that time I had youth and exceptional good looks as well as my great reputation to commend me and I feared no rebuff from any woman.
>
> All on fire with desire for this girl, I sought an opportunity to get to know her.

Chapter Four

Julia read Abelard's words twice, the second time very carefully, disbelievingly. This was the greatest philosopher of his day?

'He's so arrogant!' she said, heatedly.

'It benefits from some context,' said Arthur.

'Such as?'

He replied unusually firmly: 'That passage comes from his autobiographical confession, the *Historia Calamitatum*, which he wrote about twelve years after he first met Heloise. They had been agonisingly apart throughout that time after a terrible separation. He was living far away from her and from Paris, desolate after what had happened between them. He wrote in that high-handed—'

'Obnoxious!'

'—way to flagellate himself. He wanted forgiveness and he painted himself at the time as severely as he could. I realise that it reads today like callous hubris.'

Julia was amazed.

'Come on, Dad. You can't let him get away with "exceptional good looks" and "my great reputation".'

'I rather enjoy it. Our smug fashion for false modesty is much worse. It's rather creepy.'

'He's so calculating.'

'But is he alone in that in the courtship stakes? It's a prime time for calculation, isn't it, and exaggeration? Especially as it's his first time. And what's wrong with a bit of bounce? Boasting was his armour.'

'But he's taking such advantage of her. How old was he?'

'Thirty-five. But he describes himself as a youth.'

'And she was seventeen? What a bastard.'

'It isn't such an unusual age gap, especially not in the Middle Ages. The chronicles are littered with aristocratic arranged marriages between older men and much younger women. You find it right through society, with the early death of so many women in childbirth. Aristotle said that the best ratio was forty to sixteen. And today some predatory academics, as I know from my own university, follow him more or less to the letter – they regularly target younger women students for casual sex, which is what Abelard is honestly contemplating.'

'*Honestly?* And it doesn't make it okay that people are just as bad today. Why don't you condemn him?'

'I can't.'

'Why not?'

'I want to understand him – and what you've just read can be interpreted in a completely different way. It's either insufferable masculine boasting – which has been going on since time immemorial – or he's trying to show the world what a sinner he once had been. I think he despised his younger self and wanted the world to know it. He wasn't just a sinner but, with the then customary Catholic exaggeration, he wanted to appear as the most flawed sinner there'd ever been. Look at this terrible man, he writes, a seducer, unchristian: that was me. This is a message to God, Julia, whom he believed saw and judged all, and Abelard feared, on later reflection, that in what became his passion for Heloise, he had lost his soul. To save it he drew a devastating portrait of himself as a penitent sinner.'

'Why?'

'At that time the source of all life and knowledge was a vengeful God – Abelard believed that. And God held the keys to eternal life, which was the greatest prize for earthly existence.'

'So what had he done to Heloise to make him so ashamed?'

'That's the book.'

The conversation was over. Julia, tuned in to his ways, took no offence. What he meant, she thought, was that he would not be rushed.

Julia looked again at the passage in her father's book that had triggered his defence of Abelard. His view seemed to change its obvious meaning too much, but in his tone she had caught a plea. As if he needed to defend Abelard for reasons she could not yet uncover.

Arthur lit a cigarette. He tried to limit himself to three a day. They were in the square opposite Matthew's flat. A couple of dozen tables had been set out in front of the Odéon-Théâtre in what seemed a half-hearted bureaucratic attempt to trap tourists on their way to the Jardin du Luxembourg. Arthur liked the spot because it was in shade, and he enjoyed the desultory swish of passers-by. Yet another taste of Paris.

Julia reopened the conversation carefully. 'What makes you want to excuse him?'

He hesitated. 'Let's put aside his claim – with which many of the best minds then and now agree – that he *was* the greatest philosopher of his day. Although that meant just a corner of what we call Europe. He knew nothing about India, the Arabs or China, but you could say that Abelard was a key early voice in that roll-out of the Western modern mind.'

'But that doesn't mean we have to respect his attitude to

Heloise, does it? The one doesn't mean he can get away with the other.'

'Perhaps it does. There's a price to pay for radicalism. He was unafraid to enrage popes, insult bishops, knock venerable scholars off their perches and belittle men destined for sainthood. He set out to change the way the world thought. No less. Imagine the exaltation and the loneliness of that. But he did it. And finally they got him for it.'

'All right. But what about Heloise?'

'There's no evidence that she made any attempt to repel him.'

'How could she? He was the Big Philosopher. She was confined to barracks . . . a collector's item for her father to show off. She was just a girl.'

'Was she? Not from what I've discovered. She wasn't the seventeen-year-old that writers have lapped up over the centuries. She was more your age – at least twenty-four.'

'Where did you find that out?'

'From Michael Clanchy's book on Abelard. It's excellent – I'll lend you my copy. He proves she was somewhere towards or even past her mid-twenties. No one knows the year of her birth so she could have been even older, but for my novel she's a wholly unworldly virgin of twenty-four.'

'Hasn't seventeen always been part of the attraction?'

'Up to a point. A girl has a crush, but a young woman can be powerfully in love. And why should the years of study not have built up her appetite through a combination of restraint and imagination? She was widely considered to be the best-educated and best-read woman in France. How could anyone have said that of a seventeen-year-old? Her reading included the great Roman authors – Cicero, Seneca, Ovid – and all the Church Fathers from St Jerome onwards, the Bible, and on and on. At seventeen? But, most importantly, Michael Clanchy produces evidence that she was known to Peter who became the Venerable, the head of the Cluny order, when he was young. He was born around 1092 and writes of her as older than himself. Abelard seduces Heloise in 1117. She must have been born before 1092. The ageing lech and the star-struck student are out. Thank God!'

Julia smiled. 'Doesn't that ruin it?'

'Not for me. I think it gives it much more poignancy and fury. Own up! Seventeen's a mess.'

'I disagree. Whenever you really fall in love for the first time it can change your life. Whatever age.' She paused, hoping he would say something that might shed light on his relationship with her mother. Her impulsive decision to join him in Paris had been spurred by the hope that she would discover the truth of what had happened between them.

Her father was silent. She saw he would not be drawn. Julia took another tack. 'Why was she called "a girl"?' she asked.

'It's a fashion,' Arthur said, the relief evident in his voice. 'I've heard groups of men in middle age referring to "the girls" – "The girls will join us later." They meant their fifty-year-old wives. I suspect that certain men always have and always will use expressions like that. And women themselves use it too. And Michael Clanchy shows there's evidence that our word "girl" was an inadequate translation for the Latin equivalent in the first place. That word included an age bracket far wider than today's "girl". And remember, Abelard was thirty-five and called himself a youth.'

'Okay. I'll settle for twenty-four-ish.'

'You're enjoying this. Aren't you?'

'Is that not in the rules?' She smiled.

'Certainly not! Me too, as it happens! But look at him, Peter Abelard, whose writings had already rocked the world, who had scoured the unfashionable places in France for an education, abandoned a noble inheritance, taken on the champions of the Church, defeated many of them – what did he do now? What more did his life need? What would be more dramatic than to ruin it?'

Julia was rather uncomfortable with her father's intensity. And it was such an odd conclusion, she thought. Why should a successful person want to ruin what they had?

'And there's one more thing that hasn't been given anything like enough attention.' He finished his wine. 'Before he met Heloise he had left Paris and gone back to Brittany for three years. He said he'd overworked. I think he had a breakdown. Nobody knows what happened in those three years, but that's where fiction can go. I think he feared he no longer believed in God, in the Church, in Christ, in eternal life, or anything that provided the boundary of all thought and behaviour at that time. I think he believed that his logic had so powerfully destroyed his old religion that he feared he had lost his soul. And to lose your soul in his day was to be condemned to perpetual death, with no possibility of the eternal life Christ promised. I think he had a total and terrifying crack-up, and the fear of its recurrence never left him.

'He came back from it still, it seemed, eager for everything, but in my view, he was desperate and fearful, no longer sure that philosophy was the sole purpose of his life on earth. There was an inflammation of the mind. He had decided to use logic to study religion. Now he set out to prove that God was the fountain of all reason and only he could prove it. He came back from that chasm as wild as the wind. That is when we meet him.'

Chapter Five

Fulbert's behaviour made Heloise anxious. In the past his visits to the convent had schooled her to treat him with formality. Now she saw a kindly man to whom she owed much, a rather nervous man, at times fussing over her health, her situation, her studies, quite unnecessarily, she thought. She did not welcome such close attention. Nor did she enjoy their intense coexistence – there was a fawning aspect to her uncle's character along with his determination to show her off to his friends. She had tried to find ways to endure or evade it.

But over the past few days he had almost gloated over her. He smiled more than he ever had before, revealing big, stained teeth. He would chuckle to himself when they sat down to eat and say such things as 'Are you certain you have everything you need, Heloise?' or 'How can Paris be made better, Heloise?' He seemed to be sitting on a secret that had not quite hatched, but the prospect of revealing it made him giddy with power. Was his concern related to her having told him (too vehemently, she now thought) of her dissatisfaction? Had that turned him against her? Had he seen it as ingratitude? Later, when she repeated her request, he made no reply but chuckled even more and raised his glass of wine as if toasting himself. That was how a good uncle should behave.

Heloise retreated to her room more frequently and tried with limited success to settle her mind by rereading her favourite authors and seeking out what seemed to her to be the essence of wisdom and philosophy. But that well-trodden path could not erase her anxiety.

'This,' said Fulbert, preceding his prize into the smaller parlour designated for Heloise's education, 'is Master Peter Abelard.'

Peter filled the door frame and stood still as Fulbert, with ceremonious steps, crossed the room to Heloise, who was standing by an oak table on which were displayed a few handsome manuscripts.

She sensed that her uncle wanted her to bow and ignored the unspoken request. She was too overwhelmed and shocked to move.

'Master Abelard,' said Fulbert, addressing her while never taking his eyes off Abelard, 'is unable to secure accommodation in the Cloisters so I have invited him to lodge with us. It will be more convenient for him. In part return, he will at times be your teacher.'

Now he turned to Heloise. The precious gift he was proffering demanded a response. It took some effort to attempt a smile and to thank her uncle formally.

'There could be no better teacher in the whole world than Master Abelard,' Fulbert continued, as his voice took on a singsong enraptured tone, 'and I am sure that in time he will find that he has no more willing pupil than yourself among all who flock to Paris to hear his lectures and debates. And no better prepared student.'

Heloise made a gesture – for Abelard's benefit – to deflect this praise. He smiled, as if mocking all the claims made for them both. She liked that.

'He will teach you all you could wish to know,' Fulbert said, his eyes misting with the prospect of the joy ahead, 'because he knows all there is to know. You have asked me on many occasions to bring you a tutor, Heloise, but, like a good huntsman, I bided my time until the finest quarry was fully in sight. And here he is.'

How had Fulbert secured him? Had he bribed him? Was her uncle far more important in Paris than she had ever dreamed of while she was in Argenteuil?

Fulbert walked back to Peter Abelard and looked at him solemnly. 'I give my niece into your charge,' he said. 'She has been fretful lately, and she can be obstructive. If she disobeys you, you must strike her as you would any other pupil. I will leave you now.' He paused.

Heloise responded as her uncle clearly wished: 'I thank you for this great gift,' she said stiffly. 'No woman in France, no woman in the world who wants knowledge can be as fortunate as I find myself today.'

Fulbert sighed deeply. 'God bless you,' he said, in a heart-felt tone, 'and to you, Master Abelard, my lasting thanks that you grace my house and agree to undertake a task that I hope you will find within your time and patience.'

'Never fear.' Abelard looked over the shorter man's shoulder to the statuesque expectant figure behind him. 'God will guide us.'

As, thought Fulbert, as he left, closing the door discreetly, he has guided me. Who could have dared to think that Peter Abelard would lodge in my house to be the tutor of my daughter, the envy of my friends and the entertainment of my table?

Such wisdom, such fame and such chastity. The continence of Abelard was as famous and important to Fulbert as his exceptional mind. Though not a cleric, the man lived as a monk yet held himself as a lord. Although he was a lord he was the humble guest of Canon Fulbert, whose status in the Cloisters community would now be decisively enhanced. Who could foresee what glory would accrue to his daughter?

Chapter Six

Abelard poured himself some wine. As it curved down into the empty goblet, the blood seemed to drain out of his body. He glanced at Heloise, then concentrated on the hand that reached for the goblet. He coughed to break the silence and picked up the goblet, taking unusual care to drink soundlessly.

He had not imagined this numbing feeling. To Abelard, the thought was father to the instant deed or opinion but not here. He looked at Heloise almost furtively, as if he were spying on her. He liked the long black hair, lustred by the sun shafting through the high windows. Her skin was attractively pale, contrasting dramatically with the dark hair. Her eyes were grey, alert. He noticed that her hands were strong, locked tightly together on her lap. The long grey gown helped to reinforce the posture of a nun. He wanted to ask her why she had not taken her vows but the question seemed premature.

Still they did not speak. The encounter had silenced them.

Heloise, wholly unprepared for it, was at the greater disadvantage. She concentrated on her outward composure and barricaded her mind against the horde of questions the meeting had let loose. She knew that if she unclasped her hands they would tremble.

She had been alone in the company of a man on several occasions. When the confessor came to Argenteuil to listen to the community's meagre sins he would often request some time with her. In the Dominican fortress of Argenteuil she had felt safe; similarly when important guests had stayed the night and requested time with the girl whose Latin was so beautiful it matched that of the Roman poets. They, too, wanted to report back on this prodigy to their friends and colleagues. But they never disturbed her.

Abelard, though, was different, altogether disturbing. Just his presence threatened to unbalance her. The eyes were indeed blue, as she had guessed in the street – a sharp, flinty blue that would cut through you, she thought. And that yellow hair, like the men from the far north she had read about, the men in the long boats with pagan gods, fire and axes. She lowered her head and fixed her gaze on his hands, large gaunt hands, the hands of a hewer of trees, not those of a writer or scholar.

The nun-like gown emphasised her modesty. Abelard had laid aside his Breton finery for the plain black gown of the scholar. Nothing they wore signalled the significance of their encounter. Yet they seemed to breathe each other, to see, to sense but not to talk: just to sit, stare and drive out self-consciousness. For what could be a better start than this deep, shared silence? What was not said flowed between them, and in those few moments, they came to know each other in a way no words could have accomplished.

He had decided on this seduction. Yet nothing he had envisaged had approached the strangeness of being in the room opposite Heloise, now no longer insubstantial, no longer a dream or an ambition. His urgent fantasies had not bargained for this reality.

'The school is a hundred and twenty-eight paces from the

front of Canon Fulbert's house,' Heloise said. They were the first words she addressed to him. As soon as they were spoken, they seemed to her unutterably banal.

But he nodded gravely. 'I have not measured them,' he said, 'but it is convenient for my work here in Notre-Dame.' He took more wine. How could he be so pedestrian?

She took up her courage. 'I cannot quite believe it is you.'

Her wonder, her amazement, was so pure. Abelard began to relax.

'I have heard the students talking about you,' she said. 'How astonished they are that you can apply logic, and so wittily, to every problem. How lucky they are. It must seem as if they were in the company of Cicero or Seneca or St Jerome himself.'

Flattery released him. He laughed, a full-throated boyish laugh. 'Does philosophy mean so much to you?'

'Everything,' she said forcefully. 'The pagan philosophers, the sages of the Bible and of the Commentaries – I revere those men! They shine the light of learning on the world and the darkness retreats. Sometimes, when I cannot sleep, I recite their words aloud and the room is filled with their wisdom. Their words become my thoughts and take me into my dreams.'

She stopped as abruptly as she had begun and met his gaze directly for the first time – defenceless, as he thought.

'Philosophers are also men,' he said, surprising himself with such a humble admission. Suddenly he was physically aware of the attractive woman alone with him in this private room. What had been an abstract object was now someone he could reach out and touch. 'What shall I teach you?' he said, his voice a little strained.

'What you teach the others.'

'Shall we . . .' He looked at the display of manuscripts. 'I understand from your uncle that the pagan authors attract you most of all.'

'Depth of thinking attracts me most of all.' She spoke nervously but carefully, as if she were carrying a bucket brimful of quicksilver on her head and had frozen so as not to make the smallest movement.

'How do you know that a thought is deep?'

'When it is in my head and in my heart, both.'

'How do you know that the devil might not be in there waiting to deceive you?'

'I have no dealings with the devil.'

'And so he leaves you alone.'

'I reject him.'

'Is that enough?' Abelard smiled, and warmth came back to her. 'And how do you know he has left you? Some doctors of the Church would call that vanity. By simple rejection you leave yourself defenceless.'

'Surely not if I am on my guard.'

He let it pass. The devil was an endless subject. He must teach her something more straightforward that she could report – as he knew would be demanded – to Fulbert.

'These papers,' he tugged a thin sheaf out of his book bag, 'are the notes I am making on a new book.'

She reached out to take a page, scanned it rapidly, then hurriedly handed it back, as if her touch would sully it. 'What is it?'

'I am setting out to prove,' he began, settling into his lecturing manner, 'that by using the contradictions in the scriptures and the Commentaries – I have collected hundreds of examples – I can reveal that everything that is affirmed is also denied. I am convinced that these contradictions are the key to understanding the Bible's true greatness. A logical examination of these apparently irreconcilable differences will prove that God is not a mystery as the Fathers maintain. He is not unknowable. If logically examined, He is the fount of all Reason. God *is* Reason. But we can only arrive at that truth through an enquiry that may seem at first to reveal nothing but confusion.'

His voice had grown in enthusiasm and authority. The intensity of Heloise's attention cast a sort of spell. He wanted to touch her. Her bare neck, the whiteness of her skin, her face, which expressed such eagerness.

'So?' She indicated the papers.

He concentrated. 'Well. This you will know.' He took out one of the papers. 'Gregory the Great in his Homily XXVI writes, "We know that the works of the Lord would not excite wonder if they were understood by reason; nor is there any merit in faith where human reason offers proof."'

'So he maintains that faith needs no reason,' she said.

'Yes.' He took another sip of wine. Why had his throat tightened?

'And the contradiction?'

It was as if her sensible response had been a bolt from the blue. He scrabbled among the papers, unable to concentrate on his ideas when his body had begun to possess more of his energy than his mind.

'Isidore,' he said at last, and pulled out a second example. '*Sentences*, book two, chapter two. "Faith which is extorted by force is vain. It must be drawn out by reason and example."'

'The opposite.' Heloise paused. 'So do we choose or do we use reason to prove that Isidore is superior to Gregory, which any churchman would find difficult to accept? If so, what is your reasoning?'

Abelard took a deep breath, held it for a few moments, expelled it, and said, 'May I have some water?'

Heloise stood up immediately, went out of the parlour and returned with a jug.

He poured some into his goblet and drank. 'Thank you,' he said. He continued without further stumble.

For the next thirty minutes he worked through several of the contradictions with her.

'What will the book be called?'

'*Either/Or*.' Poise regained, he smiled at her, a cheerful *valete*. 'You will prepare answers to some of these contradictions for our next session. I have been told that your Latin is unequalled in beauty. At our next encounter, would you read me some of the hymns I'm told you write?' Then, wanting to leave her a gift, he added, 'I'll bring some of mine. I'm sure you'll be able to improve them . . . I must leave.'

He went from the room at pace and left Heloise uncharacteristically exhausted.

Chapter Seven

After she had finished working on the exercises he had set her, she pleaded tiredness and, earlier than usual, made for her room. In the solitude of her bedroom and the silence of the night, she tried to reconcile the untouchable eminence of the mind of the philosopher and the feeling of physical intensity she had experienced. Or had she misread it? Most likely, she concluded, it was the aura of the man, which proximity had intensified.

As the candle flickered and cast its shape-changing shadows on the oak ceiling, as the ancient house creaked in the dark and the last dogs howled in the night, she carefully unpicked their encounter. Every moment she recollected was precious to her. And his unexpected warmth . . . Philosophers were supposed to be distant, gods of the mind.

What could he have made of her? Clearly her uncle had pulled off an astounding coup. She had not appreciated how important he was and now, in the security of his house within hearing distance of the river, she felt gratitude deeper than she had felt before. His visits, his gifts, his surrender to her demands to come to Paris and live in his house – none had excited anything approaching the warmth she now felt for him.

She could not sleep. Her thoughts, for so long well trained

to order, were like shooting stars. To occupy herself she thought about the woman Fulbert would have presented to Abelard. What had he said? Would it have been enough to sustain the master's attention and respect? Yet into that fixed canopy of thought those flashes of light would not cease, dazzling her.

What would her education at Argenteuil mean to a man like Abelard? Now that she was in Paris she saw her old home and nest of learning as a charming but limited preparation for meeting, let alone being tested by, such a philosopher.

She let recollections spill into her dreaming thoughts. She smiled at her early pride in being one of the chosen richer girls sent to the convent to receive an education. She realised that they had all been sentenced to imprisonment until an offer of marriage would release them. So much for her pride! So much for being chosen! Yet she remembered the privileges – thanks to Fulbert – the little comforts that had been so far from the severities the local girls suffered. They were called into the army of Christ, stripped of any past comfort and pressed into lifelong service. She was glad she had escaped that. Even now, in the ease of her bed, struggling with the memories of the day, she felt relief as a presence, a shiver throughout her body: she had escaped the fate of vocation. Most especially now. As a nun, how could she possibly have become the pupil of Abelard?

Finally, deep in the night, she did her favourite thing, which was to summon up passages from her most-loved authors, who had been her true parents. When the other girls of her kind had gone to their homes for the holy festivals she, often alone save for the novitiate and nuns, had saved herself by constant study.

She had not liked to dwell on her orphan state, and whenever she let it touch her, she felt she had failed to be strong. She must never think of it. It seemed like punishment for a crime she had not committed. Her uncle had told her the merest wisps about her parents: he would not be persuaded to go into any detail.

So she had worked. The library was her home and she was happy there. Her precocity had set her apart. A monk from the local monastery had taken over her Greek and Latin studies when Argenteuil reached its limits. The classical authors became her fortress in which her intellectual solitude could be protected.

She became aware that it was the beauty of her Latin style that provoked respect. She laboured to refine it and was rewarded. The prioress took advice from her on correspondence. The abbess herself was not too proud to ask the opinion of Heloise when she was in communication with a major figure in the Church. As time went on, Heloise appreciated the contact with power this singular talent brought her. As she matured in age her style was considered 'immaculate as Cicero, as fluent as Virgil'. This was in a letter from Peter the Venerable, a master of the common fashion for hyperbole but nonetheless a supreme authority. And to seal her fame she brought into her writings copious and precise examples from the finest authorities. She had by heart Peter the Venerable's letters, in which he addressed her with the affection of a loving admirer. She also developed a gift for writing hymns, but that was of little account in the making of her scholarly reputation, which was founded on her learning, her Latin, her gender, and the exceptional nature of what was seen as a gift from God.

In Argenteuil she had neither taste nor time nor talent for friendship. She suffered her own company gladly. This, in the community, would have been forbidden, had she not been such a scholar. Even so – as she recalled from several chiding interventions by the abbess – she was by no means wholly excused blame. But as she grew in reputation she was accepted, though not without some resentment, by those in authority. The nuns idolised her, but Abbess Jeanne had publicly castigated her for the terrible sin of pride in allowing that idolatry to flourish.

When the dawn came and she rose with it, she felt no tiredness. She could not wait to meet the new day and even, she dared think fleetingly, a new life.

She went across to the table, picked out Seneca and read, 'Of all felicities the most charming is that of a firm and gentle friendship . . . It sweetens all our cares, dispels our sorrows, and counsels us in all extremities . . .'

His friend. Would it ever be possible to become his friend? His *amica*. The Latin word was so much sweeter, and so much stronger. His *amica*. She clenched her hands. If only that could happen . . .

Yet again she went over the exercises he had set her. The logic was unfamiliar to her and hard to grasp. It would take renewed efforts. But she must shine for him.

The day strengthened. The light illuminated every corner of her room. The extreme difficulty of the task he had so casually assigned her utterly preoccupied her . . . His friend? Could that be?

Chapter Eight

This time the wine was on the table and the chairs were placed not opposite each other but at either side of the table's corner. 'So that we can study the pages together more easily,' she told her uncle, who had fussed all morning over this second encounter. Her description of the first session had met with his approval. The authorities were to be tested and respected, in his opinion, as long as they emerged at the last unscathed. He was impressed when Heloise told him how effortlessly Abelard had reached out for his examples from, she said, 'the whole of knowledge'. Abelard was to move into his own room that night; Ralph, his servant, was making everything ready. Canon Fulbert was content.

Heloise heard the usual chatter and shouting as Abelard's students came out of his lecture. On some days she liked to hover outside, excited by the different languages. Perhaps Abelard would tell her why there were so many different ones when those who spoke them lived so close together, a few weeks' or even just a few days' walk from one country to its neighbour. Why was there a need for so many languages? Surely when God had made the world there was just one. Perhaps she could study them and try to work it out for herself. There was no end to knowledge.

Abelard entered the placid room. No wonder all the

women of Paris were in love with him, this handsome, noble, chaste figure. Heloise kept her composure.

She did not return his smile.

Abelard thought she was behaving coldly. 'Did you complete the exercises?' He felt guilty. 'Perhaps I asked too much of you.'

'They were hard, but I tried.' She picked up the pages from the table and the sight of her flawless script rebalanced her. 'I think I failed,' she said, 'but you will tell me how I failed.'

Abelard took the work, scrutinised it swiftly and put it on the table next to the wine. He poured himself a goblet, taking care to hold the bottle steadily. She waited for a comment on her work.

'I was unthinking,' he said. 'It was unfair to test you on logic, so severely and so soon.' He read her work again, nodding encouragingly. He smiled. 'Far better than my first attempt all those years ago.'

She kept her composure but felt a lessening of tension throughout her body. Did that mean he would still teach her?

'Who were your teachers at Argenteuil?'

She told him about the prioress, who was there throughout her childhood and into her adolescence. 'When she died,' said Heloise, 'I wept.' Clearly, the memory brought back the pain of losing her maternal teacher. 'She is always in my prayers.'

Abelard's silence was sympathetic. How sweet she was, despite the burden of scholarship. How innocent. 'And then?'

'Father Gérard – he came over from Saint-Denis.'

'I know the name. He taught you well.'

'He encouraged me to commit whole pages to memory.'

'Are they still there?'

'Yes. They are my . . . companions.'

Abelard took a deep breath. 'I have thought about how we shall proceed,' he said. 'I should begin with a short lecture, as if you were with other students in the lecture hall.'

Her smile was her thanks. He went on: 'You should know who I really am, what this new teacher of yours is doing. What currently absorbs me is the problem of universals. I want us to think together, as one.' Was that a faint blush on her cheek? Was it for him?

His attention was caught by the rays of sun coming through the small high windows, spangling the rush-laid floor with jewels. How could logic compete with sensation? He must concentrate!

'The kernel of this discussion has become a quarrel between the bolder philosophers of the day. It is this. For example, take "whiteness". Does it exist independently of particular white things, as an abstract entity in which those particulars share, thus explaining why they are similar, or is "whiteness" merely a word we use to record our recognition of similarities? Those of the first party are called realists, of the second nominalists, of whom I am one, although recently I have tempered my views a little . . .'

He expected a question, but Heloise did not lift her head from the paper on which she was making notes.

'There are two forms of realism,' he continued. 'Platonic and Aristotelian. Take the example of dogs. Platonic realism believed that dog-ness is an independent quality that would exist even if there were no dogs. Aristotelian realism stated that dog-ness exists but without individual dogs there could be no dog-ness.' Abelard outlined his own solution, asserting that universals are neither existing realities nor mere names but concepts. 'Of course I was challenged. But I had enough influential admirers and students who supported me. This is a time of new modern thought. What is new is always attacked. So,' he laughed aloud, 'when attacked I attack back.'

By now the parlour was the universe to Heloise. Abelard, too, was affected by the excitement of their closeness, the intensity of her attention and the urgency of his desire that she should know what he knew. He would ask her if she understood a particular point; if not, he would explain it further. Once, she asked him for clarification. It was a joy, he told her, that she was so intelligently curious. 'Just like my best students,' he said.

The room closed in on them; they seemed to be ever more tightly encircled, master and pupil . . .

Heloise had heard of his public jousts in many parts of the country and finally in Paris. William of Champeaux had been the prime teacher and champion of realism when Abelard had ridden into Paris after a victorious tour of the provincial cathedral schools in France. Appetite whetted, originality honed, he had demolished William's arguments in open debate. This had set off the surge of students who paid for Abelard to teach them, enriching him and impoverishing William, who became an enemy, the first of many. Abelard ignored feelings in his debates: all that mattered to him was the truth. She liked to hear of these victories . . .

When he stopped talking, there was strain in the silence.

Abelard felt marooned in that small room. New matter had infested his mind that he could not analyse.

Eventually, Heloise said steadily: 'You will have to explain nominalism more clearly. I am sure I did not understand it. And I would like you to test me on it. Above all, it is difficult for me to comprehend why universals do not speak the universal truths of the Roman philosophers or of the great Church Fathers.' She swallowed. Why was it so hard to speak?

Abelard took up the stress in her tone. 'All of this is so new to you. I would not have believed you if you had said you understood it all at the first hearing.'

'Thank you,' she said.

Once again silence became the chief comment. She tidied her pages, which needed little tidying. He shuffled his lecture notes. They avoided looking at each other.

And then – undirected, he would have sworn – Abelard moved to kiss her. Her eyes closed, her lips met his voluptuous mouth. Aside from his sister and his mother, she was the first woman he had kissed. Aside from her uncle Fulbert, this was the first man who had kissed her.

They moved away, and looked at each other solemnly.

How would they reach the next moment? In their strict virginity, where was the solution? It could be neither contemplated nor tolerated. Still the silence.

Heloise picked up her notes, Abelard his lecture. There were no more words between them. They went out.

Chapter Nine

Heloise and Abelard were walking to the door that led to the garden.

'Are you taking some air? Let me come with you a little of the way,' said Fulbert.

Neither welcomed him, but he opened the door for them and fell in on the left side of Heloise. He noted that they walked an observable distance apart. To emphasise the propriety of the arrangement, he took her arm. 'These gardens,' he said, as they steered towards the Seine, 'are a particular privilege.' He waved his right hand as if blessing them. Three gardeners were back-bent, occupied. The Seine provided a picturesque background. The mid-afternoon sun gave the water a light shimmer of silver-grey, and the boats seemed to glide of their own free will.

As they walked to the water's edge, the silence of his daughter and her tutor, though it was not aggressive, delivered a clear message. But Fulbert would not be rushed. He turned the small party to face the west and pointed out that the view of Saint-Étienne's from this vantage-point was much superior to any elsewhere in the city. He also suggested that these, the canons', gardens, were more than a match for those in the king's palace at the other end of the island. 'Not in their size,' he said, 'but we have the advantage, I think, in the variety of our flowers and the greater age of some of our trees. And, besides, our garden goes to the water's edge, much more attractive than concluding with a wall.'

There was a polite but clearly indifferent assent from Abelard, who admitted that he had seen the royal gardens and, yes, Canon Fulbert might indeed have a point.

'So I will leave you here.' Fulbert could not disguise his reluctance. It was a warm, bright afternoon, with a gentle breeze from the river and, in prospect, the company of two such gifted people. 'I must return,' he added, giving himself legitimacy. 'We have council.'

'Of course.' Abelard acknowledged the canon's demanding work.

Fulbert released Heloise but not before a kiss on the cheek. She tried to smile. The peck was a reminder of Abelard's gentle kiss but somehow threatened to spoil it. She wanted Abelard's kiss to be unblemished so that she could think back on it until she had worked out what it might have meant.

'I expect you have deep matters to discuss.'

'We do,' said Abelard.

'I have been told that walking can aid conversation. That physical effort stimulates thought.'

'Very possibly,' said Abelard. 'But there is a wide variety of opinion, and each should be examined individually.' Before Fulbert could jump in, Abelard added swiftly, 'It will serve us well here, I have no doubt.' He gave an unambiguous smile of farewell that turned Fulbert homewards.

Nevertheless after a few score steps he turned round and watched their tranquil stroll with the hope that they might look back at him for a final gesture. He wanted to be sure that anyone watching would see how close the three of them were. He was certain there would be prying eyes which would immediately inform poking tongues.

Manners made him turn away. He took deep, measured breaths of the warm, clear air and let the casual shouts of the boatmen chime him into his house.

Heloise took Abelard to the fine display of irises. Their variety of colour – purple, lilac, shades of brown, yellow – intrigued her, and the elegance of their heads, like unlidded shells, their unprotected openness to the world, made her want to stroke them. In the garden at Argenteuil she had let the sensual part of herself, otherwise untended, be warmed by such flowers. For a few moments, they absorbed all her attention.

Abelard was glad of it. The garden had been an inspiration, he thought. Now that Fulbert was gone, they had it to themselves, save for the gardeners and the occasional calls from barges and other boats. In the parlour, he had felt stifled by an inability to talk with any conviction, and then the kiss. Heloise had behaved, he thought, as if nothing had happened. He was still unable to analyse what thoughts he had – of her, of them, of himself, and of the unexpected collapse of his boastful ambition into this inarticulate, bewildered hesitation that bordered on paralysis. How could he articulate what he could not understand?

He had rarely used the garden at home in Brittany. Nature was of little interest until it impinged directly on him – rain, snow, drought, burning sun. Extremes alone engaged him. As for flowers, other plants and trees, he had left them to his mother and sister. He liked to glance but not to enquire. To his relief – for what could he say? – Heloise became the tutor.

'Do you know about these?' she asked, as she turned from the irises, her face glowing in that perfect shade, which must be from the sun, he concluded, or could it be from pleasure? Once more he felt he was seeing her for the first time and wanted to kiss her again.

He shook his head to expel the impulse and grimaced a little. 'I am ignorant,' he said.

Heloise looked at him carefully. Was this a test? Was it an indulgence? 'King Clovis?' she said helpfully.

'First French king to adopt Christianity.' Abelard rattled it out with some relief. 'Fifth and early sixth century.'

'But these flowers?' No answer. She went on: 'He changed his banner from three toads to three irises.' Again she hesitated, then, without pause – they had taught the history of Christian kings very thoroughly in Argenteuil: 'The House of Capet embraced irises. They became the House of France for more than thirty years and took the fleur-de-lis with them. It was on their coins in the tenth century.'

Abelard moved forward to pluck one for her.

'No! Please!' Her glance said, 'Thank you.' 'Picking kills them.'

He stepped back, happily checked. '"The lilies of the field,"' he said, '"they sow not neither do they reap, but even Solomon in all his glory was not arrayed as one of these."'

'And there are references to irises in pagan literature just as far back.' She frowned, summoning the facts. 'Certainly to the Romans.' The force of her concentration was mapped on her face.

He laughed. 'Let's walk on.'

'Isn't that what you say to a horse? Walk on.'

'How do you know that?'

'Non-novitiates at Argenteuil – rich non-novitiates – were allowed, in summer, to ride docile horses. We sat on the saddle as if it were a chair.'

'I shall remember that!'

They came to the trees and Heloise went to the yews.

'Are those your favourites?'

'Of course. See how dense they are. How rich in their greenness. And how old they can be.' She looked at the two

47

trees affectionately. At that moment, Abelard would have given a great deal for such an affectionate appraisal. 'Though not as old,' she continued, 'as the olive. The abbess told me that one, in the part of France she came from, had been planted five hundred years before the birth of Christ!'

He was impressed. How could they know? 'And that?'

'A prickly juniper.'

'This?'

'A large-leafed lime. We had a herb garden at Argenteuil. Can you recognise any herbs?'

'No. My education is too narrow. I see that now. So what is that?' He pointed.

She waved away any further questions. 'You're teasing me now,' she said, 'and you promised we would continue our lesson.'

'But these stretches of time,' he said, 'don't they intrigue you? Why should an olive tree live for sixteen hundred years and we for three score and ten, if we are fortunate?'

'Perhaps God likes trees more than He likes us,' she said puckishly. She was happy, in a way she had not experienced before. 'And perhaps He is right.'

'Why?'

'Trees rise up to worship Him in Heaven. Trees do no harm. They do not sin. And they have feelings. There is a poem, from the north, in which the tree on which Jesus Christ was crucified tells of its pain in being the bearer of His agony. It speaks directly to us about it. And trees bring us warmth. They bring us,' she pointed to the river, 'boats and houses. They bring us shade and fruit and flowers. They are home to many animals and birds. How could we live without them? Of course God loves them. So must we. They deserve long life, especially as we can destroy them whenever we choose. They are surrounded by enemies and devils — more than we are.'

'Would you not like to live as long as they do?'

'It depends . . . It depends on the life I was living. And, if not, then I am sure that God will keep a corner of Heaven for me . . . and for you.'

Abelard felt a wholly unaccustomed choking in his throat. 'But,' he replied, almost in a whisper, 'life is so sweet on earth.' He glanced around in case anyone might have heard him. The back-bent gardeners had scarcely moved. Otherwise the gardens were empty. He could not kiss her again, not here, not now. Or could he?

Heloise moved away, towards the eastern edge of the gardens and nearer to the end, which was like a prow, of the Île de la Cité. 'I thought we were going to discuss whether Plato could be considered a Christian, even though he was born before Christ.'

'We were,' he said, a step behind her. 'But here?'

'Nature has distracted you!'

'Yes, that's it.'

'More than Plato?' She smiled. 'Is a philosopher not worth more attention than a tree?'

'You should write a paper and we will discuss it.'

'I would rather know if Plato could be thought of as Christian. I'm sure Cicero can.'

'Will my competitor always be Cicero or Seneca?'

'Peter Abelard,' she said, as she turned away to go back to the Cloister, 'need fear no competition.'

She turned, looked him full in the face, and smiled.

Chapter Ten

'Would they have walked here?'

'I doubt it.' Arthur pointed to the flying buttresses that held up the eastern wall of Notre-Dame cathedral. 'They would be over there. Where we're sitting now was wasteland. And over there,' he indicated the crowded buildings across the water, 'that little island was all forest in their day, with a hunting lodge, a few primitive paths, deer, boar, birds – all prey.'

'Conveniently cordoned off by water.'

'Yes . . . although deer can swim, I believe, and birds can fly.'

'But basically a royal butchery.'

He nodded that one through, but under his breath he whispered, 'Different times, different customs, and it was nine hundred years ago.'

'What?'

'Times change.'

'It's the enormous cathedral that skews it for me,' Julia said. 'When you say or write "Notre-Dame", I don't think of Fulbert's Cloisters or Saint-Étienne, I see that monument, the stone carvings on the front, the towers, the bells, the hunchback, the queues for entry all around the square, just as there must have been when it was really Christian.'

'Many of those in the queues think it still is.'

'And many don't. It's just another museum, isn't it?'

'Perhaps, but built too late for my book. I wish they'd started it just a few years earlier,' he said. 'I would have enjoyed describing it. And the stained glass . . . In their time there would have been lecture schools over there but no gardens.'

'We have gardens here.'

'Much later.'

They were on a bench, facing the Île Saint-Louis. 'Odd to think of the flower of French aristocracy pelting through the forest over there,' he said, 'running down the deer, daubing its blood over the cheeks of those fresh to the chase . . . and not much later eating their victim. Soon enough we'll consider all mammals victims. We cannibalise our family.'

Julia smiled. 'I like it when you drift off,' she said. 'Maybe you always did but I never spent enough time with you to find out. You were always . . . Never mind.' She hoped for a response. She had always been reluctant to see his terrible sadness in the early years of separation.

'The fountain is Gothic,' he said briskly, 'and when they turn it on it's a treat. And if you go to the end of the island, over there, you can see those flying buttresses through the tumbling water. Did you know that after the French Revolution the radicals made it into "the Palace of Reason"?'

Julia's frustration was building – she wanted to question him – but it was such a pleasant afternoon. Now she could enjoy a rare ease with her father. Arthur had decided to take an hour or two off and go to the cathedral. The queues had been too long for them so Place Jean-XXIII had been the alternative.

'How much do you know about flowers?'

'Not a lot. Not on the curriculum, Dad.'

'They've done well here.' He stood up.

'Guided tour?'

'I suppose so.'

'Mum always said that was one of the things you were good at.'

'Like making a plan.'

'Yes.'

'Or a list. I was good at that too. Come on – it'll only take a few minutes.' She caught a rueful tone.

Her plain show of reluctance did her no good. As often before, she waited to be instructed and, also as often before, he saw resentment rise. He decided to try to overcome it. 'These yew trees,' he said, 'are, I'm sure, descendants of the great yews that were in the Cloisters gardens, destroyed when they built the cathedral. They've made them cone-shaped – the Age of Reason strikes back.'

'They look mutilated to me.'

'And white roses,' he said. 'They brought roses back from the Crusades in the thirteenth century. I could have done something with roses when Heloise and Abelard were over there but, again, they arrived too late.'

Julia stopped and looked at the site of what had been the Cloisters' gardens. 'It's . . . curious? Funny? Quite something, anyway, to think of them walking over there. Are you sure they did?'

'I'd put good money on it.'

Julia gazed a while longer at the separating bridge and the busy road to the gardens once inhabited by the lovers. 'It would be wonderful just to push a button and see the present world slide away. For a few moments you could watch the two of them looking at the flowers you wrote about and her doing most of the talking . . .'

He walked on. He was alerted by Julia's volubility on this calm but dull-skied afternoon. 'Those apple trees could have been here in their century, I think, but those,' he pointed,

'Indian chestnuts, cherries, that silk tree and the ivy tumbling down that wall and almost touching the river, no . . .' He looked away from her, unable to bear her expression of sadness.

'Sorry, Dad . . .'

The misery in her tone suddenly depressed him. He sensed it; he could predict it; he dreaded it.

'All this . . . it's good, but I want to talk about you. And why you left Mum seven years ago. And why we've never been able to talk about it for more than a couple of sentences before clamming up, one or other of us.'

He breathed out, a deep sigh, a sound so unhappy that Julia had regrets: but the resolution to do this had been too long thought over.

It was his turn to speak, she thought. She would wait.

Arthur looked around, as if hoping for rescue. He had, once or twice before, managed to evade or bat off this subject. But now, after their days together, after the renewed – or, more precisely, their first adult – emotional intimacy, he could not evade it, could not bat it off.

He sat down on a convenient bench. He put his hands on spread knees, face set firmly, almost visibly, Julia thought, working out his response.

'You deserve to know,' he said. 'It was cowardly of me to leave it so long. That must have made it worse. But, you see, it was locked up in me . . . It still is.'

Again, Julia wanted to relent. But how could she? She had been waiting so long to say this, to hear this, to understand this.

'I will . . . I promise,' he said gently.

Still he looked ahead, not at her, and she was glad. She felt tears were imminent, her own, his, and that would spoil everything. It had to be the hard truth.

'Can I ask a favour?'

'Yes,' she said.

'You'll find it very selfish, Julia. Very . . .' Once again he paused. 'It must have taken real guts to say what you've said. And what I say may seem spineless. But it isn't spineless to me . . . I promise I'll answer every question you ask and truthfully . . . but, Julia, I have to finish this book. I don't have a mission as a writer. I'm not driven in that way. I just love doing it. Yet for reasons not unrelated to your mother and myself, I need to finish this draft. And if we talk – about us, the three of us – I know I'll be blown off course. And what does that matter compared with holding out a hand to you? Or compared with your pain? It shouldn't. It doesn't speak well of me, except that you have my word, and my gratitude for being alongside me in the writing of this. What does it matter compared to your own life? Little, nothing, an insult to real life. But it's no good me lying to you. You'll see, I hope, as we go on, why this matters. To me. It will tell me what I most want to know . . .'

He's never talked to me like that before, Julia thought. To express it aloud previously would have been too disturbing for both of them. But the thought pierced her. He would hold to his word. He, too, needed help. The anger and distance she had felt, occasionally softened by affection, now shifted, like a dense cloud lifting from the uplands. Change, answers would come, she was sure, in slow degrees.

Arthur's head hung, in shame.

Julia could not bear that.

He would keep his promise.

'When did you decide to write this book?'

He looked at her. There was a glistening in his eyes; she felt loved.

'It was,' he cleared his throat, 'most likely when I was about fifteen,' he said. 'We had an exam on a novel called

The Cloister and the Hearth by Charles Reade – forgotten now, like so many famous in their day. It was set in the twelfth century and at the end of it, as I remember, he paints this simple picture of the wounded philosopher and scholar, Abelard, and the immovably loving abbess, Heloise, when they're old, walking around a garden, just talking to each other. Somehow, God alone knows why, fifteen years old, hundreds of years ago, so far out of my experience of life, it went into me, like a dart, and stayed there. Years later, I bought the book of their letters and Abelard's autobiography and that, too, affected me. I put it on a side table and liked to think it lay in waiting. Two or three years after your mother and I separated, I turned to it and knew I wanted to immerse myself in it but I didn't know why. Eventually I began. The period is not only not my territory. It's not in my department! So it was hard and stays hard.'

He paused.

'But that was not the final act,' he said. 'I see that now. You are the final act. You came here by accident, like a gift, at a time which could have been any time but it was the perfect time because you, I realised almost immediately, were the one I wanted to be my first reader, as Irene has been in the past. More than that. This book is for you. It's for you to read and return to me with you in it. With your character. So that the past and the present can unite – if I'm lucky. I saw that and daren't say it to you in case it scared you off. But it won't, I know that now.

'So if we could just go on with the book? On to the end, then talk about us, or let your questions percolate unforced through our meetings as time goes on, then I would appreciate it very much . . .'

Julia took her time. 'You've already told me a lot,' she said. 'Thank you for that. I'll do what you ask. I won't sulk, and I'm in a far better place now than I have been for years.

But if you don't mind I'll leave you now. I'll probably be late – don't wait up.'

She wanted to kiss him but held back. It seemed too small a thing.

When she had gone, Arthur took out a cigarette and considered what he had said. It had been unplanned. He was not an admirer of spontaneity as a way to deliver truths but on this occasion . . .

And it might have seemed cruel. But he could not, yet, prise himself away from Abelard and Heloise. His mind was so largely occupied by them. Even as he was speaking to Julia as fully as he could, he'd had to check the infiltration of Heloise and Abelard, their curious courtship, the path to their scarcely credible total immersion in each other.

Chapter Eleven

Yet again, days later, they were in Fulbert's parlour, ensconced for study. Occasional street cries, now and then a voice or a noise from within the house. The table set for scholarship, manuscripts, notes, master, pupil, Abelard impressed by the draining away of his original fierce and boastful assumption, Heloise easing into what she hoped might be the early stages of friendship, her most fervent wish.

He was waiting for her to finish an exercise he had set her. Usually he would leave it overnight but a curious lethargy had led him to the easier course: set a problem, retreat into your own work or thoughts and trust time will bring about change.

Heloise, less nervous now, was more aware of his moods. He must, she thought, be bored. How could he not be? What was a single kiss, a walk, however sweet, compared with the many pleasures he could find when alone in his mind?

'What we know we know differently,' she said, handing over the exercise. He glanced at it, then looked at her for more. 'I think I know the writers of the pagans in classical Rome better than you do.' She smiled. She could see that her remark had jolted him. And yet she went on: 'You have praised my knowledge of Virgil and Horace, Ovid and Cicero, Lucan, Seneca and many others. I refer to them as often as I can in my letters to prove that I have their knowledge. You use them to build up new knowledge. I, like you, know the Church Fathers, St Augustine, St Jerome, St Cyprian – but you challenge them. You are one of them. Still, at least you have said that my Latin is better than yours.'

'I have,' he said – and returned her smile. Her few words, and the smile, had suddenly altered his mood. He sat forward. He sloughed off the lethargy.

'I know the Church Fathers well, though not as well as you. You have read more – but you are older. That is not the kernel of the difference. It isn't your knowledge – which is immense. It is that you make up new knowledge.' She all but lectured him. 'You are what they call "modern". All the greatest philosophers were modern because they brought new knowledge into this world as well as clearing out the falsities that accrue to much old knowledge. So you often attack what I have struggled to understand and with your logic you change it.'

Abelard was flattered. But that vain reaction was immediately swept aside by a powerful sense of the woman within arm's reach. He leaned forward and took her hand in his. It had no tension. He tightened his grip a little. And so did she.

Peter Abelard was lost for words. He bent his head and kissed her fingers. She let go of his hand and stroked his cheek. Neither wanted to move away: it was as if a silk thread were being wound, then bound around them, until they were in a cocoon into which nothing and no one else could enter. Abelard could not name the experience. It was as if he had disappeared. Then Heloise kissed his hand, and it was as if she brought him to life.

He stood up and went swiftly around the table to embrace her. For a while they swayed as if almost dancing.

'Not now,' she said, and looked across at the door. 'Not here.'

Chapter Twelve

It was over before it had begun.

He spun away from her.

That was not as it should have been. What humiliation, what shame and anger at his failure!

He had imagined it all so carefully. He would teach her – although that had not gone quite to plan: she was less pliant than he had anticipated. He would flatter her – but she seemed immune to this, hoping for his good opinion of her intellect rather than any physical compliments – and then he would seduce her.

How he would do this was a matter to which he had given not the slightest attention. He had no experience whatsoever. He was proud not only that he had avoided eligible women but equally avoided whores. He had thought – if he had thought at all – that somehow it would happen of its own accord.

Instead there was this shameful mess on the bed. He was transfixed by it. Blood and semen. The Body of Christ. He saw the Mass. The vision swept through his mind, a new thought. This act was a sacrament. He had never considered that. They were always in the presence of God and here perhaps most intensely. Surely God-blessed, Abelard thought, and that was the sign. Heloise, face down, was trembling.

There was a tumult of murky chaos in his mind and a sense of unfairness. Above all, why had it not been as easy as he had imagined it would be?

When she reached out to touch him, he cringed. Was this pity? Did pity not seek to reward failure? And where was his mind now? Instead of being concentrated and focused, it scrambled about in disarray. A surfeit of images. Where was his mind?

He thought he heard a sob from Heloise, faintly suppressed but unmistakable. The sound took him out of himself.

Heloise was finding it difficult to control herself. Well used as she was to self-discipline, this shock had breached her sense of what might happen to her. There had been so few words after he had come into her room. For fear of waking others? In Heloise's case, for fear itself. She had known what was intended. She was compliant. But when he fondled her naked body and fiercely held her breasts, she felt her mind swim away from her. The body was permitting, amazed, upset – and there were no words to help her.

She had wanted him to love her. It was not unwillingly that she had taken off her clothes. Yet even when they stood naked together, Heloise was wholly unprepared for the action that would follow the violent surge of feeling. So, she judged, was Abelard. They were frozen in ignorance, yet aflame to consummate this irresistible sensation.

Abelard had reached out for her with a rough embrace. Skin pressed on skin, his body demanded hers and, in her swoon-like state, she returned his embraces awkwardly, as if they were clinging together for their lives.

She lay down and, briefly, he penetrated her. The pain made her cry out, but instantly she muffled her mouth with her hand. Mercifully, it was soon over and he rolled away from her.

But where had he left her? The sense of sin, which had so rarely tainted her mind, now rose, like a drowning flood. She had become, in moments, a different woman. God might forgive her, but would Peter want her to repudiate this physical love? And if he wanted it to continue, did not his mind and his eminence mean more to her than piling up sin? She knew, in that raw encounter, that she would surrender everything to him. But why the darkness in her mind?

She waited . . . She knew no way to comfort herself or Peter. It was all too suddenly strange, and stranger for being in her private room in the house of her uncle.

And where was the Peter Abelard she had so rapturously admired at a distance, who had worked with her at her studies with increasingly light flirtatiousness? She could not explain her reaction so she tried to steady her shocked flesh and gather her senses.

He turned to her, deeply shadowed in the candlelight.

She was still lying face down and still trembling as she had been when they had begun. Her nervousness had added to his.

Abelard, with, for him, unusual sensitivity to the hidden feelings of another, understood her shock of shame. His intuition told him that it was unlike his own – the shame of failing – but something other, deeper: the shame of being so abruptly used.

It was as if a sword lay between them.

Heloise was so inert she might have been feigning death, he thought.

This time he reached out for her, touched her shoulder gently and felt in his fingertips the shiver of panic.

When thoughts are so awry, what seems lost and deeply buried may emerge to help. His mind seemed to sweep across his brain, searching for any place to rest and find illumination. He remembered – in less than a moment – being a boy on his father's estate. He had been bold even then, and the men had used him to help them break the horses. The slight boy Abelard was their first choice.

They would lift him gently on to the panicking horse and tell him to lean far forward, hold the mane with one hand, stroke its neck with the other, murmur some words if he wanted to but, above all, stroke it calmly, steadily.

From that memory, Abelard reached across and let his hand rest on the tremulous glistening skin of Heloise's shoulder. Her breathing was deep and fearful. He concentrated. The skin under his fingertips gave her a reality as reassuring as any logical solution could have delivered. This was a person independent of himself who must be understood as part of himself when they were joined together. He was fascinated by the idea that the skin gave her coherence. His fingers trailed slowly from her shoulder down her spine, each stroke eventually drawing a soft sigh, which the silence of the night made the more profound. And again he did it; and then again.

Her skin in the almost darkness had a dusky gleam. Her stillness excited him as much as the sighing, yet he did not want to stop. His original bombast had been chastened into a far deeper, more slowly emerging concentration of new and unexplored feelings, and he wanted to give them time and play. He drew down his fingertips rather more emphatically so that his nails touched but did not blemish the skin.

He drew his fingers through her hair and made it more dishevelled, made a pattern of it across her shoulders, down her back, a fall, a cascade of hair, black on the dusky white skin.

Abelard felt himself being changed utterly by Heloise, by

her compliance, which had blown away his deluded intentions as easily as a child blows away the chimney-brush head of a dandelion. One, two, three puffs, and it is bare. It becomes something new. As his life now was with this woman, the first he had slept with.

When he stopped and looked on her, her eyes opened and her expression was solemn, almost holy in the candlelight. His longing for her became once more unbearable. She opened her arms to him.

Afterwards, when he moved away, he sat on the edge of the bed and now it was he who trembled but with a sense of physical pleasure nothing else had brought him. And there was more than that, much more, so simple to conjure the words, so hard to speak them aloud.

Still with his back to her, as the almost-swoon of contentment began to abate, he said, softly at first, in a murmur of self-amazement, 'This is love.' He paused and then, more firmly, he repeated, 'This is love.' He stood up and turned to her, looming above with the candle throwing a big shadow on the wall. 'It cannot be anything else.' He shook his head. 'I love you, Heloise.' He could not have spoken more awkwardly, but it was the truth that she heard.

He bowed to her. Then he nodded and went to the door, where he turned to her. 'I will see you tomorrow, Heloise.'

Once more he paused and then, as if snapping out of a dream, he deftly opened the door and was gone.

Heloise went to the door and slid in the bolt. She knew that Abelard would not come back that night and she wanted a deep security for what she must disentangle. She blew out the candle to cloak herself in the blackness.

She called on her memory to restore everything to order. He had asked her to leave her door unbolted and she had agreed. Ought she to have questioned him? He was her mentor; he was to be wholly trusted. Yet in leaving the door open she was surely complicit. Therefore by not questioning him had she agreed to what followed?

Yet it was not too naïve, she thought, to consider that he had wanted a more private place in which they could talk more freely, perhaps kiss each other. That had been her surest assumption. There was, after all, the much-trumpeted celibacy of the great philosopher. And if that were not enough of a safeguard, what could someone of the status and genius of Peter Abelard find attractive in a woman like herself, no part of Paris society, or of the court?

Furthermore, Heloise had received many compliments for her mind, but none about what she would have called her 'person'. No one had ever said they loved her. If ever they used the word 'love', it was in connection with scholarship or Jesus Christ. What Peter Abelard had spoken of was love of herself.

She lay on her back, staring into the near invisibility of the heavily beamed ceiling, her fists tightly clenched.

Why had he used the word 'love'? What did it mean?

He had not needed to say it as a key to unlock her body. She had given him that before his words were uttered. But had she been right to give up her virginity so immediately? Had he been right to give up his? In her case, though she admitted the weakness of this argument, she might have maintained there was a bond between master and pupil that could demand total obedience. This, though, was not good enough. She had given him what he had come for because she had known from the beginning that she was in love with him.

How did she know that he loved her? In her mind's eye, she saw his expression when he was telling her about his theories. Then she caught the intent glance, the kiss, the hand sought for and held very tightly. This was evidence.

If it were not evidence enough, then she had simply to believe the words of the outstanding man of truth of his age – Peter Abelard. 'I love you, Heloise,' he had said. And, as if coming to the conclusion of a logically rigorous self-examination, 'This is love.' And 'It cannot be anything else.'

At first Heloise did not know how to absorb this. It was as unexpected and vivid as a physical blow. She was transformed, she reasoned, as the night hours shortened too quickly for her. To be the beloved of her idol! To be reached out to by a man so unreachable, to be chosen by one whose choice was infinite . . .

To be loved.

Too soon, the sound that signalled the beginning of the day.

Too soon the dawn.

From this day it might be that she could consider herself loved by Peter Abelard. She was not yet ready, nor had enough time passed, to accept that unconditionally.

But of her own feelings she was, already, certain.

The lesson had been faltering. They avoided each other's eyes and chose to read from the texts rather than recite from memory. Abelard could see the burden that Heloise carried and he wanted to remove. Heloise could see his hesitancy and wanted to reassure him.

It was she who broke through the desultory scholarly chatter. She had never lacked nerve. 'You said last night you loved me.'

'Yes.'

She waited for more words. None came. 'What did you mean when you said that?'

She felt slightly dizzy after asking that question. Everything was now transparent, to be as easily denied as confirmed.

'I said it,' Abelard spoke unusually slowly, 'because I meant it. I mean it now.'

'But what is it that you believe?'

He frowned, and became more recognisably the teacher to whom she had become accustomed over the past weeks.

'I mean it, but I do not know what it is,' he said. 'For me to love you as for you, if you do, to love me seems to elude explanation. I went back to my room last night to think more on it. I know what love for a person, in this case you, is but only through my senses. It is not something that can be reasoned with any certainty, or none that I can find. But I have only just begun. I have never loved like this before. A mother, a father, a brother, a sister, one or two teachers – but not like this. This is like nothing I can explain. There is no duty, no obligation in it. It exists because I know it exists but I do not know how I know it exists.'

'I think I understand.'

'You have similar thoughts?'

'I do. But for me the proof is in the deed. Last night was love between us. In the deed and in your words. I sit opposite you now and I know that I love you, although I don't know why I know it. But it is difficult to prove. Save in the act. And in the eternal endurance of the act and in the sole object of the act – you.'

'Does it have meaning?'

Heloise did not hesitate. She spoke decisively. 'It has all the meaning we need outside the teachings of Jesus Christ. For me it means that I will do as you bid me, whatever harm that might bring me. And I will dedicate my life to

67

protecting you from harm if it is in my power. And I will be complete only with you.'

This time Abelard's pause was so lengthy that, momentarily, Heloise feared he might renounce everything he had said. But his face had assumed an expression she had never seen before, of such tenderness, a smile of almost childish innocence, it was as if a mask had dropped and a person hidden from view now emerged to claim his former place.

'So we love each other?' There was something of a plea in his tone.

'We do,' she replied firmly, as if she were taking vows, 'and we will love each other through this life and into the next.'

Soon afterwards they were taking risks.

The first was to substitute love for study in the parlour itself. This was urgent, dangerous and, perhaps because of that, thrilling. How could they get away with it? Heloise straddling the narrow table, gown hoisted high, Abelard standing over her, chief witness to their sin. Driven to this by stupidity and a madness that was out of control. One would cry out, now and then, a sound that if overheard could be put down to high spirits.

They became spies on the movements in the house, attentive to any footfall outside their door, hesitating on no reliable evidence, then persisting, *in flagrante*. Neither questioned that these deceits and risks were essential.

To Abelard, it seemed so. It not only heightened the pleasure in their action, it brought a unique intensity to it. He would consider, while thinking over this, that perhaps he wanted them to be caught. Would that force a resolution? Although it seemed beyond the horizon of the present, there would have to be a resolution. Or was it more sinister than that? Was he sinking into a world of base feelings previously unknown? He could find no meaning. Just the deepening sensation of a physical obsession.

The nights became more violent. It was as if he had to attack as well as persuade, to ravish as well as seduce. Heloise seemed as eager to be satisfied as he was. An agony of want increasingly possessed them. He would sometimes hit out unconsciously but as if further to impassion the moment; he bit her shoulder and the stroking became clawing as he sought to penetrate through excess the secret of this love-force that had such a hold over him. Only by going further and further could he understand it; only through utter exhaustion could he achieve his aim. And Heloise accompanied him without restraint. But, what was the meaning of it? Was it becoming a vice?

Chapter Thirteen

Love was not logical. Abelard walked the few morning paces to his school to teach. He had left a bed in which he had yielded to what, over years, he had disciplined himself to resist. His thoughts were all but suffocated by this insatiable quest for carnal satisfaction. He knew that his involvement with Heloise posed a risk to his work, his conscience and his position in the hierarchy. Nothing was rational about his eruptive lust for Heloise. It had crystallised into a love that was unavailable to both logic and reason.

He would torment himself but, at the same time, it did not seem to be so out of the ordinary. Young men had always sought pleasures, he reasoned. His, so far, had been philosophy, music, songs, wine, and the exhilarating risk of open debate with men whose wisdom was held to be greater than his own. Now he had picked out a woman of great learning. In that sense he was following the same path that in his youth had drawn him away from Mars, the god of war, to Minerva, the goddess of learning. He saw a pattern and felt reaffirmed.

But he had moved far away from his original intention, and so rapidly. Perhaps he should marry her. But in the growing authoritarianism of the Catholic Church there would surely be found reasons to strip him of the eminent position he had longed and waited for. And why seek out further disruption when the disturbance in his mind and in his senses was already practically demonic? And . . . *carpe diem* . . . Why not let it drift on awhile? There was time . . .

He always returned to his most pressing thought: why did he feel so? What was happening to him and why could he not explain it?

His lectures were becoming more comedy than lesson. He had always been liked for his verve, his wounding wit, employed against the most venerated Church Fathers, alive and dead – a talent that drew applause from the young men in Paris. But now he would interrupt his flow of thought to illustrate it with what his serious pupils regarded as unworthy love songs – some referring to a very lightly disguised Heloise.

Already there were complaints. Some students had travelled great distances, and at great expense, often supported by local abbeys or cathedrals, as well as their families. The Church was determined to train a more educated administrative class, and those students were to be the leaders of the future. They had to return with evidence of scholarship from the cathedral schools, and some were beginning to fear they would be unable to do so.

Abelard's favourite pupils begged him to leave references to Heloise out of the lecture theatre. Some of the more earnest deserted him for teachers they had previously abandoned in favour of Abelard's classes. His words were still revered – but in his writing rather than his speaking. He was losing control. His examples of logic included far too many references to and examples of love. Even in appearance he was not himself but a lesser, softer man, too pleased with the new silly self he had become.

Scuffles and fights broke out in the Cloisters of Notre-Dame when Abelard's favourites, inflamed by the jeering of less loyal students, set about them in brawls, which sometimes spread into the streets and consequently brought to a wider world the matter of the transformed Abelard. He became inexcusably lax. His mind fed his mouth with the merest rudiments of his themes, while feeding his memory with unforgettable images of their sleepless nights, relived in detail to his inner eye as he dawdled through Aristotle.

Now and then Abelard realised what a fool he had become: he tried to reach for his past serious self and haul it to the surface. But the task was beyond him. He was trapped in a honeycomb of such sweetness that he had become dependent on it. Yet why degrade it? Why love Aristotle in the abstract when he could make love to the real Heloise? Why spend time disturbing the interpretations of ancient commentators and sages when he and Heloise could play with each other's bodies? Why had he for so long neglected this obvious supremacy of the flesh, its beautiful demands, its oblivion?

He was no longer alone. Heloise was grafted to him. Day and night, part of his mind was occupied with her. He would imagine what she might be doing, how she looked at that moment, what she was reading, thinking – was she thinking of him? He was surrendering to her some of what he was. His world of thought, teaching and writing, which had monopolised his mind since adolescence, now had a rival planet. Heloise. He found it difficult to remember how he had lived without her. It was not only her physical presence that flared through his senses unbidden and, when he met her, utterly consumed him in a way that matched his deepest plunges into speculation, it was the aura that enraptured him until he came to believe they had become one.

The physical fact of it was just the outward evidence. But beyond that was the completeness of spirit between them, the mutual possession that effortlessly consumed his thoughts, whether he willed it or not. At times it seemed that he *was* Heloise.

Heloise acted with more propriety. Only those who studied her acutely would have noticed the difference and drawn the right conclusion. And even they would have hesitated to claim to have seen much change in this exceptionally disciplined woman. The greater tenderness of her look, the softening of her expression, the sudden looseness of her tongue, and the advent of a curiosity about the love lives of others were noted only in hindsight.

But she, too, was caught and carried by tides of feeling so high that they could not be resisted, so foreign that they could not be understood, so profoundly disruptive that she felt she had been plucked into another life. She had come to Abelard for thought. There was that, but the greater instruction was in the arts of love. They had begun as two overcharged, awkward, stumbling innocents – but soon they felt themselves to be made for the acts of love, for the love that threatened to displace everything else, her daring outdoing his, which it amazed her to discover she relished.

Yet she held him to his duty. The fondling that would lead to coupling was delayed by her determination to find what she had primarily sought in this philosopher. She would insist on an austere discussion on ethics as the prologue to satiation. She sought more contradictory statements from him and would not let him touch her until she had understood his resolution of the apparent opposites. When he whispered fierce complaints, she responded, truthfully, by pointing out that her uncle always demanded to know, as fully as possible, the meat of their discussions.

Canon Fulbert wanted to see how her mind had grown and, he said, to share in it so that he, too, could receive an education that would elevate him above his cobwebbed peers.

Chapter Fourteen

Fulbert was armoured by innocence. If his colleagues visited at a time when Abelard was teaching Heloise in a nearby room, they would try to avoid each other's eyes. He never noticed. They were too generous to their friend to present him directly with the fact that the affair was becoming part of the conversation in Notre-Dame. Even when sorrowful hints were dropped he was impervious.

Later, Abelard wrote about Fulbert's ignorance, but he also stressed the canon's love of money. Abelard paid well for his lodgings – Fulbert's glee at his catch was embellished by the rent. It impressed and amused Abelard. There was often a seam of the over-privileged knight in his character. If love of money could be scoffed at by the philosopher, how much more could it be scoffed at by the nobleman? Fulbert was doubly disdained.

But he was also won over by Abelard, and trusted his declaration of chastity with not an ounce of doubt. When Marguerite told him that Abelard had written songs about Heloise that were being sung in the streets of Paris, Fulbert praised the philosopher's talent for popular verses and rejoiced – as did Heloise – that the name of his daughter should now be on the lips of so many, that she was as famous as any of the women at court.

And so several months passed, until the day came when what was common knowledge could no longer be hidden.

Marguerite had, in her time, served Fulbert intimately. Between them they had avoided obvious dangers. She was a useful concubine, especially in those increasingly restrictive times, who took care to keep their liaison secret. Rumours were hosed away firmly. Yet, the more keenly Fulbert sought preferment, the more fearful he became, so she was now referred to not as the ambiguous 'housekeeper', but as Heloise's chaperone.

But Fulbert did not let her primary function lapse. There were times when a succession of barren nights drove him to linger over memories of the amiable Marguerite until, at a special nod, she would smile and go to bed – his bed – a little earlier than usual, and he would follow, up the creaking stairs.

Marguerite's reward was a secure situation, ample wages, and an unspoken superiority that put her above her fellow servants. This was more than she had dreamed of when she had landed in Paris ten years before. At that time she was not yet twenty, from a village near Nogent, brought to Paris in a boat owned by her brother. He had helped her onto the *quai* near the bishop's palace, in which she found work in the laundry room. Then he had left her to shift for herself. Fulbert, in need of a housekeeper, had been recommended the hardworking countrywoman. Marguerite had seen her opportunity and clamped onto it.

Either because she could not bear to see Fulbert so tricked inside his house and mocked outside it, or having kept to herself the private lives of Heloise and Abelard for so long she almost burst, she decided to tell Fulbert everything.

There was also the fear that if someone else told him, he would certainly accuse her of deceiving him. That thought arrowed into a usually repressed anxiety about the security of her position. She had to be the first to tell. It became her duty.

Abelard would be teaching Heloise that afternoon. How Marguerite envied her. She swooned over the songs of Abelard. To be near someone so loved by Abelard was painful, but she squeezed every grain of advantage from it and, in measured portions, fed her fellow servants with titbits of talk that brought her considerable benefits.

Marguerite was certain that he would lie with Heloise that night. She knew every move he made in those dark hours. She would inveigle herself into Fulbert's bed. His anxious propriety overlaid a taste for farmyard rutting, which she managed both to excite and relieve. She would tell him after he had let out the last groan of satisfaction. She would practise her words all day and whisper them while he was helpless.

Chapter Fifteen

He had given Heloise more of the apparent contradictions in the scriptures to examine, and her answers were by now as ingenious as any his best students could summon. She had read aloud her comments in Latin on Seneca, which he had asked for in order to hear the beauty of her style and praise her. He was being increasingly influenced by her passion for the classical philosophers. When she stopped reading, he clapped his hands in applause. He was drowsy as the late-afternoon sun warmed the room and the wine worked its will.

'Why should Plato not have been a Christian?' he asked. 'You have still not answered that satisfactorily.'

'He could not have been a follower of a Christ who was not yet born.'

'But if he acted like a Christian and wrote like a Christian, could he not have been a forerunner? Even if he did not acknowledge sin?'

Her reply was well rehearsed. 'William of Champeaux pointed out that the Church Fathers taught "Sin is nothing because it is not God's creation."' She had become fierce about sin. She could foresee its traps. '"Solely the intention and the will which stems from an act is evil." And the venerable scholar Anselm of Laon proposed that "God does not assess the magnitude of a sin by the magnitude of the things done, but its magnitude relative to the intention of the doer."'

Abelard was not altogether pleased that Heloise had cited two of his more prominent enemies, both of whose reputations he had destroyed in public debate. But the notion of 'intention' and her passion for it took his interest.

She gathered force. 'Christ on the Cross said, "Father, forgive them for they know not what they do." When St Stephen was being stoned to death he called, "Lord, lay not the sin to their charge." The intention is everything.'

'Who judges the purity of the intention?' countered Abelard, although he agreed with her. 'Who is to prevent anyone from using this argument to do wicked things?'

'The Lord said, "If thine eye be sound, thy whole body shall be full of light." That is, if the intention is right, the mass of works coming from it will be worthy of the light, that is, good.'

He nodded. He was in the full after-ease of love-making – quick, fierce, just a wall away from Fulbert and other canons of Notre-Dame, who could determine his fate. Yet this love made such recklessness almost a virtue. And now this discourse with Heloise. By that measure he could argue they were without sin. Love outside marriage was a sin only if it spurned God. But he and Heloise were in the fold of God. The intention in their love was to celebrate that love, which emanated from God.

Intention. He could develop that idea. Life could still be perfect.

* * *

'I can't accept *that*,' said Julia. 'Anyone could say, "My intention was good. I killed him because he was a bad man. I slaughtered them because they were evil" – it's a killer's

79

charter.' She hesitated. 'The same with Abelard. He dumped her in it and then found a way to wriggle out of his responsibility. Never mind the consequences, I'm all right. And her idea of intention gets him off the hook.'

'Only if you don't believe in God,' her father said, rather tentatively. Theology was not his strong suit. 'The truth is, I'm not sure I represented it as well as I should have done . . .' He took a mouthful of coffee to invigorate himself.

'So why bother with it? It's redundant. We've moved on.'

'On? Sideways is better. Whatever her later fury against God, both she and Abelard were enclosed in a world that, every bit of it, had to come from God. And how could they move on? That's what history is for. To find out why they were stuck, as we see it today. How could hundreds of millions of people believe in Mao? Or Stalin? Or Hitler? Or so many dictators and religious leaders – again and again and again. In different disguises. With different promises. But the same message: "Think as I think or you will be either damned or eradicated." Medieval Europe is a casebook study. You have to try to get inside that time, or history's just another story.'

'Isn't it all intimidation?'

'Partly. But what medieval Catholicism presented was the certainty of eternal life if you followed the rules. You had a soul, they said. Your chief purpose on earth was to make it fit for death and resurrection. This bit deep in those centuries, so deep that people were willing to distort or destroy their lives to save their souls. Why don't you make the effort to understand that?' He smiled, but Julia felt the flick of a reprimand.

'The entrance gate on earth was wholly controlled by the Church. Has there ever been such a controlling force? What an operation! And look at the methods they invented and employed! Spectacular ceremonies, sacred books, torture to death, if necessary, pilgrimages, Purgatory, relics, crusades, proto-cannibalism – eating the Body and drinking the Blood of Christ, Virgin Mother Mary, thefts from any previous useful religion, Christ Himself the young Apollo, the perfect man, Jesus. The invisible all-powerful God. And the confession. The best intelligence-gatherer ever invented. What an apparatus! And there was more! Cathedrals, the music, the art, the hospitals, the schools . . . And, finally, eternal life. It was terrific. It was terrible. It was meant to awe the people and it did. Moreover, many of those who did the controlling were as convinced of this practically insane – to us – world as those whose minds they enslaved.'

Julia laughed. 'Here we go again! Mr Balance.'

He frowned. 'Is medieval Paris too foreign to be understood? Or is the failure my inability to explain?' He paused, then switched tack. 'What about the Musée Cluny?'

'Cluny was great,' she said, wanting to give him some support. 'Those tapestries! And the stained glass. And what about those hundreds of figures carved in alabaster? A lot of it came from Yorkshire and Derbyshire.'

'Are you having an attack of national pride?'

'For those sculptures, yes. The Virgin Mary and all her followers or friends, going up to God – there are lots of her – and other saints and scenes, none much bigger than my satchel. I was impressed. I loved the colour. Or the non-colour. Just plain alabaster. That slightly beigy off-white, maybe cream would be more accurate. No – porridge-coloured is best.'

'When they were first made, and the Church was in its pomp, they would have been painted in brilliant reds, blues and gold.'

'Are you sure?'

'I've seen some with the remains of their original colours still clinging to the stone.'

'But they're so pure now. Just – I know they're religious but – just plain. People in alabaster.'

'Like ghosts. That's how I see them. Rank on rank of ghostly alabaster figures in the museum reminding us of the glory that once was. The Ghosts of Christianity's Past.'

'Why didn't you come to Cluny with me?'

'I will. Before you go home.'

'Ah! The schedule! What if I tore it up?'

He shook his head. 'I'd just make another,' he said.

'I knew you'd say that!' Julia clapped her hands. 'And am I still on the schedule?'

'Oh, yes. We'll get to you,' he said. 'I promise.'

'When you've finished with Heloise and Abelard?'

'It must seem rather callous.'

'It's fine,' said Julia. 'There's no room for anything but them in your mind, is there?'

He nodded. 'I'd say that at present I'm wholly taken over by them.'

Chapter Sixteen

After Marguerite had done her strenuous and sweaty best, hoicking the portly Fulbert from bedpost to bedpost, then releasing him from his groans of pleasure-pain into a relief of panting satisfaction, she waited for his breath to calm down, then dripped the poison into his ear.

'I've had to clean the stains,' she said.

'I've heard them,' she said.

'They are there now,' she said.

She laid a strong hand across his mouth and pressed it down as he bucked to let out a yell. Even when he bit into the hard edge of her palm she did not ease the pressure.

'They will be warned if you cry out,' she whispered.

His legs shook and kicked out, as they had done so recently from a different stimulus. But Marguerite had piled herself on top of him and he was no match for her.

Eventually he subsided and, warily, she rolled away.

Fulbert's mind flashed humiliation, folly and anger, then to unbearable images and scenes rapidly replayed and reinterpreted. The knowing smiles, the nods, the allusions, the street songs, and the grinning greetings of silently mocking colleagues. But mostly, cascading like an avalanche onto his frozen senses – Heloise, his Heloise, besmirched, seduced. And under his own roof – raped, he was sure of it, by the philosopher, the lying Abelard, whose deceit would never be forgiven, or redeemed, or go unpunished. The whole world would condemn and punish him.

A sob began that threatened to grow, but now Marguerite employed a different tactic and nursed him. She gathered his head to her breasts, and it was as if he hid away. Although Heloise's room was in another part of the house she feared that any unusual sound would be an alert. There was evidence to be gathered. Now was the time.

'This way,' she said. She took his hand, a gesture she had never made before. Their relationship had carried no tenderness. He trailed a step behind her, like a boy with his mother. Pausing, slowly, they went along the twisting corridor and up to the room of Heloise, lit by Marguerite's candle.

Marguerite pushed open the door and ushered Fulbert inside.

They were strewn across the bed, naked on that warm night, not asleep but 'in the act', as Abelard later reported, and could not resist adding, '*in flagrante*, as the poet said happened to Mars and Venus'.

Suddenly galvanised, Fulbert rushed towards them, his hand raised, and aimed a blow at Heloise. Abelard caught his forearm and forced him back, standing naked in front of the nightgowned canon, Marguerite in the doorway, intent, holding the candle high.

'If you strike her,' said Abelard, 'I will return the blow and take her from this house.'

Heloise stood up, the coverlet draped around her, the unbound night-black hair sweeping down her back like a cloak, her face expressionless.

'How could – you – how – you – deceive, deceive, and you – my – my niece – how – no – yes – Abelard, not Abelard!'

Fulbert began to sob, sucking in his breath to ease the tight pain across his chest.

'I will go,' said Abelard.

He turned to Heloise, who said, 'You need not go. There is no blame from me.'

'But from me!' Fulbert's voice was strangulated. 'Oh, Heloise, from me, and shame and shame and shame for ever more. For ever more. God forgive you. You – whore!'

'He will,' she said. 'Jesus Christ forgave whores. I will go with you,' she said to Abelard.

'No.' Abelard thought his brain had become numb. He needed time for thought. He would give all his learning for a thought. 'No,' he repeated. 'Canon Fulbert must go from this room and then I, too, will leave. I will see you tomorrow.'

'You will not see her again,' said Fulbert, hopelessly.

'He will,' said Heloise, 'or I will leave with him now.'

'Do not strike her again,' said Abelard. He took up his clothes and left, having, he thought, for one mad moment, won a victory.

Marguerite completed her night's work by steering Fulbert out of the room.

Had she been a nun, Heloise thought she would have prayed. Instead she bolted her door and returned to the bed to think the matter through.

Chapter Seventeen

'I think it was when they were discovered and forced to part that he realised how vital she was to him.'

Arthur had suggested a visit to the Jardin du Luxembourg after their scheduled lunch, and they were sitting by the pond facing the palace. 'That palace was a prison in the Revolution,' he said. 'It's such a strange world, the past, stranger than fiction. People were just like us – if cut they bled, if lied to they resented it, if hungry they were in pain. But then there is the time, and the context. In the medieval world even Abelard – the sublime man of reason – wholly believed that only God gave life, took life and shaped life and, above all, He could be reached. He could be spoken to through prayer. Prayer was a full-time, crowded profession. The quality and number of prayers said for you helped to save your soul, which, as I said before, was the prime purpose of your time on earth.'

'Your soul was your sole purpose?'

'What am I going to do with you?'

'Sorry. I can see what's the same about him and us. I find it difficult really to take in the difference.'

'We all do. I think it finally struck Abelard when he was forced to leave Fulbert's house without her that he was bound to her. Parting clearly caused great pain

– and a sort of madness set in. He realised that the adventure was over at the same time as he saw it was no longer an adventure. It must have threatened to destroy what he had been.'

'But how do you know that?'

'Partly because of what he did from that time on, even though some historians have little sympathy with how he behaved. But there are ways to interpret what he did as not cruel or selfish but as acts of loyalty and of a scarcely controllable passion for Heloise. In the end you have to imagine these things or they won't exist.'

'That's what novels are for, as you used to keep telling me long ago.'

'Did I? Oh dear! But, yes, I think fiction finds its own path to truth. There's more than one track up that mountain. Novels can make a unique connection – one person is alone, writing, and contact is made miles and centuries away with another person alone, reading. Receiving the message. Not from outer space but from inner space. And there's instant connection. It's a sort of magic.'

'I understand that. I really do.'

'Recognition. It's a marvel of the mind. You become invented characters – you *are* Jane Eyre, you feel for her and know her, or you *are* Bill Sykes clubbing Nancy to death. Hundreds of imaginary people inhabit those catacombs in your skull and you can be more absorbed in and concerned about them than you are for your friends. And that is just part, just a speck, of this limitless alternative universe that each of us, every single one of us, inhabits.'

'Abelard?'

'All I can do here is to imagine him on the days following Fulbert's discovery. It was a key event that helped make their story one of the most famous of all liaisons, celebrated for centuries. They were to take a self-torturing and scarcely believable course, but one that led them to a version of everlasting love.'

'Our version? The non-believer version?'

'That depends what you consider to be belief. And what you think of as everlasting.'

Ralph, Abelard's servant, found lodging for the rest of the night in a house near the synagogue. And was instructed to go first thing the next morning across the Petit Pont and up the hill towards the embryonic university's quarters to find a more permanent place there. Abelard's stipulations included a stable, a large room for himself, and a high degree of security. Ralph was given money. Nothing in life gave Ralph deeper and more visceral pleasure than to feel a fat purse of coins in the palm of his hand.

Abelard tried to work out why and how Fulbert had known and what would happen next but an orderly reconstruction failed him. His thoughts kept tumbling back to the bed, the sprawl of limbs, Heloise naked.

How humiliated she must now feel in that household. Would Fulbert beat her? Her uncle would certainly demand that she explain herself. He knew Heloise would tell the truth but also be resolute in the defence of her lover and exonerate him of all blame. She would . . . He saw her face, set and white in the candlelight, a portrait of purity in the frame of her unleashed black hair; he saw the spread of her limbs, feeling in his mind their response to his hands – he was all but there, with her again, lying beside her, whispering, as both did, and moving on to new pleasures. To his proposals she added her own variations. Nothing he suggested appeared to offend her. Everything they did, she thought, was what great love demanded.

Now, in his unfamiliar bed with the few night sounds of Paris unusually acute to his ears, which, like all his senses, were on full alert, he wanted to go back and comfort her. He wanted to reassure her and care for her, and that, surely, logically, was love.

He had not anticipated the character of love.

He had thought it had no substance. It showed itself only in feelings that could not be described or analysed with any reasonable accuracy. It was a suffusion, an immersion, a drowning without the death. Or perhaps there was a death, he reasoned, the death of continence and resurrection into a new, sensual faith. This was the heart of love, he now realised, as he lay, open-eyed, in the middle of the Île de la Cité. Was love a second baptism? It had dramatic consequences. He was totally in thrall to its competing demands. He feared that Fulbert might send her away from Paris. That must not happen. He could not live without her. But love itself? What was it? His mind could find no concept for it. It was ineffable. It seemed all-powerful, like God.

He had said as much in one of his recent lectures, for the fun of it, and set out to find proofs for it. But now, speaking silently to himself in the void of night, he meant it. It was all-conquering, like God. He could not summon any feeling that would challenge it, whereas lust could always be challenged by more lust or less. Love was indivisible and, again like God, it spread to all things. He saw now that the helpless feeling of the past few months threatened to overwhelm the logical philosophy to which he had devoted himself. It was irresistible. Perhaps the Fall in Eden gave it a unique energy, darkly rooted, fathomless in its force. For who could explain it? And love, like the life of a soul, could be perpetual. He knew that he would love Heloise until he died, and after death they would strive to meet again and love on. Love was sovereign, God's gift. The intellect could only bow down to it.

He wanted to tell her all of this immediately. He wanted to leap from his barren bed and follow the thread through the darkness back to the house of Fulbert. But the canon was in no state for such a sudden invasion.

He would find a way to see her in the morning. He would have Ralph bribe Marguerite. He would, he must, sleep now, but she populated his dreams and appeared and reappeared. She lay beside him. His Heloise.

She buried her face in the sheets and breathed in the scents of their love. She was fully dressed, prepared for Fulbert. He would return, she guessed, with increased anger. Abelard's sudden warrior fury had intimidated him but it would not last for long. He would be gathering his wits and his forces, and she must be ready.

He would be humiliated. This perfect niece, this pride of France and of the Cloisters of Notre-Dame, this flower of learning, taken up as an almost equal by the greatest philosopher of the day, had turned harlot. Gone the purity that had been the twin to her scholarship. For ever broken, the perfection he had nourished with such single-mindedness throughout her life. His ward, his niece, was now a lesser thing, the jewel of her virginity, which, with her learning, could have secured her a place among the mighty, was now lost, and with it, the fame that had been the pride of his days. She read his mind on the dark walls of her room.

She had utterly deceived him. Heloise could hear his thoughts. He had acted in what he thought were her highest interests and she had sinned against God but, much more agonisingly, deceived her uncle. Who was she now, this fallen niece? She knew him so well. He would wonder why, on being discovered, she had not wept and prayed for his forgiveness like a Christian. It must be, she reasoned, because she believed there was nothing to forgive. And so she had stood in that room like a Roman, like one of her pagan heroes.

Abelard had gone but she and Fulbert remained. Where else could she go? Where retreat? She had to see Abelard and she knew that he would not be satisfied until they were locked in love together. There had been a change, hadn't there, from the beginning? From the overgrown boy's volcanic discovery and instant compulsion to this settled love and friendship. She was his *amica* now, as much as his lover. He listened more. He cared for her more.

She had to stay here, then, in Fulbert's house, in this abandoned bed. She needed to talk to Abelard. Marguerite could not be trusted. Another way had to be found.

Soon it would be urgent.

She stroked her belly and, finally, she smiled in the dark. That touch assumed a comforting, enfolding presence. Soon enough she would be joined to him twice over and all would be well.

Fulbert had drunk too much for sleep and, in any case, he was impatient for dawn. He would do such things! But what were they? He could not wipe from his mind the multiple remembrances of those false, wounding smiles and the knowing nods of his friends. How they would gloat now!

He writhed in his chair and took yet another draught. No! No! No! It had not happened. It was a mistake to think it had happened. There had to be another explanation.

But she had not denied it and neither had Peter Abelard. To be deceived by both of them! And in his own house.

And the whole of Paris to know it, all save him. He remembered a few lines from one of Abelard's besotted songs – treacherous words, public disgrace. He heard laughter around Paris as clearly as the clopping of horses' hoofs as dawn brought in the traders.

And word would be out. Or would it? Could he put out the fire before it spread? Could there be a compact of silence? Or should he invoke the blood-laws of vengeance? Better to be silent. But so many knew. He could keep Heloise confined. He could claim that Abelard's teaching of her had come to its natural end and put him out of the house. That was his best first course. Deny everything. Order Heloise to deny everything. And send her away? Write to Abelard ordering him to redeem himself by keeping silent. Hope that time would gradually erase it. That was a solution . . .

But, oh! His daughter! And such a daughter! His one and only child!

Chapter Eighteen

After some broken sleep, Fulbert woke up suffering from drink as well as from Abelard. Vomiting, water and more wine calmed the physical pain. The other resumed its torment. The shock of the revelation; the emergence of the lordly warrior in Abelard; the unapologetic and impervious Heloise; and the drink – drink that flooded the brain, drawing it to numbness and, by a curious process of contradiction, constantly stabbing it fully awake.

Fulbert believed he was in a fight for his life.

It would blight his career. It was unbearable . . . It would never cease to be unbearable. Whispers in the Cloisters, murmurings in the Cathedral of Saint-Étienne, lies – excruciatingly 'understanding' smiles and little waves of the hand. He feared he could not endure it. He had to regain his dignity, his reputation, his character.

The imploding fury that seemed spent at one moment, only to return more nauseous and debilitating a few moments later, had to be harnessed to action.

In the emptiness of his parlour, he knelt and prayed. He asked God to forgive him for failing to protect the innocent woman in his house. He dedicated himself yet more emphatically to serve God and His Church on earth. He promised gifts to Saint-Étienne's. He swore to do everything in his power to reclaim the soul of Heloise. Once more he begged forgiveness and felt pain from the strain on his knees, but knelt on through it to prove his sincerity. When finally he rose, it was so stiffly that he all but tumbled over. The pain would fuel him. Pain and prayer together gave strength to the supplicant.

He summoned Heloise.

Marguerite made as if to stay at the door and listen, but Heloise gestured that she must not cross the threshold and closed the door firmly in the servant's face.

'I wish to apologise,' said Heloise. 'Last night proved too confusing for me. And I was lost for the words I should have spoken. You have been most kind and generous to me all my life. I broke your trust. I am to blame, wholly, for this. I made no attempt to deter him when, in the way of young men, he tested my resistance. It was then that I should have recalled the teachings of the scriptures and those whose Commentaries you led me to study. Instead I behaved in a way you might call pagan – thinking only of pleasure.'

'Perhaps you have been truthful according to your beliefs,' he said, determined to be calm. 'But your beliefs are not those you were taught to hold.'

Heloise remained silent.

'You have betrayed your faith more than you have betrayed yourself. You have broken God's holy commandment. You cannot argue against that. Prayer is the only cure, prayer and the admission of sin.'

'What sin can there be in true love?' And what about yourself and Marguerite? she thought. But respect for herself prevented her from making such a coarse rejoinder.

Fulbert waved away her objection. He had long ago realised that she could defeat him in argument. 'Such an argument is of no importance. Here we live in faith.'

'What is this faith?' She knew she was echoing Abelard. 'Without examination through reason there can be no faith.'

'Faith is sacred. What you have done is to break the faith put forward by God and supported by the finest minds God has sent to live among us.'

'No mind can go unchallenged.'

She now had that cold tone that could slice through Fulbert's propositions but the hammer blows in his battered brain drove his desperation.

'You will not dispute with me! Nor I with you. You have cast away your virginity, for ever despoiled your purity, deceived him who was set to protect you, and fed the mere lust of a man who has lied to me and to the whole world. You will listen to me and you will do as I say.'

Heloise held out a rolled scroll of parchment, like those Fulbert had received as gifts from her many times before, in which he had basked. 'This is what I wish to say to you.'

He put an arm across his eyes. 'Take it away. Burn it. Renounce it.'

'It says what I want you to hear.' She felt a rise of sympathy. What had he done to deserve this? His anguish was the result of her selfishness. Her tone was near begging. 'Please read it.'

'Does it say that you are a harlot?' He choked on the word but did not withdraw it. 'You will go back to the convent to which you were sent when you were a child. There you will stay until the time comes, if ever, when I summon you back to Paris. You will leave by noon. Arrangements will be made. That is all.'

Fulbert turned his back on her.

'No!' she said. 'You cannot send me from Paris! You cannot send me away from Peter Abelard!'

Her uncle took a very deep breath and turned to her. His eyes brimmed tears. The sight made Heloise understand the full impact on him of what she had done. She was suddenly sorry for him. He was suffering. But before she could turn the feeling into speech, he said, 'You will do as I say if you have to be bound and carried to the boat. I will declare you are in a fit of madness. Or you can choose my way and go with Marguerite and two other servants to escort you. Now. Go back to your room. Go now! Or I will have you whipped.'

Heloise swayed as she stood. She had seen whippings in the streets and heard of such punishment being administered even to rich students and not uncommonly within good families. But for her?

She knew her uncle. Fulbert meant it.

Her body cringed at the prospect. Yet it was not fear. Her Roman heroes and heroines had taught her to despise corporeal inflictions. It was finally breaking through to her that she owed duty to her uncle. But where did it take her now? Abelard blocked any course that Fulbert would have accepted.

She left the room much less wrapped in her own version of the event than when she had entered it.

She wrote a note to Abelard:

> To my only one from his unique one. Today I will be cast on the waters of the Seine to be carried back to the cradle of my learning. Between the sun and the moon there is always the giving and returning of light. I will not move away from my beloved. Reward the bearer of this well. At noon I am exiled.

She sealed it, marked it 'To Master Peter Abelard', and found an unguarded opportunity to slip out. There were always a few boys hanging around the door of Abelard's lecture hall, hoping for errands from the richer students. She found a likely courier, instructed him to be certain to hand this to Master Abelard as he came into the school. He would be rewarded well, she told him, convincing him doubly with the intensity of her look.

There would be no danger of the boy reading it. Latin, the currency of all authority, was not known to such as him.

Abelard's first thought on reading the letter was to ride hard to Argenteuil and be there to meet Heloise off the boat. But that would alert suspicion. Better to deliver the lecture first. There would be time enough to reach Argenteuil after that.

He went into the lecture with a purpose and zeal lacking in the past few months. The sudden appearance of this obstacle, this barrier to his charmed erotic adventure, jarred him into an acute sense of self-preservation. Even though his students were not aware of the discovered affair, he realised that the course he must take was first to re-establish himself as a peerless lecturer.

In front of a diminished class, a few of whom came to scoff at the plight of their once-revered teacher, he took up the most difficult aspect of his redefinition of the universals and lashed them into admiration. When he had finished, perspiring with effort, he was cheered and applauded. They had their great philosopher back.

Deftly he sidestepped the congratulations from his jubilant students and made for his new lodgings. Ralph had found a place well tailored to Abelard's demands. His chattels had been transferred to his room. The door was heavy oak, the key emphatic. He would need to look out for himself: Fulbert might well seek vengeance.

He sat down to consider his options. The success of the morning lecture had reminded him of the exhilaration he used to experience when a crowded room of clever young men listened to him as if he were not so much a teacher as a prophet. That sense of triumph mingled with the passion he felt for Heloise. He had only two candles and the presence of darkness sharpened his senses.

The first test of love is thinking of the other before yourself, he decided, as he sat, wine and empty parchment before him. Through that night he had confirmed to himself the certainty that Heloise's feelings and condition were much more important than anything else. Especially himself. Her safety and happiness came before his.

It was a revelation.

Heloise, he wrote her name on the empty page. Then he decorated the H. Heloise, he wrote again, plain, and at last he felt peace. He loved Heloise. He could teach her. Through her he could teach himself. He would turn his mind from secular philosophy to include thinking on crucial Christian matters – such as the contested meaning of the Holy Trinity. This study he would call theology. In a new world he and Heloise would flourish. Lust for her would never leave him but love had become the greater force. As he sat in his bolted room, with Heloise about to be re-cloistered in Argenteuil, he was brimful of hope. Love would make them equal. The letter would reach her later in the day. There would be nothing to provoke rumour. They must not be coerced by Fulbert.

Heloise was greeted at Argenteuil by the abbess and escorted ceremoniously into the convent. The nuns were still in awe of her learning. No base rumours from Paris had disturbed her scholarly fame in the convent. Those who, like Heloise, had been placed there for education and the preservation of their virginity while family dynastic intricacies unfolded, were strung between envy and wonder. They knew her songs. They had been forced to listen to reports of her genius as a young scholar at Argenteuil every week of their lives. And now there was Abelard. His songs! About Heloise! Songs that honoured and praised her so highly. They would sing them to each other.

And she lived up to every sentence of expectation. She was tall, handsome and magnificently arrogant. If they had wanted to criticise or in any way diminish her because of her unexpected return to Argenteuil, their plans fell away the moment they set eyes on her. She did not set eyes on them. They were, they felt, uniquely fortunate to have her in their midst.

She had been given the best guest room for as long as she needed it. The splendid chairs had been left in the will of a baron's grateful widow. There were two fine tapestries, a glitteringly polished desk, and on each wall a carefully painted scene from the life of Christ. Sitting on one of the chairs nearest the window, Heloise listened to the chanting that came from the nearby chapel and allowed her thoughts to drift back to those early years of scholarly trance. She smiled at the recollection of her earnest innocent days when there was nothing in the world save the classical language, the poetry, essays and thoughts of men of genius. How much richer she was now; how immeasurably richer.

Abelard had told her that one of the reasons he had chosen her was her learning, which had meant they had been able to write to each other as scholar to scholar. She carried the letters with her – copies of her own and those she had received from Abelard, who would often write to her two or three times each day.

He had been right, as he was about everything, she believed. The letters were alive with both their lived thoughts. They had gone between them 'hot and fast', she said, full of declarations in praise of their exalted love . . . She looked through them now, to settle herself. Her expulsion from Paris had shaken her.

Their letters were written in the unrestrained high tone of the day:

> An equal to an equal, to a reddening rose under the spotless white of lilies, whatever a lover gives to a lover.
>
> Although it is wintertime yet my breast blazes with the fervour of love. What more? I would write more things to you but a few words instruct a wise man. Farewell my heart, my body and my total love.

And on the same day, he had written back:

> Indeed your words are few, but I made them many by rereading them often. Nor do I measure how much you say but how fertile is the heart from which comes what you say. Farewell sweetest. Farewell my star, whose splendour never dies. Farewell my greatest hope in whom alone I find favour and whom I never bring back to mind because you never slip from mind. Farewell.

Then Heloise:

> To her beloved, special from the experience of the reality itself; the being which she is . . . your presence is my joy, your absence is my sorrow.

And Abelard:

> To his jewel, more pleasing and more splendid than the purest light. I have no light that does not come

from you and without you I am dull, dark, weak and dead . . .

Then Heloise:

To the sweetest protector of her soul, planted at the root of her caring love . . .

And Abelard:

To his beloved, firmly stood in eternal memory: whatever leads to the state in whose fullness nothing is lacking . . .

For some time she held onto that last letter. She reread it several times and felt calm. They could not be separated. And Abelard would never put her in any danger. What they did with his pure will and her willing consent was unassailable.

Chapter Nineteen

He rode to see her at Argenteuil like a knight on a quest in one of the new romance tales, he thought. Alone on narrow paths that trickled through sun-dappled woods and dissolved in broad meadows, always within sight of the river Seine.

Ralph had gone ahead to tell the abbess that Master Abelard was coming to visit them. He had delivered another well-argued lecture that morning and felt the better for it. No one had mentioned his ejection from Fulbert's house. The world was still ignorant and, for once, he had no urge to enlighten it. He had fabricated a plausible excuse for his visit to Argenteuil.

It was good to be on horseback, alone, under the quiet blue and white skies of early autumn, the steady ambling of his mount easing his thoughts. He could follow a line of argument uninterruptedly on this placid open-air passage through such tranquil countryside. He was convinced he could reason his way through the eruptive event.

He had learned to ride soon after he had learned to walk, when he was destined to inherit his father's title and estates. What, he occasionally thought, if he had accepted his inheritance? What if he had extended the estates, as his brother was now doing, and prepared to take some of their men on a crusade, as his brother was about to do? What if he had sired children to perpetuate his name and done bold deeds to bring glory to his house? For moments, as he sailed above the earth and swayed in his saddle to avoid the low-hanging boughs, he could see himself most unusually in armour, for Mars, the god of war . . . He smiled to himself. His mind was becoming an open gate to roads not taken . . .

As he drew nearer to Argenteuil and felt ease and warmth at the sure prospect of seeing Heloise, he found diversion and calm in forcing himself to retreat to his founding convictions. For Abelard, truth was arrived at by doubt. For about two years he had been trying to prove in his book *Either/Or* that God was the fount of all truth arrived at through reason. Doubt was the key. Without doubt, he believed, there could be no rock for faith to build on. His enemies were convinced that any doubting of the Bible was a threat. Questions were the work of the devil. Question the Church and you endangered it. Those who persisted in questioning the unquestionable authority of the Church had to be rooted out, cast out, their work, and if necessary their lives, destroyed. Questioning was a dangerous game to play. It exhilarated Abelard. To question was to conquer.

Save for Heloise. Now, as he approached the abbey of Argenteuil, he saw her not as a conquest but as a companion, not as someone to joust with but someone with whom to share a life and to whom to give part of his, as she in return would give part of hers to him.

And yet . . . As he nudged the horse into a brisk trot, he moved restlessly in the saddle. The root of love, which was lust, was not to be denied either.

Then the splendour of Argenteuil was before him. He saw a castle, his lady there. He broke into a gallop.

+ ⟶+

'Master Peter Abelard is about to visit us. What an honour for Argenteuil!'

The abbess came into Heloise's room in a flurry of delight.

Heloise stood up from her table, apparently unmoved. Visit *us*, she thought. *Us? Us?* There is no us but *me*.

'I am sure as your tutor that he will want to talk to you,' said the abbess, diplomatically, 'but his servant reports that his chief object is to examine our library. The library that served you so well, Heloise. I myself will conduct him there and answer – as far as I am able – any of the questions he may ask.'

Still silent, Heloise's inner tongue was uncheckable. '*You!* Explain the library! What do you know about the classical authors? How dare you presume to explain anything to Peter Abelard? Questions he *may* ask! Of course he will ask questions! How will *you* be able to answer them?'

'I will allow the nuns to look on him once,' she said. 'Scholars like yourself may use their discretion. After the library, I thought he could join us for our meal – perhaps after he has seen the chapel. But perhaps not. The younger nuns are already overexcited. And the scholars, as you once were here, among us, my dear Heloise, are almost out of control. Some are very well connected, and I must be careful not to snub them. On the other hand I cannot tire him with too many introductions. I will call on you when your place in the day is settled. And of course you will see him in the refectory at our meal, though not, I am sure you understand, at his table with us. I must look for some of the wine we were sent from Saint-Denis.'

When she had left the room, Heloise, by an act of will, which had been forged in the place since childhood, repressed her frustration and dismay at what the abbess had said and opened herself to the acute imminent pleasure of seeing Peter Abelard again. She sang, softly, one of his recent songs in which he compared her to the dawn, and declared her learning to be as sweet as an eternal day. Then she realised the risk he was taking. This was holy ground and they were deep in sin. They must be discreet.

She went back to her table and continued to work on Cicero's *Pro Milone*. Abelard would find her.

Perhaps it was their most sinful and dangerous coupling, a wild risk, driven by a compulsion for each other's bodies – Heloise was now as bold and impatient as Abelard in her desire to be one with him in every way. They met in the corner of the refectory when it was briefly empty, and on a table in the darkest part of it inside the sacred walls of a convent they made love savagely, in a manner that was branded in the memory of Heloise. It was to torment and also comfort her in the library of her memory for the rest of her life. As Abelard took her, she put her fingers over his mouth and he bit them so he did not cry out, yet she wanted the fierceness. Their embrace convinced them of the depth of their love for which everything else, in Heaven or on earth, could be sacrificed.

Chapter Twenty

She slept little. She remembered the day of his visit as well as she had ever learned by heart a page of Seneca. She felt she had to record the event for both of them. In the middle of the night she lit a candle, sat at her table and wrote.

She began with the style of his arrival, which she had seen from her window. He had vaulted from the tall horse and left the reins loose, knowing that a servant would lead it away and tend it. A deep breath swelled his chest. The air had vitalised his complexion, his hair was wild from the breeze and his fingers sought to order it. The directness of his smile provoked one in return from the normally severe abbess, who greeted him.

From every window the gaze of wide eyes beamed on that man, the hero of knowledge.

When he had been led indoors and out of her view, Heloise told him later, it was as if the sun had gone out. But she could 'see' him in the library, a room she knew more intimately than any other place. She guessed he would want to take down the books that she had told him she had studied and glance through them to be close to her. Perhaps the abbess would ask him about Virgil – she could hear his reply and smile at his rather rough pronunciation of that purest of Latin poets. Or Seneca. Surely he would linger on the book of Seneca's poems, the very copy from which she had learned so much. She was jealous of the abbess for being there with Abelard.

And so to the austere meal at which the nuns and scholars, Heloise observed, could scarcely bear to bend their heads to their food, so enraptured they were to have Master Abelard seated among them. All of them, she was sure, were stoking up impressions for later conversation. Now, in the candle-lit gloaming of her room, Heloise called up the previous day as if summoning an oracle again and again, until she was perfect in recollection, the technique she had used to learn her lessons.

The abbess had asked him to honour Argenteuil by saying a few words that they could carry with them throughout their lives. No one had been prepared for his supremely melodious voice, she wrote.

He stood and drained the small goblet of wine. Heloise knew that his speech would be addressed to her. He spoke first in honour of Argenteuil, he said, and of holy and learned women, of the Blessed Virgin Mary and her sister, also Mary, the wife of Cleophas, and most of all of Mary Magdalene. Heloise wondered if he had cast her as his Mary Magdalene. A woman so unjustly characterised as a whore yet none save His mother closer to Christ.

He told them that the constancy of holy women had been prophesied by Job. It was Mary Magdalene, he said, who had seen Jesus Christ before anyone else after the resurrection – a privilege that could have been granted only by God Himself – and she had been at the foot of the Cross with the Virgin. With other women she had followed Him along the shore of Galilee as He preached His holy gospel. She was the apostles' apostle, he said. And it was she who had anointed His head with oil. Heloise felt a shiver of pride and ennoblement ripple through the chaste bodies of his audience, who might have heard something of this but never before been told of it so authoritatively, so boldly. Here was the true and essential place of a woman in the story of their Saviour.

As he developed his theme he mentioned Joanna, the wife of Chuza, the steward of Herod, and Susanna, who had also been with Christ in Galilee, and others who had supported Him.

He referred to Miriam the prophetess, to the courage of Deborah, Hannah and Judith. He said that although women were weaker than men, their virtue was more precious to God and more perfect. The love of God for women was made manifest through Jesus Christ in His mother, and Mary Magdalene.

It was the voice, Heloise concluded, as she glowed in the first public lecture of Abelard she had ever heard. Abelard who loved her and was loved in return! The melody of it. The pauses, the touches of drama, the rhythm. And how rich a harvest the nuns and novices reaped from such beautifully arranged knowledge and the passion of his argument. Little wonder the students came from the ends of the earth, all said later. Who would not want to listen to this man, who radiated thought, even in the sombre light of the refectory? His words spun light around him. And, Heloise marvelled, so calm: after what they had just done together, so outwardly composed. She 'saw them' in her mind, and blushed.

When he finished, there was a deep, almost a sobbing sigh. This lecture, she knew, would bring fame to the convent. It would be boasted of whenever an eminent guest visited. He had pitched it perfectly, Heloise thought.

She wrote until the candle guttered. Just before dawn, on their way to the chapel, two of the younger, more free-spirited novices made a forbidden detour to pass by the guest room and stood close to the door to whisper-sing one of Heloise's hymns.

Then they scampered away. She smiled at their shy tribute.

She touched the walls around her womb-enclosed child in the place she had once called a tomb. 'I must,' she resolved, 'tell him soon.'

Chapter Twenty-one

They were in Matthew's flat in the late afternoon – so unexpectedly quiet, Julia thought, for the centre of Paris, as if such squares as this had been sealed off from active life. They had bypassed lunch.

'He could be quite vicious, couldn't he?' Julia produced the Penguin edition of *The Letters of Abelard and Heloise*, which also contained his autobiography. She put it on the table as if she were slapping down a legal document, a rather damning one. 'You keep defending Abelard.'

'I keep trying to understand him,' Arthur replied, patiently. 'At present I'm trying to work out how much to believe of what he says about himself. Autobiography can be a liar's charter. People generally pump themselves up. Abelard does the opposite. I think he condemns his past actions far too readily, as a way to seek favour with God by confessing to the worst.'

'So it's all about religion?'

'And equally politics. That was then. The same but they are different. Parmenides and Heraclitus. Everything stays the same and everything changes.'

'I hate it when you do that. It puts me right off. Am I supposed to ask who those two are? Am I supposed to care?

I was talking about Abelard. Was he or was he not a destructive man?'

'He could be.'

'Could be? Listen to this. His autobiography – the *Historia* – page seven. He's talking about the scholar Anselm, an old man who he says is – listen! – "the greatest authority – because of his age". That's a dig for a start. Only because of his age?'

'Anselm did have a high reputation. But when Abelard met him he was very old, and it would probably have been kinder to describe his authority as declining.'

'It's a dig. Listen. "He owed his reputation more to long practice than to intelligence or memory." That's just an opinion. So why does he write it down as if it's a fact?'

'Abelard was in poor shape when he wrote that,' said Arthur, smiling at his mettlesome daughter. 'And he needed to boast himself back into confidence in order to take on such a figure as Anselm. That meeting with Anselm was just after his breakdown. It would have been hard for him to get back into the saddle, as it were. I can see both sides. Abelard was right to challenge him but wrong to do it in such an abrasive way. But this was, for him, a crucial encounter. He was back in the debating ring.'

'Okay. You can see both sides. What about this? "Anyone who knocked on his door to seek an answer to some question went away more uncertain than he came." How does he know that? There's no proof at all. That's just gossip or spite.'

'No proof. Agreed. Julia . . .'

'I'll be quick. Last batch. Still on Anselm. "He had a remarkable command of words but their meaning was worthless and devoid of all sense." Ouch! And then, "The fire he kindled filled his house with smoke but did not light it up." There's more of the same. Just mean. Admit it. Then he goes on to humiliate the old man in front of his pupils. Why does he do that?'

Arthur was elated. 'One reason I'm writing this is to find the answers to the questions you're asking.'

'It's just a novel. Not a thesis.'

'Novels can tell truth. I promise that's the last time I'll say so.'

'But it's not the real truth, is it? That's what people want.'

She finished her coffee and for a moment he thought she might leave. 'Another?' It was as much a plea as a request.

'Okay. I'm easily bribed. And do you have a brandy? That's what we have in the other places I go to. Just one. Just now and then.'

'We', he noted. So, she had friends in Paris. He knew better than to probe. He went across to the drinks cabinet and returned with a small brandy.

'Nothing for you?'

He shook his head. 'Abelard was not admirable, in your modern view of correct public argument,' he said.

'No. He wasn't. Nor was he in whatever age – theirs or ours.'

She took up the brandy and sipped tentatively. He felt relief. Was she unsure why she was drinking it or did the taste suit her much less than the style?

'He was,' Arthur said, seeing that a conclusion was necessary, 'all but insanely competitive, arrogant, boastful and no respecter of the past. But remember the mission he had set himself. It was to challenge and change an entire system of thought that had built up over a thousand years. Maybe good manners, tact and being a nice chap aren't much use in that sort of work.'

'I knew you'd try to wriggle out of it.'

He didn't reply.

She sipped again. 'Sorry,' she said. 'I didn't mean to be like that. You're not really a wriggler. More a digger. Honest.' Her laughter drew his.

'Don't be sorry. In some way he deserves it. So do I. But you have to make the effort to put him in his time. The trick is to see the bigger story of his work and his life. That attack on Anselm was before he'd met Heloise. That was when he saw mind-to-mind public combat with the champions of the day as the only effective way to make his point or, even more than that, to justify his life's work.'

'It still doesn't justify the slagging-off he gave Anselm.' She muttered this into her brandy glass, a little embarrassed at her own persistence.

'Yes. But inside what Abelard said there was a cry for freedom. A cry to people to start thinking for themselves. He was saying, "Overthrow this tyranny of ancient authorities! Liberate your minds! You are shackled. Only reason and logic can set you free." It was a heroic task he set himself. Can't you accept that? And he committed the worst crime of all. He converted the young. They crowded into his lectures. They took back notes to every corner of Christendom. They became his agents, his missionaries. And they were the future of the Church's control system. Abelard was lighting up their minds, delivering them from darkness, as he saw it. No wonder that, to the authorities, he was dangerous. He was inflammatory. He came with an avenging sword to cut out a tyranny that called itself sacred. He had no time for public etiquette, for the widespread kowtowing. He was a revolutionary, Julia. You'd have fought for a ticket to one of his lectures.'

'They wouldn't have let me in. That was Heloise's problem.' But she nodded and raised her glass as if she were sealing a peace treaty.

'As I see it,' he concluded, 'my job is to find out, as far

as I'm able, the truth about those two astounding, complex, passionate, only half-revealed people. Why? For the sake of it.' He stood up. 'Perhaps I will have a brandy. I declare work to be over for the day.'

Chapter Twenty-two

Heloise's letter was written in a dream of joy. This pregnancy, this, as she believed, certain child would seal their union as nothing else could. The child would be the two of them in one body after their deaths, and if that child had children, their line would go on, perhaps, to an earthly eternity. This steeled her against any mortal fear. God had intended this. Voluptuousness had led to earthly immortality. Her taste for hyperbole was unrestrained. As always, she spoke truth to the event as she understood it.

She felt, she wrote, as if she had moved one step higher in the ascent of love. Whose contentment could be more perfect? Which woman would not want to bear the child of Abelard? Who would not envy her pregnant state and see, plain as the sky, that she and Abelard were true lovers? Her body had never felt more engaged with itself. It was apart from but parallel to her possession by Abelard. This was the proof of their unique love.

The letter, delivered by one of the monks who helped in the convent, ended with her declaration that she would sail up the Seine, gloriously against the current, to meet her uncle and bring to him this news.

Soon after Abelard read it, he despatched Ralph to the landing point with a note for Heloise:

> My dearest love, my only one, from your lover who is only yours. Your news overwhelms me. I cannot think for the confusion of pleasure, thanks and certainty I now feel in you, in us, in all three. But do not say anything to your uncle until I have thought further and we have decided on a course of action. I fear that his reaction will not be what you anticipate. Tell him that you have to return because of a sickness. Do not let Marguerite near you. She will have her suspicions immediately so it would be wise of you to wear your most flowing dress and also a cloak to conceal from her the state of your body, which may well, by this stage, reveal your condition, especially to a shrewd servant like Marguerite.
>
> Be obedient to Canon Fulbert in all matters. Try to be contrite. Assume humility. Deflect his wrath until we have spoken. Be prepared to move swiftly and at any time in the day or night. This from your eternal lover to his eternal love and their new love. Abelard.

Abelard had thought Argenteuil to be the ideal refuge for Heloise. By sending her there, Fulbert had done him a favour and he had rested on it. He had not needed to act – and felt sure Fulbert would surely keep his discovery a secret. Heloise's news destroyed all that.

Abelard's new plan was bold. He would in effect abduct her. He would take her outside France, to Brittany, and leave her safely with his sister until the child was born. He would face the consequences alone in Paris, consequences he knew could be severe, but the security of Heloise was paramount. Fulbert's rage could be violent.

+ –+

'So, you are truly sorry?' Fulbert demanded, his tone almost kindly despite his earlier angry resolve. But she looked so regal, this daughter, with a radiance he had not noticed before and a steadiness he was forced to admire.

'I deceived you who have protected and helped me for so long.'

He nodded, eager to welcome her in some way, to close the waters over what had happened.

'I felt some sickness at Argenteuil and thought that only here would I be safe.'

As you will be, he thought. As you are right to assume. But he was not yet ready to abandon his anger, to cast off his humiliation, to enter into normality or any pretence of it. The genuine flourish of his welcome soon evaporated.

'Go to your room,' he said. 'But not the former one. This is smaller and at the back of the house. Marguerite will take you there.'

'I know the room you mean,' she said. 'I would prefer to go alone. I need all the solitude this house can provide. Save for your company, my noble uncle. I need to find my way back through solitary thought, depending on no one but you, seeing no one but you, talking to no one but you.'

Fulbert took this as the compliment it was designed to be.

His gratitude moved Heloise. She could still see traces of how wounded he had been. Marguerite stood aside and examined Heloise closely. Heloise paid her no attention.

When she had left the room, Fulbert called for a flask of wine and sat down to brood on this unexpected development. Was he being fooled yet again?

It was her smile that began to goad him. Why was she smiling? And in such a taunting way – or so it seemed to

Fulbert. He had become accustomed to a rather stiff, tall, composed figure, unbending. But now . . . What was it? And her little inward smile, her secret joy. Joy! When she should have been grovelling in penitence. Joy! When she should have been suffering for her unforgivable sin and shame. Marguerite could tell him nothing. Heloise had banished her from the tiny quarters to which she had been confined and taken as her servant the lowliest of the working girls, a stunted, lame creature, as Fulbert saw her, more a visible sign of his charity to the poor and infirm than an effective addition to his household.

But Heloise would have no one but Marie, who worshipped her and had proved impervious to Marguerite's questioning. Either through frozen terror or absolute loyalty, which made her sharply aware of the best interests of her mistress, Marie said nothing. But Marguerite's bullying made her cry. Heloise guessed the cause of her distress, then sent her to fetch Marguerite and told her to stay outside while she talked to the housekeeper.

She indicated that Marguerite should close the door and not advance into the room. Then, the better to conceal a sudden flush of anger, she turned her back on Marguerite and spoke to the wall. This gesture curdled Marguerite's respect for Heloise. This was humiliation. And to be cast out of favour for that – dwarf! As if she, Marguerite, were a lesser creature than *that*! She saw cruelty in Heloise from whom once she had known kindness. Heloise saw a woman who had betrayed her.

'You are questioning my servant Marie. Should you do so again, or intimidate, let alone harm her, I will have my uncle dismiss you. You will never come back into the Cloisters. Your conduct with him could be made public if he tries to protect you. He will then do whatever I ask. It need not come to that if you do as I say. Now leave.'

Marguerite began to speak.

'*Leave!*' Heloise clenched her fists at this unexpected spring of fury.

Marguerite reported to Fulbert that Heloise would not talk to her. At great emotional cost but with shrewd political sense, she reined in the truth of what she had worked out to be Heloise's condition. She knew that were she to break that news she would be punished. But she watched for the opportunity of revenge.

Fulbert was not satisfied with the report. Neither was he impressed when Marguerite pleaded Heloise's famous severity as her excuse. He was used to having his way, and Heloise's secret smile, the slight upturn of the lips, the sparkle in her eyes . . . Something, once again, was being hidden from him.

With a unique act of self-control, he had told no one of his discovery of Abelard and Heloise in bed together. He could not face the consequences. Only he, it seemed, as his humiliation deepened, had held to the belief that Abelard's chastity was unbreakable, blessed by God. To confess would diminish him in the eyes of those whose respect he most wanted, whose high regard he needed to climb the ladder, which was his greatest preoccupation. But he had to find some public explanation for the end of her tutorials with Abelard.

Yet he found himself repeating – was he being fooled again? He returned yet once more to her betrayal. In his own house. And with a man he had trusted. Had there ever been such deceit?

And however hard he tried to look away from it, or ignore it, there was that smile. Where was the sorrow? Where was the self-flagellation? Where was the respect for Christ, if not for him? She walked in a self-consumed dream, of contented invulnerability, Fulbert thought. Having at first threatened to break his heart, this goading smile now began to threaten his sanity. He woke up with it; he feared to encounter it; he could close his eyes at any time of the day and, yet again, there would be that enigmatic expression.

There had to be a release. There had to be an expression of his justified rage at this insult, this foul disgrace – and under his roof.

At dusk, when the streets of Paris had quietened and the bells were the only sounds to penetrate the thick-walled houses of the canons in the Cloisters of Notre-Dame, when the students were in their taverns and brothels or around fires in crowded lodgings, the beggars were finding their beds under the bridges, the palace alone continuing activity worthy of the day, in candle-lit rooms where music was played and dancing encouraged, when devoted monks made yet more copies of the gospels and the wild dogs curled up and stopped howling, Fulbert took up a stout walking stick and went to Heloise's room. Trembling but unable to restrain himself, he beat her.

Chapter Twenty-three

Marie brought him the note. Abelard had concluded his first morning lecture and was talking to the more eager students when he caught sight of her timid presence, recognised her, took the message and read it in a rage.

The house, with Heloise inside it, was so close. He had to rescue her. He wanted to go there, attack Fulbert, beat him with the same rod and carry off Heloise. The image of her being beaten made him flinch. But he chained himself against any such dangerous reprisal.

To Marie, he said, 'Come again tomorrow. Tell your mistress I will have a letter for her. Can you remember that, Marie?'

'Come again tomorrow . . . Tell my mistress . . .'

'You will have a letter for her. Now say it all at once, Marie.' The fierceness of her concentration moved Abelard. He smiled at her. Few people ever had. She tensed herself and recited the whole message. 'Come again tomorrow. You will have a letter for her.'

'That's good, Marie. Go now and tell her.'

Marie ran back to Fulbert's house. She entered by the small back door. All the way she mumbled to herself, 'Come again. Tomorrow. Take a letter . . . for her.'

The message was delivered.

Heloise, whose wounds Marie had calmed, following her mistress's instructions, lay face down on her narrow bed.

'Good, Marie. Good . . .'

Then she waited for the pain to pass, as it would, as would all physical pain. The body would be healed and so would the soul. It was only the heart, she thought, that might be wounded for ever. There was even a form of pleasure in her endurance, as she had felt when Abelard had been barely able to contain the extremes of his passion: she knew these were one aspect of his love.

She wrote to Abelard and told him that her uncle would be away from home in four days' time. He would go to Clairvaux. His journey and his visit would take about eight days. Abelard laid his plans.

'Oh, no!' Julia shook an index finger at him. 'That's cheating. It's too convenient.'

'You've just skimmed it.' He indicated her copy of *The Letters of Abelard and Heloise*.

'I've read some of it.'

'But not page twelve of Abelard's autobiography.'

'I prefer the letters.'

'On page twelve he writes, "One night, when her uncle was away from home, I removed her secretly from his house . . ."'

'But what about where Fulbert went?'

'I made that up.'

'And for how long?'

'Ditto. But the fact of it is clearly set out by Peter Abelard. Fulbert was absent.'

'I still think it's too much of a coincidence, even if it is true.'

'Otherwise I would have had to make it up. I thought you were rather against that.'

'I don't like coincidences.'

'Not even in Shakespeare?'

'Oh! For God's sake! No one's allowed to criticise Shakespeare! But it's ludicrous that a bit of cross-dressing and mad plot lines are so often needed to push things along.'

'Are you trying to trap me?'

'Yes!' she said. 'And the brilliant thing is that I mean what I say.'

'Coincidences count,' he said firmly. 'I'm sure that one day we'll discover they follow laws of their own . . . In any event, Fulbert went away.'

'I can't believe he beat her so violently.'

'I can,' Arthur said. 'And I'm afraid I do. Beat her like a dog.'

Julia nodded. She saw the forces against Heloise more clearly.

Beaten like a dog . . .

Abelard sent a message to his home in Brittany. He wanted the two servants who looked after the horses and the fields to meet him in the village of Chartres. He gave them detailed instructions. He would attempt to match his own journey with theirs but they must be prepared to stay in the village for a day, perhaps two. They were to tell no one of this. He said nothing to Ralph who, like all the servants of the teachers and churchmen, loved to trade exclusive information.

Abelard maintained the new level of his lectures and kept his distance from the now forbidden house nearby.

He had caught no whispers of his potentially scandalous dismissal from Fulbert's house. Fulbert, he presumed, had planned to keep it secret and, anyway, would be too ashamed to talk. His servants would have been threatened into silence. All could appear to be well. When asked if Abelard no longer taught Heloise, he would say briskly that the first course of instruction was over and he was considering what might be best for her in further tutorials. Meanwhile, no longer needed in the house, her tutor had taken new lodgings.

Through friends in the Abbey of Saint-Victor, as Heloise had requested in one of her letters, Abelard obtained a nun's habit. He had arranged to meet her immediately after midnight.

At the last minute Ralph divined what might be happening but it was too late. All the other servants were asleep – and there he was with what might prove to be the most scandalous story he had ever heard! It was as much as he could do to stand by the horses at midnight outside the black-faced lecture hall and not race around the Cloisters with this inflammatory news. And he the bearer of it! Ralph – originator of what would be the roar of conversation for days on end. His head was on fire. Surely his master could have trusted him.

Abelard stepped inside the door she had unlocked earlier and there she stood, holding a candle in one hand and in the other her bag.

'This,' he whispered, holding out the nun's habit.

Heloise drew it on.

'Hurry,' he said, 'we must make some miles before dawn. Why do you insist on that habit?'

'If anyone sees me, you will be accused of abduction.

Fulbert and his family could have you murdered. That is the law. But if you are escorting a nun . . .'

'You reject the idea of being a nun.'

'I do,' she said, the habit almost secured. In the dusky light he did not notice the wince of pain as the habit caught the weals on her back.

'Will it not be blasphemous?'

'No,' she said. 'Not if the intention is pure.'

'The intention to deceive?'

'Yes. But for a good purpose.'

Her calm brought on an anxiety in Abelard he had not felt until that moment. It seemed time was rushing away, that dawn was imminent, capture certain, that he would lose her for ever. He could not face that possibility.

The soft clopping of hoofs on the cobbles was an accompaniment to their passage across the old Grand Pont. Ralph, who had followed that route many times, now took the lead. Lengths of rope linked a rider to the one behind. A half-moon gave sufficient help and the broad, well-trampled route was easily held to, a much-used way through the pastures and woods.

Once Heloise had accustomed herself to the seeping of blood from her wounds, she began to savour the journey. Night sounds, familiar to her from inside the convent and her uncle's house, were there so much clearer, each one marking some incident. Was that crash through the undergrowth the charge of a wild boar? That howl, long-held, high-pitched, must have been a wolf. She was excited by the threat of danger while remaining unperturbed: with Abelard behind her and the solid Ralph ahead, she was well protected, should need arise. And that owl: was it on its way to claw up live prey? Another life taken. She must experience the night more often, she decided. As for the phrase 'the dead of night', it was not true. She, in her camouflage and almost total darkness, felt alert, quickened in her senses – the sounds were sharper and fuller of meaning, the smells more pungent than in daytime, and the low light that impaired her vision was a stimulus to her wits. But her supreme pleasure lay in Abelard's care for her.

Abelard spoke to her, enquiries after her comfort but also postscripts to their tuition sessions. She relished this. They talked as true friends, companions, equals in the intimacy of retreating darkness. This would become a rich memory.

At dawn they rested for a few hours at a tavern. A room was found for Heloise where she slept. She did not undress. Abelard and Ralph sat on the kitchen benches before the fire. Ralph, all but distraught, asked if anyone was going to Paris in the morning. Drawing a blank, he tried to bribe the young son of the tavern to make the journey, but his father forbade it. Ralph suffered.

Abelard drew intersecting triangles before falling asleep at the table, his head firmly nested in his crossed arms.

They were away by late morning, making good progress in daylight and through the broad pastureland. After two days they arrived in Chartres where, to his surprise and delight, Abelard's sister was waiting with the two servants.

Denise was a little older than Heloise. They were, as both recognised from their speech and mien, of the same caste. Denise welcomed her so warmly that Heloise was unexpectedly moved. She had anticipated more formality, even reproach.

'You are my new sister,' said Denise. 'I wanted to meet you along the way so that you were chaperoned to our house.'

I have a sister! Furtively Heloise blinked away the start of tears. I have a family. A sister who will have children to play with our child, a father and mother who will also be my father and mother.

'You are exhausted,' said Denise. 'There is a room here in which you can rest. We have brought you fresh clothes.'

'She will continue to wear the habit,' Abelard said, 'more especially now, when we go into our own country.'

'Must he be obeyed?' said Denise to Heloise, who only smiled and did not spoil his moment by pointing out that it was her idea.

'May I talk to Master Abelard alone?'

He held her arm as they walked into the copse across from the tavern. They found a fallen tree trunk and sat on it, side by side, upright, like schoolchildren.

Heloise took a deep breath of the sweet country air. 'Peter,' she said, 'you must go back to Paris. I am safe now, with your sister. But the longer you are away from Paris the greater the suspicion and the greater the danger for you. But,' she smiled, and it was only then that he noticed the tension in her face, the pallor, 'most of all you must go back to teach your philosophy. Your position means so much to you, and too long an absence will give them more cause to attack you. And you need those young minds about you. I will be safe now. When our child is born, then you can come and, if it is safe, take me back to Paris.' She swayed towards him and her head rested on his shoulder. 'Promise me, Peter.'

Her body felt feeble against his. Abelard put his arm around her. She must not catch a chill. He stood and helped her to her feet, overcome by tenderness at her weakness in a way that he had rarely encountered in her strength. Together, he holding her tightly, they walked slowly back through the copse.

His sister immediately took charge, but before they could lead her away Heloise turned to Abelard and said, 'Promise.'

'No,' he said gently. 'I can't leave you.'

'I am well protected, Peter.'

'I will take you to my home.'

She was too faint to argue further.

Later Abelard became impatient to know what was happening and he went through the main room to the door indicated by the boy.

He saw the blood in a bowl of water and froze. Was this God's vengeance?

'The child is safe,' said Denise. 'The blood is not from the child.' He came closer. Heloise lay in sleep. Her belly was cushioned. Her lower back and buttocks were bleeding from freshly opened wounds. Denise bathed them. They would dry her skin and smooth on one of the ointments they carried with them, which would begin again the process of healing.

Abelard sat and watched. The weals and bruises, the torn skin and knots of blackened flesh. He prayed that Fulbert would be struck dead. *Thou shalt not kill*, even in thought. His intention had been the crime. He would seek forgiveness but not until she was healed.

How could she be so brave? How could that sleeping form draw so much love from him? He wanted to touch her but feared to worsen the wounds. Could nobody but himself see the force between them, like the stairways of light to Heaven that stream through broken clouds? How could love be so strong and present yet as natural as air?

How could she be so loving, placing his interests above her own? If only his eyes could look on her with an intensity that would close the wounds. If only he could find a way to express what he felt and not be so constrained to say only what he thought.

After a while he began to compose a prayer but an insistent

rhyme diverted him. It would be a hymn. The Blood of the Lamb and the perfection of the Virgin Mary. He smiled to himself as the melody came, a melody that would carry his hymn into cathedrals and churches as surely as his songs floated through the streets of Paris. A hymn to birth.

Chapter Twenty-four

'Bring Heloise to me.'

Marguerite choked on her words. She could say nothing. Fulbert, tired from his journey, irritated by his lack of success at the council and still enraged by his daughter's ruinous behaviour, had the sharpened instincts of a desperate man. Marguerite's dumb response inflamed him.

'Speak!'

Marguerite bent her head, as if anticipating an executioner's axe on her neck, and began to sob, a coarse, snorting peasant sob, Fulbert thought, in his irritation.

'What is it, woman? Speak!'

Slowly, like the early slide of an avalanche, the large figure of Marguerite subsided to her knees. It would be her fault. Fulbert would kill her.

And already, in those few seconds, Fulbert's anger was whirling into a fury.

Marguerite prostrated herself.

Fulbert, who had never before witnessed – outside the bed – any sign of dramatic behaviour from this solid, faithful servant, was suddenly struck by a terrible intuition.

It was the lashing he had given to Heloise. At the time he had known it to be too much but had been unable to restrain himself. He had returned to it constantly in his memory, sometimes with nods of self-justification and approval, but more often with the fear that he had gone far too far. Real pain. Wounds. Blood. His own daughter.

He strode urgently past the bulk of Marguerite and made for the small room to which he had confined Heloise.

There was no trace of her.

'Marie!'

His cry rang throughout the house. He stepped out of Heloise's room and again at the top of his voice: 'Marie!'

In the study Marguerite, now upright, leaned against the wall for support. It was as if all her energy had drained from her so that she could barely engage her mind to move herself. She could only stand, held up by the wall, condemned. He would surely kill her. And who would blame him?

'Where is Marie? Where is her servant?'

Marguerite shook her head. It was a small but essential movement of self-defence. She knew full well where Marie was. Two days before Heloise had disappeared, she had made Marguerite escort the fearful young servant to the Seine and put her on the boat for Argenteuil. All Marguerite's attempts had not extracted a word from Marie, whom Heloise had commanded to say nothing. She had ordered Marguerite to return to her with the name of the boat and its owner. When that was done Heloise had murmured, 'She will be safe there.' But to admit to what Fulbert would see as complicity in any act of Heloise that had not first been submitted to him for approval was too dangerous.

Fulbert accepted the shake of the head. 'Is she in the house?'

Marguerite maintained her silence.

Fulbert shouted, 'Dead? Dead? Is she dead? Oh, God, I pray not that. Forgive me. Dead?' He seemed to wither away. 'Not dead?' he whispered.

Marguerite made the one move available to her. She had kept this until she could be sure that the anger had abated a little. She would be lucky, she thought, not to be lashed herself. Her hand reached for a letter. She held it out, not yet trusting herself to leave the safety of the wall.

He took it from her hand and stared at it. Heloise's unmistakable script. His name. He appeared, for a moment, afraid to open it, but then he turned to his desk, waved Marguerite away and sat down, the letter in front of him.

Marguerite edged out and sought refuge in Heloise's abandoned room. What did the letter say? Would Fulbert discover that she had helped Heloise in the matter of Marie? Should she tell him about the pregnancy she suspected? There was that 'look' of Heloise. She had acted as if Marguerite did not exist. Would Heloise take revenge?

Fulbert would have found out about them anyway, she argued to herself, the old fool. Even for such a fool it was only a matter of time. Was it so wrong of her? Did Heloise not realise that as she grew older she had to offer her master more than the bed he now took for granted? That she needed to be the bringer of news, to be Fulbert's eyes and ears in places he never visited and on events he needed to know about? She was doing Fulbert a favour but also Heloise. Master Abelard too, she thought. She was part of it. She should be applauded.

They were all such clever people. Clever people could solve problems, Marguerite thought. Clever people lived richer lives. They bought richer clothes and food, and could afford horses. Clever people did not have to do such hard work and eat little but slops. Clever people got what they wanted, not what they were given. It was good to bring news to Fulbert: it extended the reach of her usefulness, her living, her life. But, in this case, why could they not see that she was also giving them the opportunity, at dead of night, when all Paris was asleep, to sort it out to the advantage of them all, as clever people always did?

Yet Abelard had left the house. Fulbert had almost beaten her, the messenger. To Heloise she no longer existed. This idol was no more than a spoilt rich girl.

She drew the heavy bolt that Heloise had insisted be put on the door. Then she lay on Heloise's narrow bed, threatening to overflow it, and drowned her regrets in unchecked self-pity and schemes of revenge.

* * *

To my honoured and eminent uncle, from his grateful niece.

I have asked Marguerite to deliver this to you, my guardian. I have sealed it with the seal from your desk as you will have seen. This will deter her from opening it. In any event, she has no knowledge of Latin, but my mistrust of your favoured servant knows no bounds.

When you receive this, I will be out of France and in the land of the Bretons, at the house of the family of Master Peter Abelard. I am carrying our child and I fear that your violence – witness your abuse of my person before you left – will harm the unborn one. I regret having deceived you because of the respect you are surely owed from one to whom you have devoted such special care. I do not regret having deceived you about my love for Master Peter Abelard. That would be to regret that I had been born.

Had you known about it from the beginning you would have prevented it, and I would be without what I believe to be the revelation of my life. It is wholly new to me. I am grateful to you for your blindness. Nothing had prepared me for the love and desire I have for Peter Abelard. I am joined to him for my life, both now and hereafter.

He commanded that I leave this house and go into the safety of his country. I will return to Paris after the child is born but only when my safety is assured.

Marguerite knew nothing about this before it happened. She may perhaps know something now that Peter Abelard's servant Ralph will have returned and Master Abelard himself will soon be in Paris. Do not beat her for what she could not have prevented or feared to tell you of. Your wrath is fierce as my slowly healing wounds bear witness.

I remain your grateful niece,
Heloise

* * *

'It would be within your honour to have him killed.'

William of Champeaux spoke with relish. Rarely a day passed without a needling memory of the public humiliation his pupil Abelard had poured over his ideas. It was a blow from which William's lectures, though not his subsequent career, had never recovered. His students had deserted him for Abelard. Loss of face, loss of income, and gain to Abelard of another enemy. William was one of the friends of Fulbert who had gathered together an informal council in his house.

'A killing, even a justified assassination, in a legitimate blood feud,' said the outstandingly corpulent and bibulous Gilles de Vannes, 'though it may need a degree of authorisation . . . this could be arranged.'

'No need for authorisation in the case of abduction,' said William, glad that he had decided not to drink in a company unceasingly eager for Fulbert's fine wines. 'Add to that the impregnation of an innocent pupil. Add to that several levels of deceit. Add to that—'

'Enough,' said the young Alberic of Rheims, an enemy to Abelard from the time he had humiliated Anselm. 'If we aim too wide we shall lose focus.' He was pleased with that. Generally speaking, Alberic was pleased with everything he said, especially if he could make it sound grave.

Gilles, who had principally come for the wine, nodded encouragingly. You never knew when you might need the vote of such a usefully stupid ally as Alberic of Rheims. He raised his glass to Alberic, then sank its contents and, as ever, Fulbert's man immediately brought him more.

'Abelard is not yet back in Paris,' said Fulbert, trying with limited success to parlay his all but unbearable private hurt and fury into an acceptable strategy, 'but he will be on his guard when he does return. And remember that he is from a family of Breton knights. Then there are his students, who will be loyal to him.'

'*His* students?' William pounced. '*His* students? No more than a common mob under the command of an ignorant populist! They are young men who have been bewitched by his pagan phrases, this cant of Aristotle the pagan, the windiness of Plato – schoolboy quips that contaminate the true scholarship of the scriptures and our great commentators.'

'Nevertheless,' said Alberic, 'they are a force. And many come from wealthy families.' Gilles once more raised his satisfyingly full glass to acknowledge the power of that particular sally. Alberic took the compliment in his stride.

'But what to do?' Fulbert all but wailed. 'What are we to do?'

'They have her in Brittany,' said Gilles, sadly. He had much admired Heloise. She had been kind about his self-indulged poor health and listened to him when he spoke of the virtues of Cicero's prose. Her own Latin, he had told her, was the purest of its time, and unique in a woman. 'And we know these Bretons,' he continued. 'If we harm Master Abelard they will surely retaliate by harming Heloise. If we kill Abelard, who is to secure her life? And there will be the child.'

'They would not do that to Heloise,' said Fulbert.

'Then we must not do that to Abelard,' replied Gilles, who took another sip of wine and decided, having made his point, not to speak again.

'Even the Bretons must know of chivalry,' said Alberic. 'Even barbarians have manners.'

This time Gilles did not raise a glass. He himself was a Breton.

'So what can we do?' said Fulbert. 'William – what must we do? He will be difficult to kill or harm – he will be on his guard against us. He will be armed. He will gather supporters around him. He may well – should he hear of this – decide to come here first and challenge us.'

'I will seek about,' said William, refusing to yield, although he could see that this particular skirmish was lost.

'I am in your hands,' said Fulbert, piteously.

'Our hands are the hands of God,' said Alberic.

Gilles nodded gravely.

But when they had gone, with comforting words and warm blessings, when the fire dwindled to embers under his intense, as if hypnotised, gaze and the bottle's level sank and the candles silently consumed themselves, Fulbert went into a hell of misery. Misery vomited into his mind. He had no defence against its attacks. He was sickened by failings of his own making, by the prospect of eternal humiliation, by the wreck of all his hopes, by the insupportable injustice, by this impenetrable decision of God. She who had been so pure had been led into corruption without any intervention from Him who was Himself purity. Why? The severance between Fulbert and his beloved daughter, their never to be resurrected unquestioning love, how had he deserved it? And now Heloise was in a foreign land, another body inside her own, with Fulbert able to do nothing but sink further and further into despair. Who would help him?

Chapter Twenty-five

Abelard stayed with Heloise for some weeks. His neat plans were discarded, his fears and hopes for a return to Paris quelled as he seized the chance to be with Heloise in such freedom and security. His parents were in retreat, his father in a monastery, his mother in a convent, and his sister saw that he and Heloise wanted time alone together. The place was theirs and no explanations were required.

They walked. Abelard took her around the gardens, then into the cultivated woods on the estate. Her strength needed to be repaired. The fresh air, the ripeness of summer and the grandeur of the countryside drew them away from the house, and for hours they would stroll along narrow paths, then sit beside a stream from which they could drink. Heloise was grateful to Abelard that he had refused to go back to Paris as she had insisted. This was, she thought, the true Abelard, in his own country.

It took them some days to emerge from what now seemed the clamp of Paris. The excitement and daring of the city gradually gave way to the exhilarating landscapes of Brittany. They were often wholly alone in those landscapes, yet they did not seize the opportunity presented to them with the urgency of the past. They were content to lie side by side, hand in hand, on warm grass, looking at the sky, listening to the sounds from the earth and the heavens, as one, together.

Passion could still trample the more tender shoots of affection. But there they flourished. When they made love now, both were conscious of the child and of Heloise's wounds, yet still they sought out spots in the woods to satisfy their need. The desire did not slacken. Risks were taken. But nature gave them calm.

Abelard noticed a shy pride in Heloise, in the way she gently stroked her belly when she thought he was not looking and took greater care with her hair than before, in her comments on his appearance, in small, tranquil matters. They put behind them the bombast of great thoughts or great ambitions or the great philosopher. He would fuss about the effect of a hot sun on her fair skin.

Heloise found herself in a new country in mind and body. Never before had she felt such deep contentment. In her previous life she had cultivated solitude amid the regulated business of Argenteuil and had never before allowed herself to be sustained by another person. Now she shared every moment with Abelard. At all times day and night she was with him. There was something of the character of a dream about their intense intimacy.

They talked, but without the demands of the schoolroom. Heloise encouraged him to speak of his childhood. She listened as if he were reciting ballads and romances of another age. Her childhood had been characterised by repetition, unadorned and constrained. She could not hear enough of his adventures with his brother on their horses, racing together across fields, going too far from home and arriving back by moonlight, exhausted, full of themselves and not rebuked by their generous parents.

They had foraged for small game and, he told her, joined others of their kind to simulate crusades – against the wild boars; or, if lucky, they would have spotted a wolf and, breeding courage between them, attempted to hunt it down.

Heloise listened as intently as she had read her favourite authors. Her life had been study. His was the world outside as he found it. She wanted Abelard to tell her how he and his friends had made a dam across a bottleneck in the river and how it had caused a small reservoir that then flooded a field; she wanted to know how they had climbed the biggest trees, what games they had played along the rivers, what gatherings there had been when the villagers would dance, beat drums and clap hands. She wanted so much to know the world that had made him, and experience pleasure and wonder that childhood could be such a thing.

When Abelard tried to return her interest in him by questioning her, she was conscientious, but there was so little to tell. Her mind had roved adventurously – but he knew that. Her daily life had been a drudge of unprotesting repetition. To give her more to say, Abelard would switch to the books she had read and the fine teachers who had helped her and then, with relief, she would deliver her opinions on the classical authors. But there was sadness, regret at a childhood unlived.

'You lived a childhood for both of us,' she said.

'And you studied the pagan authors for all of us,' he would reply. He would ask her to recite from memory and was moved as she delivered ream after ream of Virgil and Ovid, Cicero and Seneca in matchlessly spoken Latin. He would clap in appreciation and insist that her range was greater than his. Though she did not believe him, she was warmed by the flattery, by the impulse to please her.

To please each other – that was another strand in those slow, intimate days in Brittany. He would sing not his own but old Breton songs for her in a language she could not comprehend. He would encourage her to sing the songs she had written, and the two of them, in a glade on a hillside, would serenade each other undisturbed and rarely observed, aware that this was stolen time, full of gratitude for the day.

In that spell they became known in the district. People working in the fields looked out for them, as if to see them would bring luck. When they walked closely together, the country people thought they saw something remarkable – two fine and learned scholars, engrossed in each other's words, speaking, no doubt, of matters understood only by God.

She was not due for two or three months. At last he found the will to return to Paris. The sadness he felt was like a physical burden when, for the final time, they strolled around the garden in the early evening, stopping now and then to be still and close to each other and then went on, reluctantly, to the house.

A little distance from it, Heloise put pressure on his arm and he stopped. They looked directly at each other, holding but not staring. Her eyes began to brim with tears but she held them in check.

Then she took his hands in hers and placed all four hands over the womb.

'Thank you,' she said. 'Our child will have a mother and a father known to them. The child will have a family – your family – always to be there.' She paused and a few tears came. 'All those blessings of life, all that being in the lives of others, what better fortune, Peter?' She took a deep breath. 'And the child will be so deeply loved by us . . .'

She turned away, loosing their hands, and stood apart and looked at that place, that house, which to her was a paradise. 'Thank you,' she murmured, glancing at the broad sky, the clouds tinged with the sun's last colours fading slowly.

Chapter Twenty-six

'In the end I took pity on his boundless misery,' Abelard wrote, 'and went to him.'

This, for Abelard, was rare. He was a man who opposed opposition with opposition, unrelentingly. His love for Heloise had opened him to gentler emotions: he was moved by Fulbert's plight.

The decision he took in his transformed mood was to prove disastrous.

Marguerite led him to the study, knocked on the door, then fled. Abelard opened the door politely and walked towards Fulbert without arrogance. Fulbert squinted as if looking directly into the sun. Abelard, uninvited, but with a nod that sought approval, took a chair opposite Fulbert at the table. Fulbert's mouth was slightly open as if to speak, but it was Abelard who spoke first.

'I have come to beg your forgiveness,' he began, his expression matching the words. Fulbert did not react. 'I deceived you, when you had given me lodgings and hospitality for a noble purpose: the education of your remarkable niece. You had every reason to think I was a man of honour. And you also knew me, then, to be wholly chaste, as continent as any anchorite, without carnal knowledge. To me philosophy was everything.

'All of Paris knew that and so your trust in my honour was rightly buttressed by the common assumption that lust for women was nothing to me. I repeat this information, well known to you but now face to face, so that you know that I clearly understand why you were so confident when others might have been circumspect. After all, to leave a man alone with an attractive young woman, intimate, unguarded, could be thought reckless. But you thought you were well armed and I used your trust to deceive you. It was a treacherous act.'

He paused. But Fulbert said nothing so he continued steadily: 'It was doubly reckless because you should have known the very high regard, approaching worship, your ward had for scholars, most especially philosophers. Heloise fears your further anger and, as you know, she is now in Brittany. She will stay there until the child is born and weaned. When she comes back to Paris, you must do her no more harm. The scars from that beating will be with her for some time, and however faintly they remain to blemish her skin, they will be reminders of it.'

He stopped. Fulbert controlled his confusion of emotions but could not keep the bitterness from his voice. He spoke hoarsely: 'Why should I forgive you? You set out what happened as if you were instructing me, whereas you are simply telling me what I know.'

'Then I am all the happier for that,' said Abelard. 'Rumours have fanned this into scandal, much of it false. Now you know the truth as I know it, and we can proceed.'

'What of the truth as I myself know it?' said Fulbert, regaining his poise.

'Is that different?'

'I see a seducer, a man of fame taking advantage of an innocent woman and, with the power claimed by the famous and given to them by those, like my most miserable self, who are deluded by them, breaking all the laws of God and nature for nothing but bestial satisfaction.' (With my daughter. My flesh corrupted by yours!)

'Bestial satisfaction,' Abelard replied, 'need not always be wicked. It depends on the intention.' He hesitated. He wanted to apologise to Fulbert and a few clever words were not the way to do it.

Fulbert reached out for his goblet of wine but it was empty. Besides which, to drink without offering his guest refreshment would be discourteous. He reached for the bell that would summon Marguerite, hesitated, then decided against it.

Abelard took advantage. 'What I did was driven by the force of love, whose darker name is lust. We know the power of love since God created the earth and love destroyed the first woman. That is why we praise the Desert Fathers of our Church who saw the danger and abandoned all worldly temptations to be victorious in defying sinful lust. Alas, it transpires that I am not one of them.'

'Then you have failed.'

'In that regard, yes. But my goal is to be the master of logic. My ambition is to bring Aristotle's logic to our sacred books and liberate them from the constrictions that halt all new thought. For that I do not need chastity. But love, it seems, into which I entered, I confess, as a sport, has locked me in its embrace and I am glad of it, Master Fulbert. My life in love has given me . . .' He paused. Fulbert leaned forward: this hesitation in the confident mellifluousness of Abelard was more interesting than any of the sentences so far delivered. He waited.

'. . . Heloise,' Abelard said, surprised by his inability to discover an argument, only a name. Was her name a philosophy?

'You have ruined her,' said Fulbert, 'and me. And yourself.

Years of devotion ripped up to satisfy your thoughtless lechery.'

'I have come to make amends. I hope you will allow me to.'

'Words. You are made of words, Master Abelard. Just words. Words that fight each other and rub each other out and upset people. I want no more of *your* words. Only God's words matter . . .'

'Words are our world, Master Fulbert. The world will not exist without them.'

'God needed no words.' He struggled for clarity. 'These amends! What are your amends?' It was a challenge.

'I will marry her.'

The simplicity of the statement confused Abelard. Had he meant to say it when he came to see Fulbert? He had anticipated at best a truce, an accommodation, an argument. Where had that positive declaration come from?

Fulbert was astounded. 'Peter Abelard will marry my . . . ward.'

'I will.'

Fulbert longed for a drink and, surely, there would never be a better moment. He rang the bell.

Marguerite, whose ear had been pressed to the door, counted to five, knocked and entered.

Fulbert pointed at the bottle and nodded to Abelard. She went to fetch another. 'This is your word?'

'It is,' said Abelard. 'It is. Yes.' That way he would smooth her path back into Paris. That way he might regain allies in Notre-Dame. That way he could secure Fulbert's support and quench the voices of clerical disapproval. But, mostly, he realised, once the deed was done, he would never lose her.

Marguerite came back with a bottle of his finest wine and two heavy silver goblets, Fulbert noticed with approval. 'Pour.'

Marguerite did so, giving Abelard a measure to the brim. She concentrated wholly on the wine until the act was complete, then looked at Abelard with such a conspiratorial smile that he was unnerved. Fulbert all but pawed the goblet as the deep red wine made its curve from the neck of the bottle.

She placed the bottle in front of her master and then, with uncharacteristic speed of movement, left the two men together.

Fulbert raised his goblet.

'There is one condition only,' said Abelard.

Fulbert put it back on the table.

'This must be kept secret,' said Abelard, who had rapidly raked over the possible negative consequences while Marguerite was fetching the wine. 'To protect my position. For the moment.' He sensed danger. 'My enemies will use this against me. Especially William of Champeaux . . . They will impose the new rules – marriage is not to be allowed.'

'William is my friend,' said Fulbert, rather pleased to see that this checked Abelard. 'My good friend,' he reiterated smugly.

'My enemy,' said Abelard. 'He wants to be seen as the most eager to follow the new edicts from the Vatican, especially with regard to celibacy. There is no law to prevent me marrying Heloise – I am not a priest and I *will* marry her, Fulbert, I give you my oath, I swear it – but William of Champeaux would use this to say that even though I am not a priest the marriage would harm the good name of the school of Notre-Dame. He would see me as a prize not only for himself but for the Pope. He could make it very difficult for us.' He struggled.

Fulbert gave him no help.

'Of course I could go back to Melun, and the students would follow me, but I want to be here in the heart of philosophy, in Paris, to have my own house in the Cloisters, with Heloise as my wife. And you as a friend.'

And protector, Fulbert thought, regaining his confidence. The great philosopher is asking me for help!

'I give you my word,' said Fulbert, smoothly. 'No one will know of this marriage.'

'Not even your friends, especially William of Champeaux?'

'No one will know of it.' How soothing he found it to speak such a serpent sentence.

Fulbert came around the table, bearing his goblet ceremoniously.

Abelard, not free of the anxiety that had suddenly struck him, stood up as if to receive him. 'Will our secret be wholly safe?' Abelard heard the need in his voice and wished he could erase it.

'With me it will be safe. Trust Heloise's guardian, Peter.' Fulbert's battered brain felt such relief at this twist of fortune that tears came to his eyes. This could answer all the scoffers and doubters. The greatest philosopher in France to marry his daughter! What more could he have hoped for? 'I seal it with this,' he said. They touched goblets and drank.

And then he kissed Abelard with a Judas kiss: on the mouth.

Chapter Twenty-seven

'Mother will be with us tomorrow.' Anne spoke reverently.

'She has obtained dispensation,' Denise added, 'for Heloise.'

'She will stay for three days and three nights.'

'She wants to see you and the child.'

'Both.'

'Yes. Both.'

Heloise was touched by their solemnity. It brushed aside any tendency to be amused at their earnestness. Denise, Abelard's sister, had immediately welcomed her as a sister. Anne, who had been taken into the family as a child when her parents had died and was counted as a second daughter, had been equally welcoming. Yet again she felt immeasurably grateful to be included in such a family. 'Your mother honours me,' she said.

The birth had been difficult but neither had been harmed. Heloise had been overwhelmed by an immense surge of love for the child, and had concluded that, with these women on his side, nothing could go wrong. 'My son will feel honoured, too, when he is of an age to hear of this visit. You have told me enough about your mother for me to understand how much it must mean to her to come here.

The abbey would not wish its rules to be broken, however distinguished your mother is. You are in danger of making me proud!'

She could still be nervous when the subject of the family was introduced but there was the lightness in Heloise's tone and manner of speech that had been evident since her arrival at Abelard's home. She was keenly aware that she had never before been in this position. The newness of it had arrived like the unexpected sweet chord in one of Abelard's songs: just when the melody seemed set, a different chord would bring a new sensation, a unique sweetness that could touch the heart to tears. The warmth of Abelard's family played on Heloise like that chord.

She was dazzled by Anne and Denise. She saw warm-hearted, well-mannered and well-educated young women. Even though her own education was superior in scholarship she felt no primacy. Denise and Anne had skills beyond those of Heloise, in elaborate needlework and tapestry, in ordering and running a household. The three were equal in their knowledge of flowers, trees and shrubs, although the sisters knew more about the organisation of a complex garden while Heloise was expert on herbs. They sang better than she did but were amazed that she could compose. Soon they had her songs by heart and would often sing them with gusto and gaiety. Abelard's songs, which Heloise declared to be much better, interested them less. Both women were betrothed and the chance to practise motherhood with the child of Heloise and Abelard was not to be missed. Abelard's authority absolved them of any anxiety about sin or shame. Their brother would know why he was acting in this way and justify it when the time came. In such a household a philosopher could flourish even with a family, Heloise thought.

The house sprawled handsomely on land just beyond the

village of Le Pallet, near Nantes. It had been built over time from the local stone freely available in the crags that reared up a short distance away. There was a defensive wall, in need of repair, the gardens, which were cherished, and more rooms than the inhabitants – the family and half a dozen indoor servants – needed. Everything was, to Heloise's taste, pleasingly simple – the oak furniture, the tapestries woven by members of the family over generations, a few armaments of war hung beside them on the walls. There were singing birds in pretty cages all about the house and a large dovecote in the nearest garden. A mountain stream had been caught and fashioned into a pond with its own small waterfall and waterfowl.

For the first time in her life, Heloise felt at home.

'Father would have come too,' said Denise, 'but he is going through one of his bad times.'

'He never complains,' said Anne.

'The monastery to which he has retired is much further away than that of our mother.'

'He sends his regrets and says he is very taken with the boy's name.'

'Astralabe' was unusual. Heloise had explained it was from the Greek, transmitted by the Persians to the west. It was the name of an astronomical instrument used for taking the altitude of the sun or stars and for the solution of other mysteries in astronomy and navigation. 'He should never lose his way,' Abelard had said. Heloise loved its euphonious quality. Astralabe was a calm child.

When Lucia, Abelard's mother, arrived and walked across the large room to greet her, Heloise felt her back stiffen: she wished to present herself well to the older woman – as tall as she – who emanated gentle but unarguable authority.

'You are welcome, my child,' she said, and extended her arms for Heloise to take her hands.

My child! Heloise swallowed hard. Could this woman in some way become her mother? Would her own mother have looked like her, have been as warm, as calm? They stood holding hands, observed keenly by members of the household. It was as if they were all willing an indissoluble link to establish between the two there and then by the joining of the four hands.

'I am grateful to have been made so welcome.'

'I have seen the boy,' she said. 'He is healthy.'

'Was Peter – is he *like* Peter when . . .' Heloise stumbled.

Lucia smiled. 'All small babies are the same in my experience,' she said. 'God gives all His children a similar expression. They seem to come from one seed.'

She let go Heloise's hands. 'It's a warm day,' she said. 'That is unusual in these parts in this season. Shall we walk together?'

Heloise felt she was being initiated. This walk was its own ceremony of joining. And she could discover more about Abelard. They went out of the open door.

'I expect you will want to hear about Peter,' said his mother, indicating a bench, across the garden, bathed in the modest sunshine.

'I would like to know everything about Peter.'

His mother smiled and looked intently into the young woman's eyes. 'You have a very great love for him.'

'Yes.' Her throat was dry. The word came out weakly. She repeated it more firmly. 'Yes.'

'He will need that,' his mother said. As they walked, she continued, 'He seems to have found a clever and, I might say, handsome mother for his child.'

'Our child.'

Lucia laughed aloud, and Heloise joined in. The sound reached back to the house where Denise and Anne smiled at each other.

'What was he . . . ?'

Lucia had anticipated the question. 'He was like all the other boys. He rode ponies, he played at being a knight, and set up mock-battles with his brother. They used wooden poles as lances. He woke up singing. That was his most striking characteristic. He woke up singing or whistling and it always made my heart lift. And when he was still quite young he liked to make speeches to all of us.' She laughed. 'He was very serious about that. They were often fiery!'

Heloise smiled. She 'saw' the young Abelard preaching to his family, the small boy upbraiding his elders. 'I wish I'd been there to hear him.'

'His father was – he still is, though failing now – a good scholar. More a scholar than a knight-at-arms, although he did his duty. Perhaps he passed on that love of learning. It is so difficult to tell, isn't it? Peter liked me to tell him stories. He liked his tutor to set him tests so that he could pass them, and show off to the others. He was rather a boastful boy,' she said, 'but his high spirits would always excuse him. God compounds us from so many, Heloise. But when he was about twelve at the cathedral school they told us that his progress was remarkable. Soon afterwards when he was at home, he asked his father if he could renounce all his rights of inheritance and devote himself to study, in particular to philosophy.'

'So from the beginning it was philosophy.' Heloise's delight at such simple information shone in her expression and Lucia touched her hand.

'Yes. Though what he meant by it then I can't remember. I think it was the word that excited him.'

'But still,' Heloise insisted, 'he said it. And so young. What did his father say?'

'My husband was a kind man but he made Peter wait a year, then saw him again and asked if he had changed his mind. The boy said that if anything he was even more determined. So his father drew up a new legal settlement in favour of our younger son.'

'He never regretted it,' said Heloise, proudly.

'I am not so sure. When he was eighteen and came back here for a few weeks, I could see that he rediscovered a love for this place, his position in our limited but not inconsequential society. And then, later . . .'

Heloise sensed that a bridge was being crossed. She waited.

'He was very dutiful,' Lucia said. 'When his father and then I decided to retire from this world, he came from Paris to offer help and give counsel.'

'But that is not what you were about to say. Or am I presuming too much? If that is so, please forgive me.'

'You're right. Later he overworked and came here to recover his health.'

'That was after he had won so many debates,' said Heloise, keeper of the chronology of his life. 'They said he was too young to be so famous. It was envy and jealousy, not overwork.'

Lucia had not meant to tread so far, but the young woman's earnest devotion swayed her. 'Let me say this,' said Abelard's mother, carefully. 'There is, in Peter, something . . . strange? Curious? It is harder to define than is implied by either of those words. As a boy he was fearless, sometimes too fearless for his own good. His daring would risk disaster . . . But that is not it . . . Perhaps his mind becomes crammed, too busy for him to deal with – and then it cannot cope at all.' As she spoke, she looked straight ahead. To have had such a mother, Heloise thought.

'When he came back to us – and it was for three years, a long break early in a career – he was helpless. He could not bear to be alone. He could not concentrate on a book for more than a few pages. His speech stumbled and failed him. Only walking with Denise, walking for half the day among the most remote crags – but always accompanied – only that seemed to bring him relief . . .' She paused. Heloise knew that Lucia was pondering whether or not to continue.

Eventually she did. 'I have thought about it many times. I fear he had concluded that the God we worship was not the God we thought we knew. His father and I later put together fragments from his broken conversation at that time. Aristotle and Plato were pagans, who would never see God because they were born before Christ came to earth but they were his new idols. Most terrible of all, I thought – and who am I, Heloise, but a mother trying to understand the broken mind of her son – he had lost his faith. For all his jousting with authority, Peter was deeply pious and a believer, but at that time, it seemed, his belief had been eroded, then overwhelmed by the logical minds of unchristian philosophers through whose work he was making his way. He surrendered to their unbelief. And then it was as if one day he looked at himself and said, "What have I done?" He could not bear it . . .'

Lucia stopped. Heloise could see the toll this had taken of her. She composed herself and turned away.

'I now believe he thought he was going mad,' she said. She stood up. Before she took a step she said, 'Those words are for you alone.'

Chapter Twenty-eight

Abelard saw out his course of lectures. There was less than a week to go in the curriculum and, as he explained by letter to Fulbert, an abrupt termination might cause adverse comment. In that week he set out to repair his reputation, and success began to flow back to him. He promised Fulbert he would go to Brittany and return with Heloise for their marriage. Meanwhile he had to work hard, and while he did so, a schedule was planned and a discreet location found for the ceremony.

His ease in the presence of Fulbert was proof, he thought, of the rightness of his decision. It proved not just an impulse of pity that had moved him to apologise to Fulbert: he believed it was necessary. He had behaved dishonourably as a knight and sinfully as a Christian. It was hard for Abelard the young revolutionary to acknowledge such faults. Perhaps he feared, deeply, that by allowing one fault in, he would open the door to many others. But what he had done, he thought had been well done, and Fulbert's apparent contentment was more reward than he deserved. He saw no further ahead than that. He set out for Brittany with a light heart.

Heloise's pleasure at seeing him convinced Abelard that although he had given his word on marriage to Fulbert without forethought perhaps it had been divinely inspired. Had he not been preparing for it without being aware of it? He compared it to his writing. There were times when he was unable to see his way through an argument, and was ready to try a different route: as if from nowhere, out of nothing (which he knew could not be possible), the answer would appear and the argument gain shape. Heloise's glowing welcome, her open love for him assured him that the promise of marriage had been hidden, needing only the right opportunity to reveal itself.

Lucia – who had taken a final permitted leave of absence from her convent – observed their fond but formal public greeting with satisfaction. Soon, they looked into each other's eyes. Together, however informally posed, she thought they appeared distinguished and profoundly in love. It seemed that they would stand beside each other for ever. Lucia, who had known passion in her own marriage, recognised it as clearly as she could see the sun. It warmed her, as the sun warmed her with its bright beams, that her son, whom she had feared would be for ever alone, was now so plainly in love. They were utterly absorbed in each other, true lovers, and it moved her deeply.

Lucia's pleasure grew when she saw the eagerness with which Abelard took up his son. He was a little awkward in holding the child but so resolute, she thought, in his love and possession. Watching Heloise beside him, Lucia's confidence in their future deepened. There would be a marriage and she hoped it could proceed from her home. Heloise was his equal, she thought, and what could be better for him? Only reluctantly did he hand Astralabe to the nurse.

Then he and Heloise strolled in the garden close to each other, talking seemingly without pause, as if they were continuing a previous conversation. Lucia found it difficult to decipher who was the teacher, who the pupil. The tall, statuesque young woman had a remarkable degree of self-confidence. She smiled to herself. Her son would not, she thought, have all his own way with Heloise.

Over the days, when not with Astralabe, they resumed their intimate, perambulating conversations of the summer. Abelard neither mentioned nor alluded to marriage. He told himself he did not want to disrupt what had become such a tranquil time, that he did not want the inevitable fuss and planning of the family to unbalance matters. His love for Heloise and hers for him were, he thought, so complete between them that the longer they could stay out of the public realm of marriage, even within the family, the longer they would, in retrospect, savour the days spent together as permitted lovers. In truth he was nervous. Heloise had mentioned marriage only twice in all their time together and then to condemn it.

When the day came for Lucia to return to her abbey, Abelard took it as the cue for himself and Heloise to set off for Paris. He said it was essential that just the two of them would go. Astralabe would remain at Le Pallet. Heloise agreed with fortitude. She and her child would be parted for only a short time, and this helped her to accept it. Denise and Anne were so eager to help Heloise and Abelard, and their love for her child was so strong, that Heloise gave in despite her reluctance. Anne held the child high as the little party set off for France.

Heloise spoke little. She found the wrench from her son difficult to absorb. Silent voices in her mind called, 'Turn back! Do not leave him!' He was motherless now. How could she endure that? But Abelard said there was an important reason. He swore that she would soon be reunited with Astrolabe.

She trusted him.

+——+

Heloise's destination was her uncle's house. Fulbert, Abelard assured her, had forgiven everything. The two men had prayed together. All would be well, he declared, though Heloise was not convinced of that. Abelard had arranged that on the night before their entry into Paris they would stay at a tavern just a few miles from the Île de la Cité. They had separate rooms. He went to her after their evening meal. He had rehearsed. He had concluded that there was but one way to do this.

'I wish to marry you,' he said. He had entered after the briefest knock on the door. 'Will you marry me?'

Her expression changed, paled, grew tense. Then, in a quiet voice, she said, 'No, Peter. No. I will not.'

It was the first time that Heloise had directly opposed him. She had put forward her own views in their interrupted lessons and was unafraid to express them. But this, he recognised, was of a different order, in tone and in determination.

It would be a battle! He smiled at her, the smile that had always provoked a smile in return. But Heloise shook her head. Her lips were drawn tight.

She was tired. He had been too abrupt. It was too much of a *command*. He had reverted to his former self – the master, he thought. He had to be gentler. He decided that he would pursue it the next day.

Heloise's reply had been spontaneous and emphatic. Yet, as she reconsidered it in the comforting dark, she was certain she would never change her mind. Marriage was not for them.

Abelard, lazily confident, was rather pleased that she had rejected him. It set up an argument. Even in this matter, he thought, Heloise, supreme, never disappointed him.

Chapter Twenty-nine

The next morning he went to her room and apologised for startling her with such an announcement when she must have been distracted, unable to turn her mind from Astralabe. She said nothing but a gesture forgave him. It released him to give the explanation he thought she was owed.

'I realised how badly I had behaved and what unhappiness I had brought to your uncle.' As if he were laying it out in a lecture, he unfolded the argument to Heloise from the beginning. 'I went to see him, to confess my sins and apologise for the deceits I had practised on him, the humiliation and hurt I had caused him. I took all the sin on myself, even though I knew that you would surely claim equality in it. I wanted to win him over to our cause, Heloise.' Again he smiled; again there was no response. This time he braced himself.

'I did your uncle a great wrong, Heloise. I admit it now, though I was blind to it then. That does not excuse the great wrong he did to your person with the beating. But the greater wrong was done to him and by me. Whatever your feelings were for me, I was your master, his guest at his table. For your sake I should have restrained myself – God knows I had had years of practice – or left the house and observed the correct stages of the protocols of marriage.

'I was obsessed by you, then swept away by our love. And there was my gross vanity, the fame that came to me from my book on dialectics – how poor a thing it seems compared to what binds us now. But I was a spoilt pup. So I threw off all the disciplines of my past life as if they had been chains of straw and acted as if I were owed a reward for my good behaviour and achievements. What hubris! I sought a liaison. But lust turned to love, and I discovered that love has a unique force. It has changed my life.' Her severe silence unnerved him.

'I thought marriage would appease him, which it did. But then I realised I wanted it too. For us, not for him. Even though it must be kept secret.'

'Why secret? Why must it be kept secret?'

Abelard was not sure of himself. He tugged his hair nervously: Heloise appeared to become immobile with calm.

'It would be better for . . . It would— This new world of the Church is harsh, unlike former times. So . . . I thought it would be more appropriate for me at least.' As he said the words he felt a hollowness in his tone.

'And for me?'

'You would be married.'

'I do not want to be married.'

'But it must be,' Abelard said. 'Even though I am not a priest, I am a master of Notre-Dame. Our open married state would be enough to banish me from my position and from Paris. If we marry in secret and go about our lives it would be too late for them to act. And I am afraid for you, *un*married, of the revenge of Fulbert and his friends.'

'Paris is where you must stay,' said Heloise, with emphasis. 'You must be at the centre of learning.'

'So we must marry,' he said.

'In secret?'

'You understand?' He knew the flimsiness of his case. 'As my wife you will be—'

'It will be discovered within days.' She was firm. 'There will be rumours. No one can keep a wedding a secret in Paris and still call it a wedding. First, rumour, then enquiries by your jealous enemies – and you have made many. This would be their chance. They would swiftly uncover us. Our deceit will be held against us more than the marriage. And it will not be possible to deny it. Disgrace will follow.'

His mouth was dry: she was right. But how could he agree with her?

'And so your enemies would triumph just when you have beaten them off. You would be forced out of Paris – we would be forced out of Paris – and you would go back to being the wandering scholar, which was how you started long ago. That youthful time is past for you, my dear Peter. You wish to plant roots in the capital of learning. Your work is growing richer by the year – you are set for immortality. You cannot jeopardise that.'

'Is the proper satisfaction of your uncle not of value?'

'After what we have done, my uncle will never be satisfied. He will take your offer as a staunch, but that wound will never be healed, save by the death of one or both of us. This marriage will appear to my uncle as the merest gesture.'

'To me it is everything.'

'You are speaking from impulse, Peter, not from thought, and that is because you wish to protect yourself and also, I thank you, to give me what you think of as status. You will not protect yourself by marriage. And you will give to me no status I seek. I do not want to be called a wife. I will not be an impediment to your philosophy. You have apologised to him for what you call a deceit and that must be the end of it.'

'I want you to have honour.'

161

'What honour would a furtive marriage bring either of us? Our lovemaking needed no marriage when it began and nor does it now. Marriage could likely make it a duty and kill it.'

'I command you, Heloise,' he said. 'We must marry.'

'I cannot obey a command that will do you harm.'

'You must obey me.'

'I will not . . .'

She looked at him directly. It was Abelard who gave way and dropped his gaze.

'I will be blamed by the whole world,' she said evenly, 'for taking you into a marriage that would surely give you less time to be the philosopher all of us want you to be. Think of the scorn of other philosophers if you were to choose me above philosophy itself! Marriage would be a burden. And I would be branded for my weakness in accepting you as much as you for your weakness in wanting this fig leaf. Your reputation would be broken . . .'

Abelard sat still as a hare that sees or senses a huntsman. But the hare dashes away. Abelard was transfixed. What if there was truth in this?

She was relentless. 'St Paul says, "Do not seek a wife. Those who marry will have pain and grief in this bodily life . . ."'

'I do not agree with St Paul,' Abelard said, as forcefully as he could. 'Paul drew all his authority from the scriptures. I have logic, which tells me our marriage could flourish. We could discuss all manner of things day and night.'

'We do that now.'

'But more intimately.'

'It is impossible to be more intimate than we are now.'

'Jesus's first miracle was at a marriage feast.'

'But most of the sages, the philosophers, the prophets and the Fathers, have warned against it.' She would not be unhorsed by such a feeble example. 'Look at St Jerome,' she went on. 'In his first book, *Against Jovinian*, he writes that Theophrastes set out the unbearable annoyances of marriage. He argues that a philosopher should not marry and quotes from many philosophers in his support. And in the same book he quotes from Cicero, who divorced his wife and declared that he could "not devote his life to a wife and philosophy alike". Nor could you, Peter. Nor would I ever be forgiven if I allowed you to do that.'

'In the small time you have been as a wife I have prospered.'

'"As a wife" is not a wife. And you have not prospered! Only when I am away from you. Even then, until I became with child, you told me that your pupils were angry with you for your lack of attention and your references to love. They threatened to desert you. And think of what a sustained marriage would bring. It is marriage, not our union, that will be the curse. Think of the clashes between desks and cradles. How could you endure it, Peter? And the disorder, the dirt. The rich can do it because they have large houses and can pay servants to provide the services of child-rearing. Philosophers are not rich men. Neither do they aspire to be. The material world should be of little importance to them: it is mundane, without distinction. Even though,' she smiled, 'you sometimes enjoy the benefits of your rank. But you and the other best philosophers among the ancients have escaped from the intrusive compulsion of wealth-making and worldly business to devote all your strength to finding your pleasure and fulfilment in the study of philosophy. Seneca—'

'You often turn Seneca against me,' Abelard said, smiling, trying to find firm ground on which to counter her characteristic but exceptionally passionate deployment of her learning.

'Don't be jealous of him. I love Seneca. And he gave this

advice to Lucretius. Listen, Peter, he is talking directly to you. "Philosophy is not a subject for idle moments. We must neglect everything else and concentrate on this, for no time is long enough for it." Listen hard here. "Put it aside for a moment and you might as well give it up." I have no need to offer you more examples of men who were sages, monks or philosophers and their chosen way of life, which marked them out as singular. You know this. In my fear I am telling the master much that this pupil has learned from him but I cannot stop myself. If being a teacher at Notre-Dame is not enough to deter you, uphold the dignity of the philosopher. Some will think you have shamed your God, but do not shame your mind. And do not shame me. I will be your friend, your *amica*, for ever, but not your wife. *Amica* is the dearest word to me.'

He reached out to her. He had a sudden violent desire to make love. What else would answer? What else mattered?

But she stood up and walked to the door. 'I must go out,' she said. 'Please let me go alone. But, Peter, please – listen to me.'

He was desolate. She had never before turned away from him.

She hurried out of the tavern, and only when she had made some distance did she stop. She was just inside a wood. She succeeded in not sobbing. But she would not pray. This matter was between her lover and herself. She saw no place for God.

Chapter Thirty

Abelard had sat in a silent state of longing and apprehension. When eventually she came back, he attempted to be jocular.

'You had most of the best quotations at your command,' he said. 'But I was sorry you did not spend some time on Pythagoras, and very surprised that, in fairness, you omitted Xanthippe, the wife of Socrates.'

'She threw a pail of urine over his head.'

'Some say it was water. And perhaps such an act is included in the rights of marriage.'

'I would never do that.'

'She might have had a good reason.'

'Socrates was a philosopher.'

'That might be the reason. Sometimes even a philosopher needs a dousing.'

'Please, Peter. Let me be serious.'

He nodded but smiled, which saddened her. He thought he had done the best for her. If they made love now, then somehow for Peter they would be on the path to a resolution. Their loving still consumed him as it could her. But there were other powers in the room. For Heloise, there was the terrible pain of Astralabe's absence. More than anything at that moment she wanted to hold him. For Peter there was the necessity of a decision about the future of his work.

'You seem oblivious to the risk you are taking by returning me to Paris,' she began. 'What you did to me by taking my virginity while I was in your care will be regarded by your enemies as a crime, and my return will strengthen their antagonism. And my uncle . . . I do not trust him or his friends, or anyone who might come to any ceremony. I suspect his kiss. But I also suspect you have already planned this marriage. Then we will be pursued, or at the very least marked out, and your title as a master will be in peril . . .'

'No more of that! I can deal with it all.' His bluster did not convince her.

She heard fear in his voice and remembered what his mother had told her about the collapse of his mind. Perhaps he was spiralling into that morass once again.

'Why should I be a "wife"? I do not want it. It will not comfort me. I do not want to love because marriage makes me love. Or to love with you because it is your due from your wife: that is prostitution. I do not want the chains that are hung around a wife and husband. We have lived freely, Peter. Please let us keep doing that. Let us be free like true lovers should be. I will be your friend, your *amica* – a much happier, sweeter title than "wife" – bound to you only by love.' She saw the glaze of obstinacy in his eyes and her tone became urgent.

'If we do not marry and must part for a while, when we meet again our love will be all the more precious. Please? If you went to lecture around France I should wait for you not as a dutiful wife but as a faithful friend, wishing only that what you do is appreciated for what it is. I would have Astrolabe to cherish and see you in him every day. You have enemies, Peter. I am always your friend.' She was growing more desperate. She could see prison walls closing on her.

'To have such a friend. Does that mean nothing to you? Please?

'This word, "wife", let it go, let us bury it here before we reach Paris. For me now it would be a punishment. Oh, please, let us be friends, Peter. That is a noble and honourable state. Marriage will destroy us. You cannot see it. You, who see so much, cannot see this. I do not want it, my love. Is that not enough for you? It would do you no honour and I know I will lose you. Have I asked anything of you? Let this be my sole request.' Still she saw no yielding. Her voice rose.

'I tell you, Peter, if Augustus, emperor of the whole world, thought fit to honour me with marriage and conferred all the earth on me to possess for ever, it would be dearer and more honourable to me to be called not his empress but your whore!' She waited for a response. In vain. He was not moved. He stood absolutely still. She remembered what his mother had told her. It flashed into her mind that to save him she would have to make a sacrifice.

'I beg you,' she whispered. But even those words accompanied by an involuntary gesture – arms forward, palms upward, a supplicant – were met with no response.

It was over.

Her pity for him moved her where argument and appeals to love had failed. His need overcame hers. He was incapable of saving himself. She gathered up all her strength and said, 'We shall both be destroyed by this, Peter. All that is left us is suffering as great as our love has been.'

The marriage had a funereal air. In the small church of Saint-Julien-le-Pauvre, just across the Seine from the Cloisters of Notre-Dame, they kept vigil for six hours through the night and left before dawn. The small congregation solemnly swore secrecy. There was no joy. Heloise was escorted back to Fulbert's house. Abelard went up the hill to his lodging. As they parted she did not look at him.

For some weeks the secrecy was maintained. Abelard and Heloise were like ghosts of themselves. Though married, their meetings were fewer and more fearful than they had been before entering the state of matrimony. Now married, they behaved like surreptitious lovers. When they embraced it seemed to be in memory rather than in the present. When they found the time and place to make love, the act was drained of much of its former urgency. The secret marriage seemed to freeze them.

But their thoughts of each other floated through the air from the Montagne Saint-Geneviève, across the river and into the Fulbert house, then wound back again. The complications and excitement of intrigue had fallen away but so had the energy. Sadly weaving their story in the indifferent heart of Paris, waiting on events, they were bound together, yet rarely together in their open prison.

Heloise waited in expectation of an ending. Abelard bent all his will to the teaching of his new work on the dialectics, already applauded for a brilliance it was agreed far outshone the work of his former master, William of Champeaux. It was being compared, favourably, with the defining work of the immortal Boethius. Who, he thought, could want more? Yet the success gave him little satisfaction.

Heloise again, but sadly now, heard the exuberant chatter of the students as they came out of Abelard's lectures, excited by his ideas, eager for all that life could give them: free.

Chapter Thirty-one

'Why does it have to be such a tangle? Why did he have to marry her? Then why did he insist on keeping it secret?'

'I've given my explanation in what you've just read.' Her grilling could become galling.

'I'm not sure how much you've made up.'

'All of it is in the *Letters*. They are the key source, but there are gaps.'

'What happens then? When you fill in the gaps. How do you attempt to find out the truth about them?'

'It has to be imagined.'

'And you think that can get at the truth.'

'I do. Imagination is the undiscovered physics in the minds of all of us.' He laughed. 'What do you make of that?'

'Go on.' They were in the flat in the late afternoon. 'There's time.'

'Are you sure?' He paused. 'Okay.' He topped up their glasses. 'For what it's worth I've tried to work this out for myself. I believe that imagination is the least known but most powerful part of the brain. When it was activated I think it marked our essential difference from the great apes. We began to be able to work out what might happen in the abstract – what if? What if we used those large round stones to move the heaviest weights . . . say with tree trunks laid across them? Then what if we used fire instead of running away from it as other mammals did? Our species became engaged in using imagination for inventions and we went on from the wheel until now. World domination.

'Imagination is faster than the speed of light: we're told that our brain has more movements than there are atoms in the universe. People talk about language being the initial drive to *Homo sapiens* – but birds have language. Chimpanzees, whales and dolphins have language. It's everywhere. We gained language as the others did – as Shakespeare said, out of "the air, the thin air" and "gave it a local habitation and a name". By breathing in and speaking out. But at some stage our language became a unique complex of words and we use them to an extent immeasurably beyond that of any other species. Perhaps that comes from some chemistry of curiosity we have. An itch to add to all forms of knowledge. Maybe to appease a hidden god of imagination squatting inside our minds.

'Einstein said that imagination was the greatest gift of all. We are just at the beginning of understanding it. There are regions in the brain, like dark brain planets, about which we know nothing – more than a hundred of them – and within those regions there will be many sub-divisions. You, sitting there with your coffee, are perhaps thinking or imagining what you will do later today, remembering what you did yesterday, what the news implies . . . what made that man you were with so suddenly unattractive. James Joyce tried to capture it and that's just the tip of the brainberg and the thousands of nerves. Who can count the thousands of comets and fragments and stars and, similarly, who can count an hour's sensations and thoughts nudging consciousness?

'So I think about what I know of Abelard and Heloise,

Marguerite and Fulbert, and try my best to summon up authentic feelings, and conversations I find nothing about in any records. It's a cliché but it contains a truth to call it creativity. It used to be thought of as some sort of magic. But it's all over the place. Technology is its favourite child at the moment. The magic of one century becomes the commonplace of the next. But the even more extraordinary fact here is that all of us are in this "ocean of unknowing" together – this is not a zone reserved for experts. If it were, how could discoveries of any kind in any medium transfer from one mind to another, which they do every day?

'We all make it up. You and I make up and remake our lives and reorder our memories all the time. As do thousands of artists, scientists, artisans, labourers, idlers, gardeners, song-writers, engineers, shop assistants, biologists, physicists, *everyone*. Every moment we are looting the past, putting together the present, then projecting it into an unknown future. It's being alive. One stride and we're in a different world. And now the internet, the iPhone, artificial intelligence, robots are taking us further and further out of ourselves. We are giving what were thought of as essential bits of us to machines. Less us, more them. Soon the question will be, what is a person?

'Yet we eat, we drink, we starve, we fight, we bleed, all that in ways Abelard and Heloise's world would recognise. We are stratified. We contain multitudes. And this is just the start of it. For I think that what is happening today is not unlike the radical alteration in our place on the planet, which began about seventy thousand years ago. When we parted company with the great apes. And then when the Industrial Revolution came it made muscle redundant and changed the idea of space and mass, of time and energy, and set us on a course that may now be reeling out of control.

'Your generation, Julia, will be borne along by this Silicon Valley newness, and I envy what you will be able to know. Fasten your seatbelt. Imagination is where we are all equal, private, connected and free. Whoever learns to control it could become as powerful as God or gravity. Meanwhile, I find the past just as fathomless and majestic as the future.' He raised his wine. 'Let us now depart in peace.'

'Is that one of your lectures?'

'Yes and no.'

She shook her head. 'I loved it,' she said. 'Did you teach like that?'

'No, this is part of what I do in the vacations. But in the last few years I've hooked up with a rather ambitious book club. The members are all local and I enjoy their company. Each of us gives a talk now and then. That was my amateur effort. In that unpretentious and uncynical company, I found it easier to air ideas that matter to me, even though I'm no expert on them. A sort of amateurs' night with nothing on the line. I enjoyed doing it. And it gave us something to discuss when we went for a drink afterwards. I've made a couple of friends there over the years. It's always nice to be with nice people – my mother used to say that.'

With an instant leap of imagination, Julia suddenly saw her father's loneliness, his sparse life. So that was who he was. Her silence invited one last comment.

'If I could come back in five hundred years,' he said, 'apart from wanting to see if there were any traces of us around, I'd want to know if they'd cracked imagination. That would be something to know. Don't you agree?'

'Why? What does it give you as a writer?'

'For some reason it gives me satisfaction I get from nothing else. I see these imagined people and I hear them. That's strange, quietly exhilarating, and the voices you hear may reach others – a silent, secret conversation. Or,' he shrugged, earthed himself and threw off any solemnity, 'you could say it passes the time. Like so much else we do for no material purpose. But, then, who knows what will turn up out of self-indulgence?'

'It's rather like lying, isn't it?'

'Lying's okay,' he said, 'if nobody gets hurt. Most artists lie.'

She nodded rather warily. She had to step away from this. There was a sudden sadness in his voice, which upset her. He needed her interest.

'Why did he not just brazen it out? Why not just live with her as a friend? She kept saying she wanted most of all to be his *amica*. What stopped him?'

'I think he was afraid of the revenge that Fulbert could deliver. Fulbert was connected with a family who would not have been pleased to be disgraced by a lecturer, even if his name was Abelard. We are in the age of the blood feud – in some parts it was often the only law there was. An eye for an eye. And there was fear. I think Abelard masked it but sometimes it escaped his control.

'Most of all, I think, he had convinced himself that he was right. Abelard's life was devoted to solving problems. Once they were solved, there could be no further argument as far as he was concerned. He thought he had solved the problem of Fulbert, Heloise, himself, Astrolabe, their future – all done! So Heloise's opposition could make no impact. He had made up his mind and it could not be unmade. Perhaps a sort of madness took over. You could say that his obsession with the truth of logic met its limitation.'

'How do you know?'

'Because it makes sense of him. He wanted to be master of all he undertook. He had to be in control, I think. It's not unusual with highly ambitious people in all walks of life but it's a question of degree. In Abelard's case, it was absolute – he was a chronic controller. And we must never forget the strain of the colossal task he had set himself.'

'And Heloise?'

'She loved him, Julia. Without reserve. There would never be any lessening in her intensity. But, if this is possible, she loved the philosopher as much as the man, perhaps even more. She thought that everything should be sacrificed to preserving the philosopher. That is why the two of them magnetised attention for centuries. She loved him through his philosophy with a formidably obstinate and sexual passion. You could call it alarming. But I don't think it's entirely unusual. People *have* died for love. People have shackled their lives to unrequited love. They have burned out their lives in unsuitable love, risked everything for it, found it and been unable to cope with it, needed it and wasted a life for the lack of it. Heloise's love was, you may say, impossible and magnificent, both. She even took on the God of the Middle Ages and blasted Him for denying her this love. She loved Abelard to death, after death and to the furthest reaches of her heart. She was even willing to put her soul in peril.'

'And he used her.'

'No. No! I want to prove that claim to be false. He loved her more than he had ever or would ever love anyone else.'

'But he made her lead that terrible life after they married. Locked away with her uncle, as she thought he was, and cut off from her child. What future did he offer her?'

'I think he hadn't any idea. There are those whose minds are so intense that the outside world commands little of their attention. A quick decision has to do. His way was to try to act decisively, then to repair any damage afterwards. In his work, he would spend months in solitary study to test a handful of propositions. So I agree – he didn't take care of her in the ways he could have done.'

'You say he feared he would have been expelled from his job if he'd gone public. Is that true?'

'He was certainly convinced of that. I'm not so sure. He was loved in the lecture hall. Had he publicly declared the marriage he might just have got away with it. The Church's high moral gates were closing but he might have squeezed through. What Abelard had was a reputation that was key in maintaining the scholarly eminence of Paris and had a great value. It was Abelard above all who drew the flocks of students into Paris. And Paris wanted them. I think he had no idea of his power. He was utterly pathetic at any sort of politics so he ducked a confrontation he could have won.'

'Does that make him a coward?'

'No . . . an ostrich.'

'If he ignored it, it would have a happy ending.'

'Something like that. But which of us could not lead a better life if we got a second bite at it? Or, of course, make an even bigger mess.'

'Did you make a mess of it?'

'I think I did.'

'With Mum?'

'Yes. But we live in the moment and sometimes it's the moment that seizes us by the throat. We're told that a small fall of snow can start a great avalanche. Your mother and I had bad moments.'

'Is that why Abelard attracts you?'

'No. He attracts me for other reasons. It was Heloise who drew me into this. It was the – how can I put it? – unbearable constancy and force of her love that made me want to write this. To try to understand the feeling she had. How she held on to it. How she found the strength.'

Are you talking about yourself as well as her? Julia left the thought unspoken. Out of a past she had feared buried, and which she had been hoping to open up, her father was coming alive to her.

Chapter Thirty-two

'Iam not married,' said Heloise to Marguerite, who simpered with pleasure at the pain her words had given her haughty mistress.

'But they all say so.'

'Who? Who?'

'People. At the market. Along the Seine. They say that you and Master Abelard were married at Saint-Julien . . .'

'We were not married!' Heloise rarely raised her voice to such a pitch as she did for this lie. Had they not all sworn themselves to secrecy? It was a further twist of the knife to remember that she had predicted this. But she would not break her vow of silence.

'I am only warning you,' Marguerite said relentlessly. 'I am trying to be a friend.'

'You are no friend, Marguerite. Nor will you ever be. I do not need and will not heed your warnings.'

'And they say you still meet. In dark places.' Marguerite relished that last phrase and gave it a guttural suggestiveness. She had Heloise by the tail. It was, Marguerite thought, a blessing from God to feel superior to her. She had never anticipated that it would give her such satisfaction.

'Leave me.'

'You're no better than I am,' said Marguerite, as she left.

But she spoke only to herself. Caution was too branded into her to be thrown away carelessly.

Fulbert was her next unwanted visitor. 'Who spread this news?'

'This rumour,' said Heloise, locked into the oath they had all sworn.

'William of Champeaux challenged me with it in the Cloisters this morning.'

'He is Peter's enemy.'

'He is a man of authority and distinction. You do not appear to realise how your actions dishonour me. The deceits, the flight to Brittany, the child – and now this talk of a secret marriage.'

'But,' Heloise needed courage, 'you agreed to the marriage. You were present. You swore an oath to secrecy in Saint-Julien. So did the others.'

'It could never be kept. These rumours prove that. I was blinded by my concern for you.' His face was tense with fury. 'Abelard has twisted everything. Now we are impossibly placed. We are accused of deceit. You have ruined yourself once again,' he was close to her, 'and you are ruining me. Harlot!' He slapped her across the face. She stood her ground, held his eyes for a moment, then turned away.

'You must stop denying this marriage,' he said.

'On my oath I was not married.'

'I too swore that oath.' He whispered the confession. 'But God will forgive me.'

He waited for a reply. 'How dare you not speak to me?' Fulbert took her by the shoulder, pulled her round and, where the marks of his rings still showed, he landed another, even harder blow, which made her stagger. 'That is for the bastard you left behind in Brittany,' he shouted as he swept out of the room.

She locked the door and lay on her bed. If she closed her eyes tightly and sank into the dark, she could see her son in the arms of Abelard's sister. She saw him smiling and smiled painfully, as if returning it. Her right hand went across her stomach to where the child had been. Perhaps it would be a fine day in Brittany and the boy would be outside and happy. When would she see him again? Would she ever see him again?

* * *

Abelard saw the bruises when next they met. His stomach watered to fear when she told him what had happened. He produced an instant resolution. He would meet her the next morning and by boat they would travel downriver to Argenteuil where she would be guaranteed refuge, although he said they would not describe it so dramatically. Once again he would bring a nun's habit. She objected but he would accept no demur. Save for the veil. He relented over the veil.

So, once again, they fled from the Île de la Cité as if they were thieves, hunted people rather than recently married, widely fêted for their learning and ornaments to France. Once again, Abelard seized on an instant answer. Later he blamed himself for allowing the crucial suspicion to be unleashed that he had deliberately taken Heloise to Argenteuil in order to abandon her.

But as they sailed downstream, there was no hint of that. These were moments of amity and quiet companionship, talking without touching, while the four other passengers and the crew were content to be about their business. A master – it was Master Abelard! – and his pupil, speaking sometimes in Latin, the sacred language, the sound of scholarship, quietly going with the stream, not knowing it was the last journey they would ever take together, the last time they would quietly talk to each other, the beginning of the long ending, the end of that inflamed beginning.

It was a matter for Fulbert's kinsmen to decide on. He would not want and could not be seen to act alone. Responsibility had to be shared and dissolved into unassailable numbers. But first he summoned his friend, Abelard's relentless opponent.

'This time there can be no mercy,' said William of Champeaux, who had responded immediately to Fulbert's request. His reciprocal request was that they meet alone before others were admitted. 'He has tricked you as he tricked you before,' said William, his ascetic features stripped to the bone by excessive fasting and self-denial. 'His life is founded on trickery. He has not the depth of intellect to study the authorities in the way recommended by the prophets and the Fathers. He pulls out tricks from the pagans to trip up the Word of God with low wit. His pupils neglect true scholarship for what they think is cleverness.

'And with your niece it is the same. He tricked and deceived you. He abused and assaulted her. He ran away to Brittany when the consequences were becoming obvious, and now he has tricked you into believing a secret marriage will solve all problems. Why secret? Why marriage? And now it seems he will make her a nun. She was seen on the boat in a nun's habit. I want you to swear an oath that this time the punishment will be in blood. He has taken her to spite you, to silence her for ever and to free himself for more malpractice. We cannot let him go unpunished and it must be savage. We need to make a public example of him.'

Fulbert, infused with gratitude and a re-stoked fury, rang for Marguerite to show in his kinsmen. William of Champeaux would be obeyed.

In their dreams and half-awake memories they knew each other again. There were three nights after the transport of Heloise to safety. Three nights in which Abelard slept fitfully in Paris lodgings, disturbed but more often willing himself to stay awake and revisit the times of their earliest passion. He recalled that he had once thought it would be a brief dalliance supplemented by letters and continuing more in words than in fornication. But the words had been in scalding letters that had fired their lovemaking, which had become a passion far beyond any expectation.

Now, in the safety of his bolted room, the last candle snuffed out, the smell of the tallow still in the air, the streets quieter than the countryside, yet again he dreamed of her. He saw her fully clothed and naked, he saw her reaching for him and urging him to take her, he saw in the darkness flesh, his, hers, and felt the clasp of her arms.

Then this half-dream, half-memory would melt into shapes and sounds not so well defined. She was his night and day. It would be as if he and Heloise were entwined in eternity, one light from two flames mingling, the darkness banished. And all would be well. The agitation around the marriage would fall away. What they had would survive. In solitude he resurrected the truth of what most mattered. He remembered words he had written and heard words she had said as, together, they sealed this unbreakable, eternal union.

+ ─+

And Heloise? She lay on her narrow bed in Argenteuil, hands by her sides, refusing to clasp them in prayer, her thoughts winding through the night sky along the Seine into Paris, into the mind of Peter Abelard. She smiled to herself in her dark, unlit room, and reflected on what endless incomparable pleasures they would have, her unpicking his knowledge, him finding the fathoms of her devotion and desire. Surely there would come a time when Abelard would be all hers, she all his, and Astralabe would join them. Let her not doubt it this night. Let her fretting fall away. There was in Peter and herself not a divine spark – they did not need that – but such splicing of spirits as would give them the blessing of eternal happiness.

It would be kept between them and shared between them, with no one else. They would call up all they knew, they would draw out all that love offered, they would twine together in scholarship and friendship, and their world would be like no other. And they would live together in the peace of love without end.

Chapter Thirty-three

Ralph encouraged him to have more wine than usual and into the final goblet he slipped soporific powder. He waited until he was sure that Abelard was fast asleep, then waited a little longer.

They came in soon after he had left the room. Four of them, bearing candles. Two to hold him down on the bed and bandage his mouth with a gag. The other two to perform the operation.

The surgeon found the testicles, pulled them towards him and slid a noose of catgut around the top, which he tightened until the flesh disappeared inside the encirclement. His apprentice held the candle in one hand, and in the other a large wooden bowl for the blood. One fierce snap of clippers as used on young bulls and the castration was done. The testicles fell into the bowl followed by a spouting of blood. The wound was swabbed with alcohol-saturated linen. The veins pumping out the blood needed to be stitched up. The surgeon staunched the flow, which threatened to over-brim the bowl.

Initially Abelard had struggled, gagged sounds coming through the bandaged mouth, his legs rising to protect himself but instantly clamped down by the hirelings. The room stank of alcohol and urine. The surgeon observed the bleeding closely and appealed for fresh swabs, more alcohol, then smeared a paste, his own recipe, on the wound.

Abelard made himself lie still. His breathing was now almost regular. He was to say much later that it had scarcely hurt as he was so deeply asleep. There was within him the code and honour of a nobleman. A nobleman did not admit to physical pain. He dealt with it by referring to it lightly or not at all.

When he was sure he was alone he opened his eyes to the future. It was a just punishment. God had wounded him where he had sinned. But how would Heloise react?

And how was he to live with the shame of it?

Ralph finally responded to Abelard's call. He had lain awake throughout the night, deliberating. Should he flee with the fat purse and take the earliest boat upriver to his home village and be safe, or at least safe enough to consider his next move? But flight would be proof of guilt. The boatman would surely know him – Peter Abelard's servant – and just as surely report him when the outrage was discovered. If he stayed in Paris – a new Paris with his fat purse, a Paris at last open to all his appetites – it would be less suspicious or, if he were clever, it need not be suspicious at all.

The hirelings had made a fair job of tying Ralph up and gagging him. He would claim that he had been silenced and managed to slip out of his bonds only after hours of struggle . . . Gradually as the darkness thinned, he grew comfortable with his plan and even grabbed a snap of sleep before he heard Abelard's call.

And then! Ralph thought he excelled himself. He ran down the stairs, shook the boy awake and sent him for Monsieur Floriot, one of whose trades was medicine, then raced down the hill to the Cloisters and aroused to high excitement the drowsy early birds with cries of 'Master Abelard is dying! Master Abelard lies in a bed of blood! You must save him! Help me! Help me!'

And up the hill they went after the galloping servant, now in a state of frothing self-confidence.

The students rushed up the stairs in such numbers that they soon became glutted. The fortunate ones who had led the charge gathered around the bed with wailings and lamentations that would not have disgraced the mourning over a martyr.

They wept; they cried out for revenge; they vied with each other in their love of their master; they competed with ideas for the most barbaric vengeance. They were young students under the spell of the man, madly excited to be present at such an event, the wound both humanising and sanctifying him. To see their master so stripped of manhood, his body so violently desecrated, gave them the opportunity to express most fully an already besotted devotion. There was no measure to the depth of their feelings now released onto the street and taken up by a gathering morning crowd.

Abelard longed to silence all of them. Every adoring lamentation was a spear of humiliation. Pity was a lash. Voices raised to the heavens gave his shame wider currency. Abelard had been castrated! Like an animal in a slaughter-house or in a field or in a pen. Let him be!

'The doctor must get through!'

The students made way clumsily for Monsieur Floriot, who demanded that 'everyone except the loyal servant, Ralph, and you and you' – he pointed to four students – 'leave the room. Master Abelard needs air.' They did as he commanded.

The doctor changed the crude dressing with care but he

still could not help causing jabs of pain, which Abelard forced himself to ignore. His mind which, when he was surrounded by the baying of his students, had threatened to implode, reassumed its disciplined character whenever physical pain set in.

But terrible thoughts tumbled down in an avalanche of dread. What if his voice rose in its register, became thinner, a squeak, this admired rich voice of his with its Breton twang and its melody in every sentence? Where would his lectures be then? Could he ever again sing his songs? He wished the doctor away so that he could speak aloud and hear if the instrument was already showing damage.

And how could his reputation sustain such a blow? 'Abelard? Isn't he the man who is no longer a man? Where are his love songs now? Who can believe them? What authority is there in logic piped by a eunuch?'

And Fulbert! How God had blessed Fulbert. To exact his vengeance on the part of the body that had brought him such humiliation. A perfect response. And how Fulbert and his kinsmen must be laughing. They had struck down their despoiler by depriving him of that which had ruined their prize.

How would his parents and sister react? How could they bear the jibes, which would certainly be worse in the wilds of Brittany than in Paris where so much happened that dramas were soon forgotten. When would Astrolabe be told? Years on, perhaps, but what humiliation lay in wait for the boy.

It would no longer be 'There goes Abelard the philosopher' but 'Look! That's Abelard the castrated.' And then there was the law. He called it to mind. A eunuch is an abomination to the Lord, he remembered, and is forbidden to enter a church. Even animals were turned away. Leviticus wrote, 'Ye shall not present to the Lord any animal if its testicles have been bruised or crushed, torn or cut.' And in Deuteronomy: 'No man whose testicles have been crushed or whose organ has been severed shall become a member of the assembly of the Lord.'

Now after his death he was to dwell in perpetual purgatory or most likely to be thrown into the flames of Hell and with all the foul fiends of the earth to suffer unrelenting torment and know there would be no reprieve.

Abelard cried aloud at that thought. The doctor looked up, shrugged an apology and began to stitch up the wound.

Did that mean he had lost his soul? Or could his soul be kept despite the mutilation of the body? That was all there was to know. Surely if he lived the rest of his life in the service of God, his soul would be valued even though his carcass would be thrown on the dung heap of Hell. He must save his soul.

He would study the history and the fate of eunuchs as soon as he was well enough. Surely God's infinite goodness must at some point have shown itself in an acceptance of eunuchs. He must find authority. He tried to get out of bed but this time the pain provoked a yell and he fell back.

'The faster you go the slower you will get there,' said the doctor. 'This wound has been well cut but it will not begin to heal for some time and meanwhile you must stay here in your bed. Your servant will bring you what you need.' Floriot looked up and smiled encouragingly. 'When you need to piss, just piss as you do normally – that is, as if you were normal. Always have a pot beside the bed. There will be blood and irritation but time will heal.' And he returned to his sewing.

Only later, when Monsieur Floriot had gone and sternly instructed Ralph to let no one, save himself, enter for at least three days, did Abelard allow himself to think of Heloise.

There could be no more lovemaking. Here was pain. The pain of knowing that he would never again have what he wanted and now wanted more than ever. He was already missing what would not be there in the new future.

There came a rush of images. He saw her. He saw them. In detail he remembered the times. The scenes tormented and taunted him. No more the Heloise who had been his as he had been hers. No more the Heloise who had been as bound to him as he to her. And then a sense of dread possessed him. Would others come to take her?

How much of the security of their love lay in the acts of love itself? This sudden dread, which, from its inception, he knew was without any foundation nevertheless swept through his mind, driving out all reason. For now that Heloise had so powerfully tasted this potency, why should she not wish to pursue it? And where was the eunuch then?

However hard he tried to rein in this fear, he failed. Yet at the same time he knew that their love would survive. His observation and his logic convinced him of that. But this dread would not be beaten away. Perhaps this was the true pain, he thought. Perhaps this was God's cruellest punishment. He could not shake it off. The bed was a rack.

How could he live without her? And with her available to others? He would go mad.

Chapter Thirty-four

Heloise did not falter. The bestiality, cruelty and illegality of the act were unpardonable. She had immediately sought out her authorities. She found that such a punishment as castration was not appropriate for what they had done. Castration, she read, was the punishment for two people openly caught in the act of adulterous sex, their organs clearly visible, witnesses to be called, and this sentence to be pronounced only after the third sighting. Fulbert had acted illegally! But who save herself would challenge him?

She would never forgive God. The pain – although she herself could scarcely bear the thought of it, Peter would endure the bodily pain. She knew that. But the lasting humiliation, the public shame . . . Why had God picked on him alone? She, too, was responsible. Why should she go unpunished? The blame rested more heavily on her. Eve was her ancestor. Peter's demands on her were natural.

Above all, though, she now loved him even more deeply, if that were possible. Now he could serve philosophy without distraction and they would find ways to love each other that would never go. She had worried over the scoffing of the students and the disapproval of some of Peter's contemporaries at, as they saw it, the damaging digression of marriage. There would be no more of that. This punishment cancelled their criticism. She and Peter could study side by side in celibate unity. Astralabe would come and live with them. Peter would write all the books he had discussed with her.

But even that idealised picture could not block out the shocking image of castration. Would there be an infection? The wash of rumour she heard said that men could die of this crude operation.

But she was confident that he would recover and it would not impede him. She would not let it. He would go on to conquer more of the mind. He was its foremost explorer, she thought, the chief voyager into the unknown. In her room at the convent, she was alive with a love and duty to him even more powerful than before.

She wrote:

> To my dearest husband, my sole love, from his ever-loving wife.
>
> Greetings. I will be with you whenever and wherever you want me. The very thought of such brutality makes me score out thought itself. I will renounce my uncle.
>
> We were never adulterers. We were lovers. Now that we are married we are blamed as never before. I am very guilty and yet very innocent. It is not you alone who should have suffered in this way.

She listed heroes in ancient and biblical history who had overcome adversity and later used it as a spur to reach undreamed-of heights. She wrote of love that had lasted through fire and fury. She dedicated herself to him and vowed that she would remain his friend for all time. He was her unique and only love until and beyond death.

As she wrote she kept hearing the songs he had written for her, and found that she was weeping.

+— +

The students, denied access to their master, pounded through the streets of Paris calling for 'Justice' and 'Death to the assassins!' In narrow streets already cluttered with traders and buyers, they ran down the slits of alleys and into the squares, and swept up to the walls of the palace. The people of the city were ignited by the fire of youth. As the morning lengthened, Paris became a scene of righteous riot.

Fulbert was loudly accused of being the chief culprit. He had to be! Outside his house they gathered in a mass, chanting, hammering at his heavily locked doors, allowing no movement but theirs in the Cloisters. The canons of Notre-Dame cowered in the sanctuary of Saint-Étienne.

Then the assassins were found. One of those who had held Abelard down had betrayed the other hireling and gained the time he needed to smuggle himself out of Paris, never to be seen or heard of again. The captured man then accused Abelard's servant, Ralph. Ralph, in a bubble of complacency, was holding court in the tavern nearest to Abelard's house. He was dragged out, bound and, like the hireling, castrated, blinded and left in the stench of the gutter.

Fulbert was surely the instigator! Fulbert was their prey, and the students of Paris, intoxicated by their impact, set out to arrest him.

Fulbert had already retreated into the impenetrable reaches of the Cloisters of Notre-Dame. For days he lay low, protected by the canons. But when the tumult refused to subside and the canons feared for their reputation, he was stripped of his position, his house and possessions. The students had to be satisfied that an act of justice had been done. After a year or so, his possessions and privileges were returned to him and the canons of Notre-Dame combined to agree that Fulbert had not been directly involved, that he might have been a little negligent in his duty but he could surely be readmitted into the ruling cadre without enduring loss of any kind.

Some of Abelard's contemporaries disagreed with the students. His enemies fed on his humiliation.

One of these was Roscelin of Compiègne, who had been Abelard's first and most influential philosopher-teacher. A brilliant man, who for years had been a famous wandering scholar, though not as famous as Abelard, his one-time pupil, Roscelin sent out a public letter.

> Dear Peter,
> Or can I still call you by the name of a man?
>
> I have seen indeed in Paris that a certain cleric called Fulbert welcomed you as a guest into his house, fed you as a close friend and member of the household, and also entrusted to you his niece, a very prudent young woman of outstanding disposition, for tuition.
>
> You, however, were not so much unmindful as contemptuous of that man, a noble and a cleric, a canon even of the Church of Paris, your host and lord who looked after you freely and honourably. Not sparing the virgin entrusted to you, whom you should have taught as a student, and whipped up by a spirit of unrestrained debauchery, you taught her not to argue but to fornicate.
>
> In one deed you are guilty of many crimes, namely of betrayal and fornication, and a most foul destroyer of virgin modesty. But 'God the Lord of Vengeance, the God of Vengeance, has acted freely' (Psalm 93: verse 4). He has deprived you of the part by which you had sinned.

Did this mean that, in God's plan, such earthly love as theirs had no place? Neither Abelard nor Heloise could accept that.

After the wound had healed sufficiently Abelard walked, slowly and almost steadily, with a student at each arm, to his lecture hall in the Cloisters of Notre-Dame.

The room overflowed. The doors were kept open to let those outside hear. Abelard sat down and waited until the applause was spent. He then began: 'We were discussing the *Dialectica*, I have been obliged to interrupt the argument but I assume I need not repeat what I have already said. You will have your notes. Therefore I will take up where I left off.'

The voice was quieter – but, then, he was still convalescing. It might have been a shade lighter, but that made it more melodious, surely. The students, in their fevered discussions on castration, had arrived at the conclusion that a voice was changed substantially only if the castration happened before puberty.

He spoke with his accustomed authority. His thesis was scintillating, purest Peter Abelard, the best logic they would ever hear. Once more they were enraptured.

After this lecture, he had decided, he would renounce the world. And to protect her and to save her soul, his logic ordained that Heloise, too, must renounce the world.

Heloise, he had concluded, though she had no vocation, should remain in Argenteuil, not as a guest, nor as a student, but to take the veil, to become a nun, to become a Bride of

Christ, there to serve and worship God for the rest of her days. He, similarly, would become a monk. When he was sufficiently recovered he went to Argenteuil by boat, alone to inform her of this.

He walked like a man drained of life. Heloise felt like Mary Magdalene seeing Christ after He had been three days in the grave. He was so stricken and fragile. Was this the ghost of him? She saw and caught his humiliation but held back her tears.

He trembled. What would she think of this no-man? And how could he be as he once was when he was so much less than before? They embraced each other carefully, briefly, as if they had lost the habit or, worse, the will to be close. For a while they did not know what to say or do. It was Heloise who broke the spell. She suggested they walk in the garden.

The day was overcast and chilly. They walked slowly. She interpreted the pressure of his arm on hers to be in itself an act of affection.

He looked so much less himself, she thought, his face much thinner, his movement so much slower, his speech and manner without the quick charm and vitality that had dazzled her.

She was even paler than usual, he noted. But her arm was steady, her body easily able to bear any weight he put on it. She was attentive, he thought, to every whisper that crossed his mind.

As they walked her confidence grew: they were together as they had been, as they could be again, and she felt the bond between them no less than before. And as they walked, Abelard's confidence ebbed – for how could he carry out his plan without seeming cruel, and how could he give up all of this?

All this priceless normality. The two of them walking together. Talking of Brittany and Astralabe and Denise, agreeing to suppress conversation about Fulbert and Abelard's enemies. They talked of ordinary matters, of the days spent in Brittany, of the landscape and the gentleness of his family, and of their adventures, but lightly, without regret, for Heloise believed that this was the beginning of their new life and Abelard was convinced it had to announce the end of their life together.

Yet in this interlude in the garden they were observed by some of those in the abbey as an all-but-sanctified couple, tenderly embraced arm in arm, bending their heads to listen more attentively to the other, loving and loved.

As the cold bit in and they turned back to the convent, he grew silent. She feared she had overtaxed his strength.

He was gathering all the strength he had for what he must say the next morning.

He stood beside the window. Like a wild creature she moved erratically, violent, in the cage of the guest room.

'I cannot do it, Peter. Please don't make me, I beg you. By your love, by our love, I entreat you. Do not do this to us. If you do, I may never see you again. I may never see our son again. Do you realise what that means to me – that you are burying me alive? From you, from Astralabe. Peter! Help me!' It took Heloise every bit of her courage not to break down at this terrible prospect.

'There is no other way to be safe.' She saw that he trembled. Again she remembered what his mother had told her about his fear of madness. He looked distraught but his eyes were hard, set on his purpose.

'No other way? For you, Peter, or for me?'

'For both of us. I have too much shame for anyone to bear to live with me,' he said.

'I will help you.'

'Only God can do that.'

'God? God is cruel.'

'God was just.'

'He was not! He should have treated us equally. He has separated us. I will never forgive Him. Please, Peter – don't leave me like this.' She saw, as in a vision, a vast cavern of darkness and of utter solitude waiting for her. How could she bear it?

'I must become a monk,' he said. 'To save my soul, I must serve only God.'

'Though not for the love of God,' she retorted.

'Not solely. And not yet. For my safety. I am too raw in the world now. I want the peace the Church can give and there I will teach myself to love Him.'

'You will hide! But why should I, too, be for ever hidden away? What peace will I have without my husband?'

'You must become a Bride of Christ. There is no greater purpose in life. We have had profane love. As a nun, a Bride of Christ, serving only Him, you will know sacred love. You will be closer to Him than any others – as Mary Magdalene was. You will be one of His chosen and so near to Him that you will have the purest influence on Him to save the souls of others. And to save my soul, Heloise. But most critical of all to expiate your sins, to redeem your life.'

'Our love was not sin. You redeem my life.'

'We were blind. Our love, like Eros, was blind.'

'It is eternal, Peter. It is the finest thing on earth.'

'You will find greater love, greater riches, in the love of Christ.'

'How can I? How can I have greater than I have now?'

'He will teach you.'

'I have no vocation. I will lie and God will know that I am lying. Everyone will know I am lying – and how can I bear all those rituals, that immersion in prayer to a Being I do not respect? But, most of all, how can you expect me to embrace life without you?'

'What would you do otherwise when I take orders and join Saint-Denis?' he said, his speech firmer now that the argument was engaged. 'Who will guard you? Who will nourish you?' And who, he did not say, will not want to take you from this convent, from the unmarried state to which my conversion will return you? Who would not want to marry you? I could not bear that. It is entirely selfish and entirely loving. 'And you will be praised,' he added.

'I want no praise but your friendship.'

'Heloise. We cannot live together in the world. The world tells me that every day. Every day I am taunted – are you a man, Master Abelard? Every day I would be mocked or resented, and we would be humiliated.'

'But every day we would be together. Without you there is only a void in my heart and mind. Why should I fear what the world says of us? Why should you, Peter? The world is what we will make of it.'

'Do you not understand the shame, Heloise? It is a curse for life, this nothing that I am as a man. What good is that to you?'

'To me you are everything a man could be. And you, too, have no vocation, Peter. You, too, will be lying when you become a monk.'

'At the beginning, yes, I will be lying. But I will learn my vocation. Fear for my soul will help me. I have fear. Fear for both of us.'

'Can I not help you conquer that fear?' she cried. '"Perfect love drives out fear," said St Paul. Can our love not help you? Has that become so weak which once appeared unconquerable? Did you ever really love me, Peter? Please . . . please . . . do not let me go . . . Do you love me?'

He could not answer. To say yes would be to bind himself to her. To say no would be to lie outright and wound her spirit as brutally as his body had been wounded.

'How do I interpret such a silence? Such a silence from a man of so many beautiful words.' You must not go! You must not leave me! If only she could pray, she would: God, let us not part. You joined us together. Let us never part. I will serve You and give You all You ever wanted from me if You will answer this one prayer. 'Can you answer?'

'No,' he said, and he could say no more.

Pity mixed with love but he dared not yield. His head was a thinning shell and he feared it would crack. He saw himself standing dumb before her. The Abelard who was outside himself wanted to give her all she asked. But the mind was rigid with a force that seeped through him, like deepening darkness through a thick wood. His blight of breakdown had returned.

'I don't think that I can do this, Peter.' She spoke very softly and carefully. 'I want you. And Astralabe. Not Christ. There is no life for me without you. You cannot be replaced.'

'You will be safe,' he whispered. 'No one will be able to reach you.' The fractured, all but unrecognisable tone sent out a small alert, which took Heloise yet again to the words of his mother. 'You will be safe,' he repeated hopelessly.

'Immured, disciplined, not free. I will stay here but why must I become a nun and renounce the world for ever? Is that to be safe?'

'I ask you to become a Bride of Christ with all the treasure that will bring to you,' he said, with an effort she saw and was moved by. 'I am too weak to command and too proud to beg. But, Heloise, my unique love, let us leave this world together.'

'No! Please! No! Please. I am not too proud. I beg you,

I beg you. Let us be free together, Peter. Stay with me in the world. I will remain in this convent but do not force me to take vows.'

Once again he was silent even as the tears ran down her cheeks and her body grew rigid with strain.

He knew in his heart that this was wrong. This was a sin against love. But his reason had concluded that it was right. The conflict in him became unbearable. How could he lose her? Why? But how could he save her? He had to leave the world. And in his fevered logic, only if she did the same could they survive. He bent his head as if an unsupportable pressure weighed harder and harder on it. She took his arm and helped him to a seat. Then she turned away from his blind tears.

They were robed as monk and nun side by side in the convent of Argenteuil. Abelard would later go the short distance to Saint-Denis to be accepted there. Heloise would be first.

Those present could scarcely bear it. The painful low sobs of this most disciplined and noble woman made many shed tears of their own. Abelard now wore armour of stone-faced certainty: only by doing this, he kept telling himself, could their souls survive. And no other man would ever be able to touch her.

The moment before she was called to take the veil, Heloise broke into Cornelia's lament from Lucan's *Pharsalia*:

> '. . . O noble husband,
> Too great for me to wed, was it my fate
> To bend that lofty head? What prompted me
> To marry you and bring about your fall?
> Now pay your due, and see me gladly pay.'

After that speech, Cornelia takes her own life.

Heloise strode quickly to the altar, swiftly accepted and put on the veil, then fled into the tomb of Christ.

Part Two

Chapter Thirty-five

'How can I forgive my shame?' Heloise cut across the elaborate welcome from Abbess Jeanne.

'What is your shame?'

'That I pleaded with Peter Abelard as I did. That I begged and entreated him. That I lost my character at a crucial time. Instead of behaving in the Roman manner, instead of being strong and true to myself and to philosophy, I cried like a child. Difficult as it was for him, I made it more difficult.'

'It was hard for you as well, my dear Heloise. There were those who said it was cruel of Master Abelard to demand it of you.'

'He did not demand it . . .' Heloise paused: she saw a trap. 'He must not be blamed. I now agree with his wish that both of us leave the world.' She could not sustain the bravado. 'But did I have to take vows? And when he asked me to lead, to be the first to take those vows, perhaps, I thought, he might not trust me to follow him. But he knows! He knows I will follow him into the jaws of Hell if he commands me to. He is all my love on earth. All I want in another life is to be with him. I love Peter Abelard before God.'

'God is the only one who can command total love.' Steel

entered the tone of the abbess. Heloise was to be cherished, admired and favoured, but not on any terms. 'You have entered this convent to serve God, to exalt Him and pray daily, from dawn to dusk.'

'How can I pray to God when God allowed the person of Peter Abelard to be so unjustly assaulted? Why was I not equally punished? He and I are one body. God made us one body.'

The abbess braced herself for the struggle. This could not be allowed. 'One of our great philosophers said that on entrance to a monastery or a convent you must "Leave your body at the door; here is the kingdom of souls. The flesh has nothing more to do with it."'

'How can you deny flesh?' Heloise countered. 'That means you deny love. In my mind I constantly see us together.'

'Denial,' said the abbess, grimly now, 'can be taught and it can be learned.'

She was too wise in the politics of religion and the experience of novitiates to confront Heloise with the obvious question: why then did you take the veil? Perhaps intuitively she feared the answer. At present Heloise, she reckoned, was too volatile to be confronted. Time would break her in. Argenteuil was rich in time.

'There are moments,' the abbess continued, as her response seemed to have checked Heloise, 'when even the strongest have doubts. I was no exception. Especially at critical times such as just after the taking of the vows, the putting on of the veil. But obedience soon follows and such sacrifice as you have made will grant you the assured reward of eternal life.'

But I want earthly life with Peter, Heloise thought. Her silence was anguished. Faced with the intractability of her future, she was overcome by what she had surrendered with such finality. All that she could never now do surged up in her mind to goad her. And Peter – would she ever see him again? Her heart bled with fear.

And her son . . . Until now Astrolabe had been part of her. But now, faced with the walls of her future, which barred him, images of him lined her mind. Her child was no longer hers and never would be. Had Abelard thought of that? He had seemed to love Astrolabe so much in Brittany, but now he had stripped their son of his mother. How could he be so cruel to his child? She struggled to understand that.

This place, this convent, was now to be her entire world. And why? Why had God let that happen? Why had she been punished after she had obeyed His laws and married, when, unmarried, there had been no punishment?

'Peter Abelard is not just a man,' she said to the abbess. 'You must understand.'

The abbess tried to let that pass: she was unused to being lectured.

'He is a philosopher. He was born to bring truth to the world.'

'Christ brought all the truth we need.'

'Yes,' said Heloise, doubtfully, and then, with emphasis, 'but also no. Peter Abelard says that the Commentaries on Christ and the ancient prophets and sages are corrupt and misleading and must be re-examined. Prejudice and ignorance call sacred that which is often a mistaken or false report. He corrects the mistakes, cuts away the falsehoods and teaches the truth. His logic reveals what has corrupted so many – even the most distinguished: acceptance without real examination. False prophets are everywhere and our eyes must be opened. Peter Abelard opens the eyes of the world.'

Abbess Jeanne had the clear feeling that she was included in the batch of ignorant believers Heloise dismissed so brusquely. She was not pleased. She thought of herself as someone who was exceptionally clear-sighted and learned in textual and traditional matters. She steadied herself.

'Philosophers, like prophets, must be alone,' said Heloise, solemnly, irritating the abbess even further. 'I knew that to marry him would be to destroy him. I agreed – who was I to contradict him? He required me to agree, even though I warned him, because I knew that he was possessed by the agony of doubt. But his mind is too valuable to the whole world for my feelings to be an obstacle. And it has ended like this.' She looked around, rather bleakly, at what the abbess considered to be a well-appointed room. 'I now have to serve God.'

'You do,' said the abbess, briskly, 'and for the rest of your mortal life.'

Abbess Jeanne was perturbed. This was not the Heloise of legend. This was not the Heloise of wide report as a scholar, the muse to a philosopher, who was bold but still under the canopy of the Church, still inside the faith.

There was a terrible physical restlessness about her. And something deeper. The abbess reviewed their encounter minutely. There was the unhealthy agitation of the flesh, and a profound, undeniable conviction of her own rightness on the matter of Abelard. Heloise, she concluded, was possessed by the absence of Abelard – of his mind, which could be excused, but also of his body, which could not.

She had seen young women come into the convent far more willingly than Heloise could ever have pretended and still they would, of a sudden, encounter absence. Those they most loved were not there. They would never be there again, so much common familial history gone. All shared past life lost for ever, save in memory. The force of absence could make the strongest quail while for the weakest it was heavier than the closing of the monumental convent gates. 'For ever': an executioner's words.

Heloise was not weak. It was her strength, the abbess knew, that was the deep cause of what she let pass as her thoughtless talk. The dangerous strength of her love for Abelard, which the abbess was now beginning to appreciate.

Her spirit had to be broken. Heloise had to be tamed.

The next morning Heloise was summoned to the abbess's presence. She was not invited to sit.

'You were afforded a privileged entrance to this distinguished convent,' she began. 'You will know its history as well as I do – better, I would expect, than anyone alive. It is a place that, for more than fifty years, has not only trained novices to become the most prayerful nuns of our age but privileged girls of distinguished families, such as yourself.

'But now that you have taken the veil, I have the duty to guide you to God. Privileges that you took for granted, although they may in some measure be restored at some future date, will now be withdrawn from you. You will lead a life of total obedience. We are here to pray. Paradise lives in us, in spiritual exercises, regular prayers and holy meditation. As you know – but now you will know it in a different way. You will begin the day with the midnight office, and follow seven further stations of prayer and worship until compline in the evening. You will attend all these services throughout every day and night. You will have observed our routine when you were here as a scholar. Now you will follow it as a nun. Correction will be severe if you fall short. There are no exceptions.

'You will also have observed that the nuns often complain because they are not allowed to sleep more than two or three hours at a time. This is essential to our discipline. If you have difficulty in sleeping, the solution is to recite the Athanasian Creed seven times. Your bed will be a pallet; your pillow is a book.

'Your food is not that of a scholar – it will be bread, water, vegetables, and very occasionally a little meat. Your chief duty is to pray, for the mercy of God, for your own soul, for the souls of your sisters in Christ, for those whose endowments enable us to live as we do, and for the strength to resist the devil who never ceases to tempt us.' It was the only time the abbess paused. 'His favourite trick is to show us the past, to exaggerate its beauty, and to take our minds away from God and back to the wicked world we have abandoned.

'You may write a letter today, in the library, if you wish. You will join us this evening, at compline. You will follow our rule for one year, after which we may talk again. You are now a Bride of Christ.'

From then on, Heloise cultivated hypocrisy. She praised the simplicity of the rough, scratchy, misshapen garments that were too heavy in summer, inadequate in winter, and always insufficiently washed. She said that the meagre food was perfect for the mind and sharpened the spirit. Short spans of sleep she declared to be the finest training for the soul as it could busy itself in salvations for more waking hours and thus be better prepared against the devil. She would sing her own songs but only when permission was given. She encouraged the younger nuns with their reading and volunteered for the most disagreeable tasks. Above all, she was shy about taking a place near the altar and this was presumed to be the crowning glory of her humility.

It was before the altar, especially when Communion was served, that her spirituality was most visible. She could scarcely raise her eyes to the Cross. She trembled. What her observers did not know was that when she saw Christ on the Cross she also saw Peter Abelard, and when she saw him she saw the two of them merged into one: Christ's opened arms opened hers to him, his straining face looking down on her now more as Peter, not in crucified pain but abandoned to lust. This was sacrilegious and she was aware of it. Appropriating the passion of Christ for the passion between Peter and herself was undoubtedly a terrible sin. But she would not resist it.

She all but fainted with longing at the altar, a state the nuns saw as certain proof of her immeasurable devotion to Jesus Christ, their Lord.

Chapter Thirty-six

'How could she feel that she had no option? How could she agree to it and leave her son like that? Knowing that Abelard would be locking himself up as well? It was a terrible thing to do, Dad. How can anybody respect her after that?'

'I know.' Arthur again felt personally responsible for the defence. 'All I can say is that's part of what makes this unique and, ultimately – the story is not finished – so memorable and, I think, in their way, extraordinarily true and admirable. They were on a different plane.'

'All that happened was that she was locked up for life to pray.'

'That is one way of seeing it.' Arthur was wary of Julia in her 'rampage' mood.

'A waste of breath.'

'Is it?' His tone was sharper than he had intended it to be.

'Yes. I read about it. Somebody in history did an experiment with hundreds of people praying for something and it didn't happen.'

'Perhaps God was rather busy at the time.'

'Dad! It's rubbish. You know it's rubbish. I know it's rubbish. If it's a help to people that's good, but it's still rubbish. There's nobody up there listening.'

'But is there somebody in here,' he tapped his forehead, 'inside here, listening? In the cellars of the mind, in the still unexamined undergrowth of the brain? Perhaps somebody in here is listening to us. We're told our own dark energy could be in there. Could there be something of God in that? Could we listen to it?'

'Like yoga?'

'Nothing at all like yoga!'

'I meant meditation.'

'That's better. The Middle Ages had meditation as well as prayer.'

'Who did?'

'The people I'm writing about, many before and after them. They believed that they had a connection with God through His Son and His saints, so if they prayed in purity of spirit, they would be listened to. They produced many examples to support that view. It's believing in belief that's crucial.'

'But you don't, do you?'

'No.' He spread out his hands. 'But I respect much of what the Church brought. And I seem to be perpetually condemned to see the "other point of view".' He smiled. 'It's probably because I'm a Libran – the balance.'

'That's the pits, Dad. You're just giving yourself wriggle-room.'

'Guilty as charged.' He took the first sip of his lunchtime glass of Chablis.

'It seems to me,' she said, 'with the lack of sleep, the routine, the cold and the starving, more like one of those Soviet psychological hospitals that set out to break people's will.'

'Possibly, but there were those who argued for centuries that only by destroying the desires of the flesh could the spirit be released and the soul fly up to Heaven.'

'That was still just an excuse for controlling people. Wasn't it?'

'Yes and no.'

'There you go again.'

'Yes, the Catholic Church, in the Middle Ages especially, was a uniquely effective control system. But prayer was even more vital, and more important to them than control. When rich, powerful people feared death they would donate spectacular sums of money, lands and treasures to a monastery or a convent in exchange for prayers after their death. Many were intelligent. They were convinced that these prayers would help them avoid Hell and speed up their passage through Purgatory. And they were assured that if their donation was large enough they would ascend into Heaven at the earliest opportunity while those unceasing prayers back on earth would keep them safe for eternity.

'So pray, pray, pray – which they did, in psalms, in hymns and chants, in saying amen again and again to readings from the Bible or from the Commentaries. The abbeys were factories of salvation and wealthier than emperors and kings. And they believed utterly that prayer kept the world of God going. The more prayer the better, and the better the quality, the more valuable. Argenteuil would have been regarded as a prize prayer site because chaste and virtuous holy women were best at it. In my view, prayer is the biggest factor that distinguishes most of us today from most of them back then.'

'And Heloise pretended to go along with it.'

'She had no option. Once she had decided to stay, which she did, for Abelard's sake, she had to go along with it.'

'So she was a hypocrite.'

'She was. She is open about that from the start in her letters. She tells us that hypocrisy was her only way to survive and keep a measure of internal independence. It worked.

Praise for her sincerity never stopped – such a devoted, committed, holy woman! She was to rise far up the Church hierarchy. I see her as a secret agent, undiscovered, a traitor to everything she publicly professed. And look at the way she took her profane love for Abelard to the altar rails in the service of Holy Communion. The Mass was her Purgatory.'

'Poor Heloise. Why did he put her away? How could he be so cruel? And separating her from her son. Just think of it. Day and night. Alone. Inside her head. It would have driven me mad in a week. Why did he do that to her?'

'I think he did it for love. A spiritual love. A love that's foreign to us now. Abelard truly believed that to be a Bride of Christ was the highest calling for any woman. He also writes that he loved her so much he could not bear her to be with anyone else.'

'Is that not just selfish?'

Arthur carried on: 'But my conviction is that he did it to save her soul. He now saw both of them as unredeemed sinners. He wanted her to live on. He sacrificed their earthly love for her eternal life. So it seems that he behaved badly, but the idea that love conquers everything was its own religion at the time. Don't you believe that?'

'No.' She paused. 'Sometimes.' She hesitated. 'What about you?'

He dodged the personal aspect her question raised.

'I'll go with "sometimes". But at the time I think he was breaking down again and felt threatened with madness. His mind was losing its order, its authority. The castration, the unrelenting shame of it. He had prided himself on his manliness, after all, and that is partly why Heloise reports that "all the women of Paris, high and low, swooned over him". That was gone. He had a rich singing voice, we are told, which was probably much diminished. His post, the

213

master of the Notre-Dame Cathedral School, so long craved for, was gone. He was a proud aristocrat. Now any wretch in the street could call him a eunuch and run away. He thought he had brought dishonour on his parents, his family, on the future of his son, and in this weakened state – with his enemies scenting blood – the attacks on his writings and lectures increased and those writings were now the sole support of his existence.'

'You're still making excuses for him,' said Julia. 'He should have stood by her.'

'I think the Middle Ages would have suited you, Julia,' he said, 'the tablets-of-stone argument. There's right. There's wrong. There's nothing in between.'

'Well?'

'Perhaps. Perhaps after all to try to understand everything is to forgive everything and therefore permit everything.'

'You don't believe in Heaven, do you?' Her question suddenly jumped at him.

'Do you have your suspicions?'

'I think you do.'

'I used to. When I was a boy in a Christian country called England, long ago, I was as fundamentalist as they could make me. I liked singing the hymns – I still know some of them by heart. The virgin birth? Resurrection? Of course! Ascent into Heaven and eternal life – that was inevitable if you behaved. But adolescence and reason took over, and soon nothing was left, save a memory of a young person who was once me. Church history, names, miracles, above all phrases from the Bible linger on. Maybe that's why my secular loyalty to Christianity holds on in those phrases. And Heaven persists, like a small irremovable scar, even though I no longer believe it exists and abandoned it decades ago. Yet I don't resent those who do believe it exists. For me it's become a cultural inheritance.'

Julia shook her head. 'It makes no sense, Dad. It's senti-mental, that's all. It's your childhood that lingers on, not God's Heaven.'

'Could be. And you?'

'No. Nothing. No. Never. Dead is dead.'

For a few moments they sat in silence.

'Was Abelard a believer?'

'Oh, yes. Implacably. But there's another problem with Abelard.'

'All of him is the problem for me.'

'I'd hoped I was changing your view. But the problem I'm talking about isn't the man himself but what he did. He was a prolific, radical writer and debater. There's just too much material about him.

'Heloise was leading what proved to be a double life of secret hypocrisy and, yet, remarkably, she proved to be unequalled in public success. But we know next to nothing about the details of how she achieved it. Abelard wrote an autobiography that gives us so much in such a short space we're dazed by it, the variety and the vivacity of the infor-mation he delivered. Until the letters, she was silent for thirteen years. For thirteen years, she wrote, he made no contact with her nor she with him. The two don't balance in the information we have about them.'

'Oh, Dad, not balance again!'

'It matters. I want to write about Heloise and Abelard. Not a pound of Heloise and a ton of Abelard.'

'So make up more about her.'

'Yes and no.'

'Groan.'

'Sometimes you, I, one, just can't make it up. Whatever I make up, the tramlines of her repetitive life in the convent can't hold a candle to what he did in the thirteen years before the letters began to pass between them and we have a sense of equality again. She did much the same thing every day and gradually was steadily promoted for being so good at it. Whereas Abelard . . . he lived in volumes.' Here Arthur opened a file of notes. 'These are just the bullet points.'

'You don't have to tell me everything. Something would do.'

'Okay. Abelard was inducted with unusual speed as a priest in the Royal Abbey of Saint-Denis just outside Paris. The abbey saw him as a great catch. Being Abelard, he went on the offensive, first of all about the state of eunuchs. He cited Origen, whom he called the greatest Christian philosopher – Origen was self-castrated. He found sentences in the Bible in which God tolerated eunuchs. But most of all he set out on a lifelong mission to use his logic to *prove* that the word of God itself would be clarified by logic, that faith was fundamentally a product of reason. It proved impossible. But he never let go.'

'I suppose you have to give him that,' she said, and felt pleased when he nodded. It was good to agree.

'He took on the most abstruse and mystical aspect of Christian thinking – the Trinity – and wrote about it in a book called *Theologia*. Two years after he had become a monk he was put on trial at the Council of Soissons. He challenged them on what seems to us to be nonsense: God – three in one or one in three with Christ and the Holy Spirit. He out-argued them, which was the worst thing he could have done. He was blustered into submission and made to throw his book onto a fire and watch it burn. He said it hurt him more to watch his book burn than to be castrated. A mob was waiting outside the courthouse and he just escaped being stoned to death. Imagine that! The classic biblical execution after a sophisticated medieval disputation. What did that do to him? The arguments and outcome of that trial alone could occupy more chapters than seven years of Heloise's progress – amazingly stubborn, hypocritical and successful though it was. Where she was outwardly static, Abelard was like a comet over the turbulent intellectual and theological skin of Christendom.'

'But he didn't give in?'

'No. He rewrote the book at greater length. Much later that book was the central exhibit when he faced yet another show trial.'

Julia took her time to respond. When she did she spoke quietly, with a new respect. 'I hadn't realised he was so persecuted and so . . . brave. And so indestructible.'

'I think he was destabilised, badly, after loving Heloise. His intense concentration on Christian doctrine was, I think, because of her now being a Bride of Christ. He wanted to justify what he had done and what he had made her do. He was comprehensively restless. He found a way to insult the Royal Abbey of Saint-Denis by – correctly but stupidly – questioning the canonisation of Saint-Denis himself. They threw him out. He fled to the court of Count Theobald, an old supporter. Then Abbot Suger of Saint-Denis offered him a piece of land in a forest not far south of Paris and he declared himself to be a hermit. The forest was to be his Old Testament "wilderness". He went there with one clerk and embraced isolation. But his fame skewered that plan.'

'You make it sound as if he was permanently on the run after abandoning Heloise.'

'I think he was. And *because* of Heloise. But he wasn't alone for long. Crowds of students deserted their masters and sought him out in his wilderness. It became the fashion. He felt hounded, and after ten months yet again an object of widespread envy in the place he called the Paraclete. The name itself got him into trouble. No one, it seemed, recognised that "the Paraclete" meant "the Comforter", by which the whole of the Trinity could be named. Or they used it as an unnecessary stroke of pretentious scholarship with which to criticise him. Norbert and Bernard – both to be sainted – criticised him from the beginning and would not let go of the judgment of Soissons, even though a more considered view had exonerated Abelard. Envy was the spear in his side again and again, and who can doubt it? He was a threat to all of them – to their livelihoods, their reputations, their sacred texts, their increasingly zealous and extreme Christian fundamentalism. Abelard could not bear these stabs and neither could he tolerate the refusal to debate the truth. I see him as a man wild with new conflicts.'

'You see him . . . ?'

'Oh, yes. In that forest. Surrounded by admirers but cut off from Heloise, utterly tormented by what he had done yet determined to justify it.'

'So he's on the run from her.'

'Yes. And somehow to find a way to close his mind to her.'

'Why couldn't he go and see her?'

'God alone knows. I can only guess that he now regarded her as beyond him, of Christ rather than of Abelard. I don't know. But he was, you were right, on the run. His next home was disastrous.'

'Not again!'

'Again. He put himself forward as abbot of Saint-Gildas-de-Rhuys, a rich but barbaric monastery on the coast of Brittany where his attempt to bring logic and understanding to old-fashioned monks happy with their concubines, money and children made them turn on him, taunt him, scoff at his learned ways and set about trying to murder him. They nearly succeeded. He was wholly unsuited for the post. At one stage he was so disgusted with his treatment at the hands of the Christians that he wrote that he considered going to live among the pagans. It was at Saint-Gildas that he was to write his autobiography – full of violence, in words, in ideas, in actions, no regrets.'

'Why don't you write a separate book about him?'

He shook his head. 'It's not what I want to do. They have to be together,' he said, 'even when they were apart for so long.' Just the listing of a few of the chief markers in Abelard's life disturbed him. How could he accommodate all those facts? How could he not accommodate them? There were the multiple events of Abelard's life and so much that the man stood for in that twelfth-century renaissance. And then there was the unquenchable passion of Abelard for Heloise, which never ceased to consume him.

'He seems so different when she's out of the way,' Julia said, 'almost mad but a bit of a hero. Won't give in. Speaks his mind. Takes them all on. Hunted around France, a wanted man. The burning of books.'

Julia's new sympathy for Abelard – although he guessed that soon enough she would turn against him again – pleased him. But . . . 'It's always a question of balance,' he said, and held up his hand. 'Sorry.'

'Just tell the readers – don't worry, Heloise will be back on page a thousand and one, or whatever. Meanwhile, look at what this man does. He's a philosopher, he's castrated, he's treated like a red-hot revolutionary, he's "modern" and the anti-moderns are out to get him. So are the sacreds, or whatever they call themselves.'

'And they do.' He paused. 'They do get him.'

'But not his mind! Not his thoughts, Dad.' There was a hint of yearning in her tone.

'No . . . No one could stop him thinking his own thoughts and making the public listen.'

'There you are, then,' said Julia, and the barely audible sigh of relief was his reward.

'But after he'd left Heloise, it was his soul that became

his prime preoccupation. And she could save his soul, he was sure of that. He wanted more from this Bride of Christ and once wife of himself. He had taken it for granted that the life he led would find enough favour with God to allow him to share in eternal life. Now he was unsure. Sometimes he was desperate. He became obsessed with salvation. His logic and now the power of prayer were to support that. Her prayers most of all.'

'Oh, no! And she didn't believe in prayer. And he struggled with it.'

'But their independent struggles to believe in it bind them together. I want to keep them together.'

'Why?'

'Because that, for me, is the unique story. A man of principle hounded for his beliefs is not this story. A man tormented by his wound is not this story. A man who has known unlimited lust and the deeper plunge of love and is unable first to comprehend and then to deal with it, despite his being the "greatest philosopher" and her being "the cleverest woman", *that* is the story. *That* is what I want to tell. And all this . . . activity of Abelard's is, I believe, just that, "activity". Neutral.

'I believe absolutely that he has a continuing love for Heloise, a love that dared not speak its name because of fear for his soul. She belongs to Christ now. But there is eternal life. Where they might meet again. Where he aims to meet her again. That's the story! That was the drumbeat under the noise of their lives.'

'How do you know that?'

'Because of his selfishness over her, his fears for her and for himself, his subsequent actions and help for her, and the nature of the man as I have come to understand him. All of these point me to that conclusion.'

'How did you come to think you understood them?'

'By thinking about them continuously.'

'How do you think?'

'Who knows? I could say that some of him was me – a very, very little. But more of me is she. But there are those bits of me – my experience is a minuscule part in the scheme of things. It's the same with everyone. I am my outward life but I am also what I am to myself, and someone else to those I know. I am those I read and meet, I am what I hear and hope for and regret. I am what I dream and imagine, what I envy and desire. I am, we all are, as Whitman said, multitudes. Everyone comes from everything.'

'But where does it go?'

'Okay. I tried the best I could to get to know him by reading and thinking about him for months and making notes on him, and most of all just trying to put on his skin.'

'That makes sense.'

'Good.' He reached out and touched her wrist. 'Emotional intelligence is hard to come by,' he said. 'You're good at it.'

The unexpected compliment made her blush. Rather brusquely, she said, 'And what about Heloise all this time? A ball and chain in that terrible prayer-factory. Up at midnight for the first shift, up again a couple of hours later, and again and again. What was she doing while he was being a philosophical nomad?'

'Nomad!' He smiled. 'Maybe I can use that. She – she's harder to find. She seems to live both outside the world itself and the world in which she finds herself. The convent is a sealed-off God-castle. Her world is enclosed in God and Jesus Christ and total outward obedience to the Rule of St Benedict. From which she detaches her inner self. But then the outer world crashes in.'

Chapter Thirty-seven

'I will not speak to him.'

'I thought that a year in submission to my instructions would teach you humility.'

'It did,' said Heloise.

'And obedience.' The abbess felt a spurt of anger. How was it that this woman, so seemingly endowed with every fair gift of God, could grate on her nerves so quickly? Heloise's aspect was calm, nothing about her issued a challenge, and yet, the abbess knew she was being flatly opposed. This was not as it should be. 'We stress obedience in Argenteuil.'

'And I have obeyed you.'

'So you have.' The truth of it galled the abbess and again she thought, Why? Why should truth so annoy her from this mere nun, more a novice if the usual protocol had been observed? Yet Heloise faced her as an equal.

'And,' Heloise added, cutting across what she sensed would be another attack, 'I have done so in a way that has been noticed by the whole convent.'

'So you have!'

Heloise's behaviour over the period of what had been set as a punishment had been too successful. She was jubilant in a way that disturbed the abbess. Even mocking, she suspected, mocking the authority of the convent and, dare she even think it, of God Himself.

Most dangerous of all, she thought, Heloise had become an idol to the novices and the younger nuns. This, the abbess was certain, could have been avoided. Such a crush of popularity was easy to nip in the bud – she knew this from her own rather less lustrous experience. She was sure that when it swelled to the force she saw in the case of Heloise, it was because Heloise must have encouraged it. It was like the devil: you opened the door a crack and he was in, and once he was in, confusion and panic took over from control and devotion. Heloise was now celebrated by the young in a way that was inimical to all the traditions of monastic life and yet . . . what had she actually done that was wrong?

A glance of defiance, an attitude of independence, a presumption of superiority, a lack of fear, a transparent refusal to be humbled, save in a manner that implied she was doing God and the abbess a favour.

'You have still not renounced Peter Abelard?'

'How could I? Peter Abelard needs my prayers to support him. Whatever he is doing, he needs my prayers. And I offer them to him.'

'You will offer them to God!'

'And direct Him to use them for the safety of Peter Abelard.'

'God is not your messenger.'

'He is a messenger for all of us,' said Heloise, ready for the argument she suspected the abbess had neither the time nor the inclination to take on.

'He is not solely a messenger,' the abbess said, in a tone that closed down the discussion.

Heloise held her peace. Any mention of Abelard took her onto a different plane. It was as if one skin had suddenly been cast away and another, raw, still bleeding, had been exposed.

The abbess composed herself with a few moments' silent prayer. She reverted to what she had announced at the beginning of their conversation.

'I called you here,' they were in the principal guest room, once Heloise's private room, 'to tell you that Canon Fulbert is to visit us tomorrow. He will be confirming a generous endowment. He has asked to see you.'

'I have already said I will not see him.'

'You will see him, Heloise. It is my wish and command that you do so, that you engage in a conversation with him and that you remember the forgiveness of sins.'

'His sin is not forgivable.'

'Remember Christ on the Cross and the thief hanging beside him, to whom Christ said, "This day you are with me in Heaven."'

'That was Christ,' said Heloise. 'I do not have His charity.'

'Have you not learned charity while you have been among us this last year? Been truly among us, not here as a rich scholar to be educated and privileged, but among the common nuns, some from the poorest families in the district, innocent souls but believers: they know how to forgive. Have those who idolise you not taught you and chastened you to give up this pretence that you are different from others?'

'It is my uncle who is different from others. Against all laws he had my husband most cruelly wounded. This was done to satisfy my husband's enemies, not to save his soul. To destroy what made him a man, not to teach him and help him to be a better man. And who is a better man than my husband? They violated his person to satisfy their revenge. They destroyed his manhood, attacked his reputation, maddened and hurt him so much that he did not know what he was doing. He was not in his right mind, and look at us now! Myself entombed, forsaken, Peter Abelard cut off from me, no word do I hear of him but I know, for I see him in visions and dreams, that sometimes he can barely suck in breath, so maimed is he by what this – Fulbert! – this despicable canon of Notre-Dame, this—'

'Stop! Stop this! I will not hear such talk! Silence! Canon Fulbert has suffered too.' The abbess continued more quietly: 'I could punish you but you would see it as a sort of martyrdom and so would those silly girls who elevate you. I could cast you out of Argenteuil with such a name that no one would take you in.'

Here the abbess checked herself. Heloise, she realised, would not be schooled by punishment. The 'punishment' of making her previous year as menial, grinding and harsh as possible had merely strengthened her position in the community. Neither was it remotely true that 'no one' would take her in if she were to be cast out of Argenteuil. She was unique and Argenteuil was fortunate to have her. Other convents would rush to embrace her. This wholly obstinate woman was still indisputably the cleverest woman in the land. Among much else she received regular letters from Peter the Venerable of Cluny, who had made her his favourite. No, that threat would not do. And then God brought her the inspiration she needed to unlock this insulting obstinacy.

'You sent us your servant Marie,' she said, 'and you have befriended her, I am told.'

'I have.'

'She has proved to be a fine drudge in the laundry.'

'She is happy here.'

'I will punish her, even to the point of banishing her from Argenteuil. This will be to her certain danger – as you know, she is not very capable. I will do that unless you do as I say and talk to this convent's good friend and revered benefactor – your uncle, Canon Fulbert.'

'God will never forgive you,' said Heloise, wildly.

'Oh, but He will,' said the abbess. 'He will.'

She was thinner, Fulbert thought, but it did not diminish the distinction of her appearance. She was facing the window, looking out into the garden when he came into the room and, for a few moments, lost for words, Fulbert feared that she would never turn to face him. This, he said to himself, was his daughter. Should he tell her that? Would that help him? Or would it more deeply contaminate him in her eyes?

'I have come to ask for your forgiveness,' he began.

She did not respond.

'I believed you had been abducted by Peter Abelard. I thought that I would never see you again. I wanted revenge and there were many who urged me on. They said it was my right. Some said he should be murdered. I said no. And that he should be blinded as well as what happened. I said no to that as well. How would he live, I said, if he could neither read nor write? I stopped them blinding him.'

Heloise finally turned to face him. 'Do you ask me to forgive you because you did not murder my husband or blind him? How can I forgive you for what you did not do when I will never forgive you for what you did?'

'I have offered prayers day and night. I have gathered together a significant endowment for your convent where they will pray for my soul.'

'Who will pray for your soul?'

'The community,' Fulbert said, rather shakily, 'the nuns.'

Heloise's direct stare was as strong as a punch in the face. Clearly it registered. 'Not this nun.'

'What more can I do?' he pleaded.

'What have you been doing?'

226

'God's work,' he replied, in a penitent tone.

'Why were you not blinded and castrated like the two unfortunate servants?'

'I was not present at the scene.'

'It was your intention that caused it to happen. Your intention was the wickedness. Much more wicked than those you paid to carry it out.'

'The matter got out of hand.'

'Out of your hands – is that your excuse? It was instigated by you, your family and Peter Abelard's greatest enemy, William of Champeaux. All of you are guiltier than Ralph and the other culprit. You suffered nothing. You lost nothing.'

'I have lost you,' he said.

'Yes. And for ever,' she replied.

'Your mother . . .' Even those two words seemed too much for him and they dwindled into sad air. 'You look well,' he said.

Her silence, he saw, was final.

'I came to see you and I have seen you.' His voice broke in sorrow and self-pity. Heloise was unmoved.

'I will enquire after you,' he said. In desperation, he added, 'I treated you as my daughter.'

His silence was no match for hers and, no longer able to withstand her contempt, he turned and went to the door, where he paused for a brief moment, his back to his daughter, and thought that one last plea, perhaps even the revelation that he was her father . . . He thought better of it and left.

Heloise returned to the window.

The abbess had granted Heloise the one concession she had asked for, which was to send and to receive four letters a year.

Her letters were to and from Denise. They touched on her life in the convent, briefly and circumspectly. The abbess would read them before sending them to Denise. In the final paragraph Heloise would thank her for what she had reported about Astralabe and send blessings to them all.

Denise was dutiful. For many years, until her death, she sent reports of Astralabe to his mother. They were concise but for Heloise full of the knowledge she craved. His education, his health, his growing love of riding, his singing – though his voice was not as good as his father's had been as a boy! – his looks, black hair like Heloise, the smile of Abelard . . . Although she knew it was in vain, she tried to picture him . . .

When the pain was all but unbearable, as it was now, Heloise would take out one of the letters and read it as if her life depended on it, then read it again although she knew it by heart.

Chapter Thirty-eight

It was the turn of Heloise to suffer from the corruption of the Church. Abbot Suger of Saint-Denis, who had given Abelard the land for the Paraclete, now further exercised his ambition through a local warrant of authority by taking over the convent of Argenteuil through suspect ancient land rights. This would substantially increase his estates. He fortified his legal position by claiming that the nuns in Argenteuil under Heloise, since she had become their abbess, were behaving immorally and deserved to be stripped of that wealthy and landed convent.

Heloise and her nuns were ejected from Argenteuil and scattered across the region. A few dozen stayed with her. This expulsion left them as refugees. The accusation, the absolute authority of Abbot Suger in that region, and the ease with which a community of women could be mistreated, combined to send them out on a path towards extinction.

It was a scandal. As soon as news reached Abelard he formed a plan to save them. He set off immediately on the journey from Saint-Gildas to the Paraclete – a journey that would take him up to ten days and just a few miles from Paris.

+ →+

When Abelard arrived at the Paraclete, he found it had become a desolate space. He had left a thriving community of scholars, with buildings in clearings in the forest organised for the purpose of housing students and servicing their needs. Now he discovered that after he had left for Brittany, attempts to keep it going had been half-hearted, then minimal; eventually it began to be reclaimed by the forest and its animals. It seemed that his great project had wasted away.

Yet he was full of energy. This, he thought, would be perfect for Heloise and those of her stranded community she had kept together by her willpower and through the generosity of a scattering of admirers. Abelard had written to her to tell her his plans. The peril in which she found herself at last motivated him. He took great care that his tone was formal, his style elaborate; no personal feelings were allowed to taint the pages. He forestalled a reply by insisting that it was not necessary: he would inform her when he had made the Paraclete ready for her. Their distance from each other was useful, he thought. He needed to be more organised when he met her. The Paraclete was in his gift: he would give it outright to Heloise and her nuns.

He was accompanied by his trusted monks and five others from the abbey – two gardeners, two builders and a cook. He had also brought funds from savings built on the rich abbey's generous recompense.

He had sent a messenger to Abbot Suger; the same messenger went to the local bishop with a letter from Abelard, requesting a meeting. It was granted and Abelard convinced the local bishop to support the new settlement of nuns. The bishop was not only flattered by the attention Abbot Philosopher Abelard paid him but also delighted by the gift of a silver chalice Abelard had brought from the treasure of Saint-Gildas, and flattered again when Abelard asked him to sign a joint letter to Peter the Venerable, pleading the cause of Heloise and her nuns. This would enclose a similar letter for Pope Innocent II.

Abelard felt a renewed zest for life. He would see Heloise! He began by preparing a permanent house for her. He hired boys and men from the local villages to weed and scythe and thatch, to help the builders find stones and build in the dry-stone manner. The oratory, the centrepiece of the Paraclete, remained half finished but Abelard's men cleared it of weeds and debris and laid up long logs for a later push to complete what Abelard had so enthusiastically begun when he had first arrived there.

He went out to local villages to preach to the people. He spoke of the women in Christ's life and of other women who had served God. He prepared the way for Heloise by being her John the Baptist, proclaiming her arrival as that of an exceptional servant of Christ. He urged them to help the nuns seeking refuge in the forest that lay near their own secure homes. He knew, he said, that it would be strange to have a convent in such a place, it had not happened before in their country, but to welcome and help the women would be to please God: their prayers of thanks would go directly to Him and the nuns would bring them glory.

There was reluctance. There were some – clerics from nearby Saint-Denis who came to sniff out Abelard's latest move – who doubted the legality of the new Paraclete and would do so until the papal authority arrived. There was still debate about the circumstance behind the expulsion of the nuns from Argenteuil. What was the immorality they had been accused of? Surely Abbot Suger would have evidence, would have reasons. Abbot Suger had to be respected and feared. He had connections in the royal household, his ecclesiastical estates were increasing by the year and . . . Who was this Heloise?

Then there was the talk: the child, the castration, the marriage, the scandal . . . What would Heloise be like? Abelard had won the respect of some in the wider neighbourhood and there would surely be new students, but Heloise . . .

There came a time when Abelard decided to leave. He had extended his planned stay by a month. Saint-Gildas, whatever his difficulties there, remained his prime responsibility. But, most of all, he had decided that his presence might disturb Heloise: it was essential she stayed untroubled by the past and by him. It was a sacrifice.

But as he walked around the reconstituted Paraclete on the final evening, as he saw order where there had been ruin, a bright readiness where there had been a death rattle, he imagined Heloise there. He hoped it would be good enough for her. If not, he thought, she would make it so. He had sent word that the place was ready.

His time at the Paraclete had given him the liberty to think about her continually. He could see her everywhere in those dwellings for God's purpose in a clearing of the forest.

As he wandered around in a euphoria of expectation at the pleasure she would find in what he had done, his deepest feelings were given space to surface. How could it be that, despite his unmanned state, he still longed for her? How could it be that Fate, God and his own stupidity had split apart two lives that had become one? Yet there was no way back. That was the intolerable prospect. There would be no more love. Save in the mind. Save, with grace, in the soul.

He strayed from the Paraclete into the darkening woods, and by the broad stream of the Ardusson, he sat down and mourned for what should have been.

+ —+

When Heloise arrived with her score of followers, gaunt from hunger, fearful from persecution, she was greeted by the three men Abelard had left to usher her into the Paraclete. He had left her a letter of instructions, with papal support promised. The letter seemed to stop her heart. He still loved her. That was what it said. That was what the Paraclete said. She, too, went into the forest to find calm and returned resolute. She would not let him down.

She looked around again and saw the work of another self, her other self, Peter Abelard, who had put such thought and labour into her needs. She repressed her tears. She could not be seen to be weak.

The next morning she organised for what would be more than a year of labour and a meagre income. Peter Abelard was thanked and remembered in all their prayers every day. Was this his final act of love? She found it inspiring. He had been there! She could walk in his footsteps. In her greatest despair he had appeared as her true friend.

Chapter Thirty-nine

Abelard's second visit to the Paraclete excited him in prospect far more than the first. Heloise would be there.

It was six months since his initial visit. As the father of the Paraclete he was an expected, though not a required, presence at the main holy festivals. This autumn event would, so the message, which came from Heloise's colleague and 'sister in Christ', had informed him, celebrate and praise the Lord, the harvest, their survival and Abelard's unique generosity.

He took six monks and the present of a silver cross from the treasury of Saint-Gildas. They bought food and drink along the way, but Abelard made sure that at their penultimate tavern they loaded themselves with meat, wine and such fruit and vegetables as would keep. His correspondent from the Paraclete had been unembarrassed to detail their needs. She had also pointed out that they hoped he would stay for some days to preach and gather in more of the local people, some of whom were still unsure about the black-clad nuns so openly in need of alms. In his reply he promised to do that.

The nearer he drew to the Paraclete, the lighter his heart. As if the climate of his body had been transformed. She would be there! Thirteen years since he had seen her, but in his mind he could see her as plainly as he had those years ago. She was real and she was a vision. He hummed and occasionally sang, rather quietly, some of his songs as they picked their pilgrimage way along the narrow paths, across meadows, through woods, over bridges. His companions encouraged him and he sang again, as if the words and music were an overture for their meeting.

They arrived late in the day, when the convent was busy. Other guests from religious houses sympathetic to Heloise had come. Two huts had been reserved for Abelard and his men. Some villagers were still there, with harvest gifts, waiting for the next service, cheerful in the small crowd. The nuns were at prayer. The horses were fed and stabled in the woods.

At the harvest service of thanksgiving Abelard stood at the back. He had been invited to move to the front of the congregation but he refused. Shyness, almost paralysis, seized him. Thirteen years. Yet he had lost not a grain of his feeling for Heloise. He waited, practically breathless, for her entrance. This was noticed.

And when she came in, he was transfixed. They were once again breathing the same air. The simplicity stunned him. He recited the words and heard the chanting, he joined in the prayers and said many amens, but everything he was, every ounce of him was locked onto Heloise. It was difficult to bear. How could she be so close and they not hold each other? How could she look out at the congregation but seem not to see him? He looked to trap her gaze in his own and say, 'Here I am, Heloise, at last, with you, together. That is enough. Look at me. Look at me as I look at you . . .'

The service ended and the nuns dissolved into the night as they made their way to their dormitories, and Abelard was left with the small congregation. One or two of the bolder ones greeted him. Others gave him a close look, the better to describe him later to their friends. His own monks waited, and eventually he collected his senses and they went to their quarters.

When he prayed he was vividly aware that, just a few steps away, Heloise would also be praying. Or would she not have changed in that essential and be pretending to pray? The thought reminded him of her resolution. Even so, their words would be the same. And would they ask God to relent? How could they stay such a small distance apart? What laws were they obeying?

Heloise had seen him from the moment of her entrance. The first look had filled her with painful pleasure, which squeezed her heart and stopped her breath. But there was not a break in her stride, not a stumble in her voice: the discipline and solitude of years had steeled her. But how fine he looked! Older, of course, thinner, but so fine, she thought, so very fine and noble, and the eyes still searching, for her, she knew that, searching for her as she longed for her eyes to gaze on him. But the service proceeded as it always had, and as she always had, she went out before her flock, leading them to the next station of devotion.

Abelard stayed for seven days. He preached; he talked to inquisitive strangers; at appropriate times he wore the robes and jewellery of an abbot. Always his eyes sought out Heloise and always she evaded him.

People could see his fascination with her. They talked to each other about the pillar of stone he became whenever Heloise was in his vicinity and how intently, how hungrily he looked at her.

But she neither beckoned nor approached him. On his way back to Saint-Gildas he concluded that this was because she was adhering strictly, as she would, to a protocol that decreed he was so far above her in rank, and so exalted as the founder of what was now her convent, that she could not make the first move. Moreover, by her attitude she had to be sure that nothing she did indicated affection or the longing for him to approach her. It was so very strange, he thought, but such reasoning was not beyond her. And he could not breach her bridal state without her invitation.

In her sleepless nights, Heloise tried to unearth why this nothing had happened. She was wholly ignorant of the last thirteen years of his life. In the absence of information, her imagination had raced from unsupportable hope to despair. She had spent so much of her energy remembering, in anger, in affection, every colour of her moods that his mere presence was too hard to absorb. There was too much of him in her thoughts, of him with her, too much to be able to tease out the single thread that would begin to unravel the years of knotted regret and fury, and somehow heal or at least bring understanding to this unending love. Silence was the only response she could make.

And so it was when he returned some months later to the Paraclete, one final time. Once again, words, on which they had built their lives and reputations, appeared to fail them.

Chapter Forty

Arthur was certain that when Abelard went back to the Paraclete he had not yet written his *Historia*. Yes: it must have been composed a good time after his return to Saint-Gildas. It was from this primary evidence that Arthur had to work. In many ways the Paraclete episodes puzzled him most.

On the same page in his *Historia* as Abelard recorded his visits to the Paraclete he gave a shining portrait of Heloise – whom in this instance he called his 'sister in Christ'. It was warm, admiring and loving. So – he was there!

He reported that after she had endured the first hard year or so at the Paraclete, money had begun to come in from neighbours and benefactors. Soon, Abelard wrote, Heloise was given more funds than he would have accumulated in a hundred years. 'Bishops loved her as a daughter, abbots as a sister, the laity as a mother.' Yet in a later letter, after she had read his autobiography, Heloise wrote that she had had 'not a word' from him when he came to prepare the Paraclete for her. Nor did she talk to him. Arthur had to accept Heloise as a truth-teller. So what had happened?

'I have to believe her,' Arthur concluded to Julia, 'although it seems beyond belief. After thirteen years they did not speak to each other. And he had rescued her from destitution.

Surely she would at least have sought him out to thank him. And would he not have asked her what her plans were for the Paraclete or shown or discussed with her his own former plans for the completion of the oratory? Or are we speaking of two people with apparently fathomless resources of self-control and a paralysing, rigid respect for protocol? Yet both had been capable of breaking out of their prisons to make love sacrilegiously, to regret, to rage? Why was there none of their former passion?'

'Perhaps there were letters, which were lost,' said Julia.

'There would have been references to them.'

'You would have thought,' Julia said, rather reluctantly, 'she would thank him. It was very generous of him.'

'And Abelard, who talked for France, dumb?'

Arthur scrutinised the passages in Abelard's *Historia* once more. They must contain an explanation, he thought.

He read Abelard's account of going a second time to the Paraclete after Heloise had taken possession. He went, he said, because people had begun attacking him for not extending to the nuns the help he was capable of giving them. His preaching, his lectures would, they said, bring to the Paraclete wealthy students, whose funds would have assisted the women in their struggle for survival in those early months. Once again it looked as though he had risen to criticism, but to Arthur it seemed not much more than an excuse to see her again. The scent was up.

But he had returned on the respectable mission to teach and help. Would that not have entailed conversation? Surely he would have asked her advice on how best to direct his efforts? Nothing of that was recorded by either of them. Possibly Heloise and her nuns had found a way to be hermetically cloistered. That, perhaps, could be a reason for their silence. But that Heloise did not talk to him when, from her own later letters, it was clear that her feelings for him were ready to erupt, was so weird, Arthur thought. How did they *not* talk being so near each other, working on the same project? But he had to accept it. Given that the facts were as they were, he couldn't dodge it by making up another version. The only way was to dig deeper.

He thought that Abelard's own explanation offered at least a possible reason for the silences.

Abelard wrote that he had been criticised for not going to the Paraclete often enough. He responded by going again. Then heavier and more damaging criticism rained down on him. That he could not keep away from her. That clearly he still lusted after her. That this was a way to resume in some form that which had driven them to such carnal excess in Paris.

It was no surprise to Arthur that Abelard was wounded yet again. It was that, he concluded, that eventually drove him away. How could he be seeking carnal pleasures when – as he protested in his autobiography – God's mercy had released him from all sexual temptation? He was a eunuch.

But it was possible that he had kept his distance from her because he was afraid of what might be the consequence of any form of public touching, or talking. He did not trust himself. He did not trust his body. Did he ignore her to save them both? He was prepared to give, to serve, to help, but not to compromise the sacred integrity of Heloise. This was the boundary of his new spiritual love for her. Perhaps he was convinced she could never love him as much as he wanted to believe that she loved Jesus Christ. She was no longer his wife but the Bride of Christ.

Yet to Arthur their silences remained incomprehensible. Love had been blind when they were young: had the separation blinded it in some other unfathomable way? Did they not dare to make contact? For what would result from it? To see and not to touch – was that not enough now?

And Abelard did revisit the Paraclete. Was it out of a sense of duty or guilt, a form of penitence? Was seeing her enough for him or could he afford no more? But Heloise, bold, fearless Heloise, why did she not walk up to him, touch his arm, talk and stand alongside her lover, however fleetingly, however poignantly, however painfully?

Arthur could find no final explanation. Yet the absence of expression between two such tormented and expressive lovers only added to the mystery, and the terrible power of their bond. Such elements of mystery, he concluded, were at the source of their fascination.

Chapter Forty-one

'Matthew was always the lucky one,' her father said of his older brother. 'He fluked into Oxford because – or so he says – at the interview he happened to have rehearsed the questions they asked. He got another lucky break when the foreign correspondent he was working with was badly wounded and he took over. And then he bought this place.' He looked around the ample apartment.

Julia sensed her father wanted to drift into chat. She wouldn't let him. She picked up her mug of coffee but only to nurse it. 'That's the big thing,' she said, in a quieter mood than usual, 'isn't it? What's really going on between them when they don't see each other for all that time? Do you know? Or has it to be another of your let's-imagine episodes?'

'A little. But this time I'd rather tease away at the few facts we have. There is no evidence for her encounters with the abbess – but both are consistent, I think, with her character and her subsequent actions. You have to leave it to the reader. It's a quest, Julia, and I'll go along any track that will help to get me there.'

'But what do you think was *really* going on between them? You write about this unique love affair, taken up by writers and historians for centuries. What was it?'

'We haven't discussed the letters between them yet. And, as I said, when they meet at the Paraclete, Heloise knows nothing of what Abelard has gone through at Saint-Gildas – the attempts to murder him. When she learns about that, their story enters another dimension.'

'That's odd, though, isn't it? That she knows nothing. Especially him having been forced to throw his own book onto the flames at Soissons and crying while they made him say a creed. You tell us how celebrated he was. Wasn't that a famous event? You'd have thought she would have heard of it.'

'I agree, but I have to leave it as another unsolved puzzle. And for her to have known would completely undermine the letters, as you'll see. They are my chief evidence. I have to rely on them.'

'Even so, you must have a well-worked-out view of them by now.'

'I think both of them had access to an unusual depth of passion, which brought them from sex to the soul in his case, and to a lifelong inflamed fidelity in him and what might be called a perilous sinful slandering of God in hers. And both of them had, equally, the discipline and the need to conceal it. It's an exceptionally fierce and unique love story. It's that which drew me to it.'

Julia could restrain herself no longer. 'Is this to do with Mum?'

He had prepared for this. His tone was wary. 'Partly. With what we had and what we lost and why we lost it.'

'I thought you'd got over it.'

'I think you never do. Nor do I want to. It's an open wound for ever and you go back to the matter or it comes back to you again and again. And just a nudge of memory can replay the whole . . . let's call it drama. It never lessens. If anything, time feeds it. Love can be indelible. And it

243

can still grow after it's physically over. Or even after death.'

Julia was silenced. What did he mean? She had no response, save 'Is that why all the best songs are about it?' or 'All the best clichés are about it' or 'So, after all these years and books and thinking, you came up with "It's love that makes the world go round"?' All that seemed too light for the occasion. Yet she felt she had to answer.

'"Love is all you need"?' she said. 'We used to sing that in the car.'

He nodded.

'Go on,' she said.

But he looked weary.

'You promised to tell me everything.'

'I will,' he said. 'But . . . it's hard. Next time.'

'I can't let you off. I'm sorry, but I can't.'

'I understand.'

'So what you yourself experienced led you to write this book?'

'Directly. I remembered the story when the time, my time, was right for it. I was immediately drawn to the two of them, and the attraction just grew and it's still growing. I want to find out the truth about them. My version of it.'

'And about yourself and Mum?'

'Perhaps. But Heloise and Abelard were – are on another plane.'

'They never let it go?'

'Not, I believe, for one moment. We have their secret life. Then we get the letters. And then there is this cry from the depths.' He paused with relief, grateful for the reprieve. 'Although . . . Let me predict that you will once again take serious issue with Master Peter Abelard.'

'And you will defend him.'

'And her. I'll try to explain what I see.'

Julia nodded. She was moved by what her father had said. But it was not enough.

Chapter Forty-two

Heloise read Abelard's *Historia Calamitatum* as soon as it came into her hands. Her first reaction was of terrible disappointment. Was this superficial chronicle of what they meant to each other, then, now, and for eternity, all he had to say? She reread what she considered his meagre references to their love as if rereading would reveal new meanings. It was so little! They had had so much! He had been the book of her life. She appeared little more than a passing chapter. That could not be all. This was not her Abelard, yet his name was on it. Was this all she was? Was this all it had been between them?

She controlled her despair and read it another time. She forced herself to be calm. Its intimacy and directness were, in Heloise's experience, wholly new. Abelard had laid open his life and hers. She noted with unhappiness that this confession was directed to help not her but a friend, never named. What friend could be closer than her? What friend needed more help?

He did not spare himself. Her Abelard was fearless. Here he stood, a modern man, stripped of all pride. Who could this 'friend' possibly be? She could not accept it. That must be a trick to muzzle his and their enemies.

The book was for her, so why had it come to her by a

mysterious accident and not directly from him? It spoke to her as to no one else. It was meant for her.

At last he had called to her out of his peril at Saint-Gildas. Yet he had said nothing of it when they had met at the Paraclete. That would have changed everything. Now she had to answer that cry. But how could she silence her own cries? He was so brutally dismissive about their love. He was so cruel. He trampled down all that they had built up. He gave her nothing in these words whereas, in the early letters when their love had begun and while they were together, his sentences had given her all the passion in the world. Was this what he really thought? Had he been false to her all along? She needed all her strength to stay steady. This *confession* ripped up their past, her past, her love, her life. How could he do that? And why? And in words not even addressed to her. She wanted to howl, to destroy her memories.

The salve was to write to him immediately.

Heloise had her own small room in the expanding convent. It overlooked the herb garden, the vegetable garden and the limited patch for flowers. The Paraclete was now a substantial scattering of buildings, mostly small huts, but the oratory was completed and there was a refectory, a dormitory and a small library. She studied in her room, wrote there, and it was there that her community believed she talked to Christ.

The only time she could be uninterruptedly alone was the three hours after the midnight prayers. She had new tall candles brought to her room. After considering the matter carefully, she allowed a small fire to be lit and logs laid alongside it to feed it through the night. Intense cold would be an unnecessary distraction. This would be the most important letter of her life. She had no doubt of that. She waited patiently in that white room, looking at the flickering yellow and crimson flames of the fire, breathing in the scent of the burning wood, listening to the wind disturbing the trees. Waiting for the moment to begin.

She decided that formality, impeccably correct procedure, would best usher her into an uninvited and apparently accidental correspondence. Fortune had blessed her. She had to seize what she saw as the first and probably only opportunity she might ever have to rejoin him.

With her newly sharpened quill, she began:

> To her lord, or rather father, to her husband, or rather
> brother, from his handmaid or rather daughter, from
> his wife or rather sister, to Abelard from Heloise.

By tightly intermingling the relationship they had in the Church hierarchy – abbess to abbot – and the relationship she had to a monk as a Bride of Christ, and in their earthly married past, she netted him comprehensively. He could not, she thought, ignore such a greeting.

She began in sorrow that he should have undergone such miseries and perils at Saint-Gildas and was still undergoing them at the time of the writing of his *Historia*. She could see no good reason that he had become the prey of the murderous clergy. At first sight, she had hoped she might find encouragement and strength in this letter for herself but instead she wept at his suffering. And as she wrote she felt her heart beat with fear at what might happen to him.

In writing to him she was speaking directly to him for the first time for so many years and it hurt. A pain in her chest seized her and she laid aside her pen until she could compose herself. To fortify herself and her letter, she quoted from Seneca on the welcome value of a letter from a friend.

She tried to hold in check the resentment that threatened revolution in her calm cell. But it was to prove beyond her. Yet she began calmly.

In telling this 'friend' of his misfortunes, she wrote, he had reopened and redoubled the unhappiness she herself felt. And it was all very well, she could not help but point out, to write to a good friend but what of his 'dearest friends . . . your daughters', those at the Paraclete who owed him so much?

> It is you alone, Abelard [she wrote] who built up the Paraclete. You gave it to me when I had nowhere to take my flock. It was you alone who shepherded us here. You secured it for us. We are in your debt but you are also in our debt because of our constant prayers for you. Yet we have had no letter from you. Nothing after you visited us. No comfort through the early difficulties of survival on this land.

How could the *Historia* – which she saw as a confession – *not* be for her? She paused. Her fluency deserted her. She sat inactive, waiting for the bell that would summon her to prayer. There was to be no more writing that night. The simple act of sitting at her table, with paper and pen, had exhausted her. It was as if a net were being dragged through her body, scooping into the open all that she had forced herself to subdue for so long. But Heloise was not to be stopped. The following night, she went back to the *Historia*. In it, she thought, he had reduced and damned their lives. She would not accept that.

He had destroyed what they had been, she wrote. He had taken no full account of all that had happened to them. He had listed events in a cold-hearted way. They had been as one. Then and now. How could he so casually repent that? What was left of her without their past?

You must know that you are bound to me by an obligation which is all the greater for the further close tie of the marriage sacrament uniting us. You are deeper in my debt because of the love I have always borne you, a love which is beyond all bounds. How can you not love me when I love you so completely? My love will serve for both of us. You know that. You know, beloved, how much I have lost in you, how at one stroke of fortune, Fulbert's supreme act of flagrant treachery robbed me of my very self in robbing me of you.

You are the sole cause of my sorrow and you alone can grant me the grace of consolation. You alone have so great a debt to repay me . . . I found strength at your command to destroy myself. I forced myself to seem to change my mind along with my clothing in order to prove that you are the sole possessor of my body and my will alike. You do not acknowledge that! Why? Where is the man you were?

Her arched back was stiffened by her concentration. She had not wanted to blame him. How could she when he had suffered so much? But the accusation could not be withheld. And worse! In making it she saw a cascade of images, those pictures of Abelard and herself nakedly entwined, which never ceased to torment her. But never with such force. Never like this. The images took over her mind. She walked around the room, aching in agony.

She had to respond as powerfully as she could. In his *Historia* he had dismissed their passion. But . . . She began to realise that came from a new state of mind, a different Abelard, a man bent on desperate repentance.

She would not let him do that. She could understand that he might be seeking salvation, but Heloise wanted the truth.

She would not let their past be diminished by his fears for his future. She would challenge him.

The bell sounded but she ignored it. The fire was low. She could scarcely bear her body. Then, abruptly, she returned to the table, possessed. She wrote swiftly, not a waver in the lines:

> I will tell you what I think and indeed everyone suspects.
> It was not affection that bound you to me, but the flame of lust rather than love. You hold me cheap.

She sat back, paused one final time, checked her tears, overrode the clutching grip in her heart and ended,

> I beg you, think of what you owe me.
> Farewell, my only love.

She put the pages carefully to one side and then, for it gave her some relief, she laid her tormented body on the stone floor and waited for the next summons to the prayers she now longed to believe in.

Chapter Forty-three

'How could she bear it?' Julia said. 'And how could she bear it for so long?' She paused and tried to imagine what Heloise had gone through, then shook her head slowly, as if a less gentle motion would dislodge her disturbing thoughts. 'And him,' she said softly, 'how selfish can you get?'

'Many people would agree with you,' Arthur said, 'especially nowadays. But again, sorry, the past really is a foreign country.'

'How could he not write? After doing all that to her! How could he not just write a letter?'

'He says in his reply to hers that it was not lack of feeling on his part but he was so confident of her own "good sense" that he thought nothing else was needed to pull her through. He was not wrong. And, besides, she had, as he thought, dedicated herself to God and become a Bride of Christ and therefore, in the scheme of things at that time, she had access to all the comfort she might need from her Bridegroom. She could receive help from Christ Himself, which was far superior to anything he could bring to her. I don't think he understood that he had long ago replaced Christ in her credo.'

'Very convenient.' Julia stirred her coffee, which had

already been sufficiently stirred. She did not want to look her father in the eye. 'I'm shocked,' she said, still speaking quietly. 'I'm shocked by what he did or didn't do,' now she looked up, 'and I'm a bit shocked that you're on his side.'

'I think it isn't as simple as you would have it.'

'Which means you'll complicate it so that he gets off.'

'Gets off what?'

'His responsibility. He should have looked after her better.'

'Does she not have responsibility for herself? Might she have been a willing collaborator?'

'He dazzled her.'

'She wanted to be dazzled.' He paused. 'I've known two people like him, one man, one woman. In both cases, once they had worked out what they thought was the best course for a relationship, that was the end of it. They saw no point in further discussion, let alone any interference with the way things flowed. And Abelard's mind was quite extraordinary, Julia. I wish I could describe it better. I believe that the energy it took for Abelard the philosopher just to be Abelard at this stage in his life exhausted his resources. Heloise is the sole exception to this throughout his life. Only she can divert his mind. And I believe he genuinely thought that what he did was a way to solve the problem. By, as it were, giving her to Christ.'

'And blocking anyone else from seeing her.'

'That's additional. He wanted to save both their souls.'

'That's not the point.'

'I think it might well have been. And there's another aspect to Heloise. She wanted him to be hers. She had loved the public glory of being in his songs and poems and, most of all, being in his life. She saw herself as and wrote that she was finer than any queen, any lady, any woman in France. She'd believed they all envied her. She'd been a scholar who had lacked all worldly ambitions and experience. Then suddenly she had her great philosopher, not in books, not in ancient times, but with her in Paris and publicly devoted to her alone.'

'You've been setting him up to be liked all along, haven't you?'

'I've been setting out to see him as a man of the Middle Ages, not a lecturer in a contemporary university.' He spoke rather sharply.

'This isn't a tutorial!' she said. He thought she was about to walk out. 'Sorry, Dad. Why do you like him so much?'

'Perhaps . . . I'm – and from the start of this I always have been – overwhelmed by the man's courage and also full of sadness for the isolation his thinking and impetuosity brought on him. He needs friends.'

'But it's not just that, is it?' Julia persisted. 'You need to make him someone others will accept despite what he did to Heloise – despite abandoning her and sentencing her to a living death. Is that it?'

'How others interpret what he did to Heloise, yes. But it's her as well as him. I can't see them apart.'

Julia heard a new note in his voice: distress. When she looked at him directly, he had the eyes of a beaten man. She switched the conversation. 'So you've never found out how she got his autobiography?'

'As far as I know, nobody knows.'

'Isn't there a clue?'

'None! It drives you mad!' He began to regain his poise. 'People have said that the *Historia* was really addressed to her anyway. But why then would he go through all the business of this unhappy friend of his? And why was he so cruel and superficial about their early life together?' He threw up his hands. 'It's nowhere on the radar. Was the document being passed around? We don't know. All we do know is that Abelard wrote it when he said he did, and Heloise got it when she said she did. Not much of a paper trail. And why should all the responsibility be his? Why didn't Heloise write to him over the years or talk to him at the Paraclete? Why not?'

'Maybe she did.' Julia leaped in. 'You made up a letter he wrote and never sent. Why didn't you do the same for her?' She looked closely at him. 'I'll tell you why. Because you wanted it to be loaded in his favour.'

'Not really. I just want it to be fair.'

'So why didn't you make up a letter from her? She might have sent one.'

'And he would certainly have replied. And we would have that reply! When she began to write, he always replied. But there's no trace of an earlier letter from her. And with these historical letters we must start with what we have.'

'Poor Heloise. I still think he was a bastard. She didn't ask to be a Bride of Christ, did she? He let her down – didn't he?'

'You're a tough jury.'

'Did I cross a line just then?'

He tried to reassure her. 'I also think she's blameless and wonderful. Heloise won't let go, now she's begun again with this letter. She won't give in.' He spoke urgently. 'But what can anyone do when someone loves them more than they can take? To love someone too much can be a barrier. Love is rarely fifty:fifty. You can't love someone just because they love you. Even if they love you passionately. That can make it worse – a conquest rather than a convergence.' He paused. Julia waited. He went on: 'Heloise wants it all remembered as she herself remembers it, and she wants it *back*. I know about that. And she knows she can't have it back but that doesn't stop her. And all the time she's building up the convent, the Paraclete, and being successful, but she's still criticising God, and she'll never let Peter Abelard go whatever he's done because she loves him unreservedly and for eternity, and that, she insists, earns her his love in return.'

Julia nodded. 'Yes, I suppose she's had what you might call real love. How many people have that? Sometimes she makes me want to cry. And she's so brave out of so much pain from that bloody philosopher of hers! But she won't give in. Not to him. And not even to God. I love that!'

Chapter Forty-four

Abelard instructed that the messengers be well fed and housed and given good provisions for their long trek from Saint-Gildas to the Paraclete. He put Heloise's letter inside his work satchel and continued the day as if nothing out of the ordinary had happened.

It had to be given time. He himself had to be given time to absorb it. He would spend the day imagining what she might have written. He was stunned to receive a letter from her.

He continued on his rounds on another dismal day in Brittany. The winds gusted across the endless ocean and brought in fleets of heavy clouds, which unloaded their rain on the rocky shores. He walked from the service to his chapter house and then to the refectory, accompanied at all times by his bodyguard of monks. Abelard now prepared his own food after the attempt to poison him. He avoided those more raucous and scornful monks, who flaunted their concubines, made feeble jokes about eunuchs, which always provoked heavy laughter, and relished the knowledge that their ever-imminent violence against his person unnerved him. They enjoyed seeing him frightened. But they underestimated his toughness.

Abelard was braver than they were. He had a good grip

on their Breton language and insisted on schooling them to as high a degree as he could manage. He still had an aristocratic manner of command, which, at times, could check them. He never gave in to public despair.

But he was desolate. Yet again he had not taken sufficient thought. Another of his apparently clever hasty decisions had proved to be disastrous.

Intellectually unstretched, physically threatened, morally repelled, as a spiritual leader disregarded, as an abbot ridiculed.

Yet still he wrote radical books and essays and that activity soothed him. Abelard wrote as other men breathed. In the solitary security of his cell he reached back to the early philosophers and commentators, some of them the hermits he most admired. Here he could do God's work. And here, above all else, he could save his soul, grind away his sin, atone for the fornication, the deceit and the lust, which had so consumed him that he had given no thought to the most important matter of all, the only reason for existence: the preparation of his soul for the next world.

Heloise, to Abelard, was now the key to his salvation. When he had visited her at the Paraclete, he had asked the community to commend his soul to God in their numerous daily prayers. His body had sinned with Heloise, and God had punished and resolved that. No more could he sin there. Every day he was thankful to God. But no day passed without a memory of the sweetness of physical love.

And as he wrote his treatises he was attempting to salvage the souls of all who read him. His enemies, who were the increasingly intolerant hierarchy, condemned him for the very work he believed would cleanse Christian teaching and save the Church. Abelard's distress was deepened by this opposition to his religious works that were based on logic.

How could they not see the reason in what he was doing? He strove to show the truth behind unexamined contradictions. For this the only instrument was logic, and for using logic he was condemned.

He suspected that Heloise's letter would soothe the wound in his soul just as God's merciful wound had healed the gross fault in his body.

Alone, after compline, his guardian monks close by in their cells, he opened her letter, read it swiftly, greedily, then again more carefully, and could have wept.

Was that all she thought of?

Was the reclamation of a lost and sinful passion to eat up all that remained of her life?

Heloise, a Bride of Christ, as near to the Redeemer as anyone could possibly be, had delivered a list of complaints on an earthly matter he believed had been settled years ago. How could she not be proud of her vocation and, from what he had seen, of her work and influence at the Paraclete? But this! This moaning!

He wrote back.

He had not written to her, he said, because he knew that her resources and intelligence were capable of managing without any encouragement from him. She had been given the greatest prize of all and he was now outside her needs. But he assured her he would respond immediately to any letter she wrote to him.

But the central matter was prayer and his soul, which occupied the greater part of his letter. She was the outstanding abbess of her day, admired by all, but far above that, she was a Bride of Christ. What more could he give her than she already had?

He requested that she and her whole community pray for him. He sent her new prayers they could chant. He wrote about the special providence that came from women's prayers. He gave as examples the two men resurrected in the Old Testament because of the prayers of women. He returned to the women who followed Christ, whom he had talked about in their early days at Argenteuil, and how special Mary Magdalene was and how God preferred the prayers of women.

You, he said, have privileged access to Jesus Christ. Use it for others but also for me. This, he intimated, was not only so much more important than carnality, however warmly remembered. This, if she loved him, was recognition of what Christ most wanted from His creatures on earth: the proof of His divinity – in the salvation of their souls. What else could compare?

Just before dawn he met those sent by Heloise. Rumour had spread the news that a letter had come from her, which had encouraged Abelard to race through his reply. He wished to forestall any attempt to ambush her men along their road home and seize it. He was safe at dawn, he thought. The Bretons were not early risers.

The letter concluded:

> Live, fare you well, yourself and your sisters with you.
> Live, but I pray, in Christ be mindful of me.

At the end of that day, he went to his favoured place for meditation. He absorbed the sound of the sea breaking on the black rocks, the surge and drag of the tide. The mesmeric repetition of the waves lulled him into a drift of sensations. His mind was so drilled that little escaped analysis. Here there was respite. From here he could see the beginning of eternity. From here he could sense the majesty of God. On evenings such as this the sun would fall below the earth, alive with fire, and soon out of darkness would come the moon and the stars, and still the surge and drag of the waves, still the spray as they attacked the rocks, still the majesty that, in the darkness, became biblical.

He had tried to cut off thought of Heloise from the moment they had parted. He had failed. Memories of her were too strong. He could not confront the loss of what he saw as her beauty and fierce love. In the mornings when he woke up he reached out for her. At night before sleep, he spoke her name. Just seeing her, as he had done when he went to the Paraclete, had disrupted the order into which he had disciplined his thoughts. She ought to have been for ever outside him, but the mere sight of her embraced him. Her letter moved him in ways he dared not express: he feared that to admit the feelings they called up would be to lose his battle with himself.

He had learned to love the whip of the salty west wind on his face. His companions stood some distance away, leaving him in respected isolation. 'He is thinking of what next he will say in his lectures,' said one.

'He is planning how to counter the next attack,' said another.

'He is waiting for God's words to be sent down to him,' said a third. 'He likes the sea,' said the fourth. 'He just loves the sea, this sea that goes on into eternity.'

As the horizon brightened and the near light failed, as the sting of cold began to numb, prudence warned him against being so vulnerably in one place for so long. He bowed his head and composed, as he could, a hymn of thanks for the day.

The sun began to dip, as if bowing to the earth, leaving with the promise of return, golden in its last downward glide.

+ ⁃+

'I still can't get the praying,' Julia said. 'It's got under my skin. It's so odd and there was so much of it, every few hours of every day the same prayers. And Heloise so clever?'

'People still do it today. Millions of them. And not only in the most hopeless situations. Look at the billion Muslims. Hear the prayers of the millions in Catholic countries, in South America, in Africa, in India . . . Even in small pockets of Britain there are prayers.'

'I know. But so?'

'Prayer can be a private consolation for those in unbearable circumstances,' he said. 'But prayer for the soul? That's what worries you, isn't it? What soul? People like you and me can't subscribe to the soul. But Plato did – and who has thought harder than Plato?'

'But Plato was back then, Dad. How could somebody like Peter Abelard, the modern man, be so convinced by it? He talks about logic. Prayer isn't logical.'

'The logical Greeks and the logical Romans prayed. So did and do many logical Chinese and Indians, and the majority of us Europeans did until two or three generations ago.'

'So what? It's all over now.'

'I think we have lost many important parts of ourselves along the way. What's gone is a part of the past that once appeared full of meaning and mystery and is now, to you and me, incomprehensible and redundant. Maybe what has really gone is our understanding of it. Or our innocence. Like the dreamlines of the Aborigines. It can't be dismissed but it's hard to accept. And because we pride ourselves on being able to analyse and prove everything, we're angry that we cannot even discover how the likes of us thought several centuries ago in Paris.'

Julia let it go. Perhaps she had been in too many churches in Paris over the past ten days. Perhaps some of the atmosphere had rubbed off. She quite liked the idea of the soul – that was the problem. She thought it might still be there, somewhere, waiting to be brought into another life. It made her feel uneasy. What if it hadn't gone away?

Chapter Forty-five

Arthur got up from his desk and went to the window that looked across the square to the theatre. He pressed his forehead against the cold glass. How many tragedies had been performed in that theatre in the name of love? Maybe love could be the most profound tragedy of all.

He found it easier to generalise in Paris. He would pass that on to Julia. He enjoyed turning over matters with her. He wanted to tell her what he had never before told her. He had never talked about what was essentially important to him about this work. What he had said was obvious to him but not perhaps to her.

Those views on imagination, and fiction! However simple they were, he wanted her to know how he saw things. It was a time for the two of them to share, a time that might never be repeated. And soon he had to tell her what she most wanted to know and he was almost prepared for that. He could trust her, after their days together, and he could trust himself.

His impulsive invitation had turned into an encounter with his daughter that he would want her never to forget.

+ —+

Heloise seized on Abelard's answer to her letter to go back into battle.

She began by criticising him for, as she saw it, putting her name before his in the greeting at the beginning of his letter. This contravened protocol. Correct protocol was essential. Then in her own greeting she produced a mini-masterpiece of a correct address: 'To her only one after Christ, from his only one in Christ'.

After taking him to task for not giving her the comfort he ought to have shown, she set out her own psalm of lamentation.

She wrote that she wept for him. And her 'daughters', her nuns, followed her in tears. They did so, she said, partly because Abelard had referred to the strong likelihood of his death. But mostly because if he died soon they would have to bury him instead of, as Heloise thought proper and ordained, he, their patron, her husband, burying them. God would surely not allow them to outlive him. They should be sent ahead of him to Heaven so that he would be untroubled by his obligations to them. 'We shall not be able to go on living when you leave us.' She brought to bear a mystical certainty as well as her absolute love.

'If I lose you what is left for me to hope for?' She cried out her fear in her beautiful script. He had left her, she had been denied him in every way, and now God, 'cruel to me in everything, threatens through these murderous Bretons to take you away for ever'. How could she bear it?

It was not enough for her to curse God. In her bleak lamentation she turned on the goddess of her idolised pagan authors, Fortuna: 'The higher I was exalted when you preferred me to all other women, the greater my suffering over my own fall and yours . . . What glory Fortuna gave me in you,' she continued, 'no other woman was my equal, and now, through you, what ruin!' Fortuna had made sure that 'the happiness of supreme ecstasy would end in the supreme bitterness of sorrow'.

It was so unfair! So unfair! The primal cry expressing the agony from within. Unfair! Unfair! When they were lovers, God and Fortuna had spared them, and their locked bodies, coupled with free minds, were unchecked. But as soon as they did what the Church and God wanted, and married, God and the Church turned on them! Adultery was not persecuted. Matrimony was. And then, in full anger, she complained yet again that, for what both of them had done, God had punished him alone when they were equally to blame.

She accused the devil of malice. Having failed to destroy Abelard and herself through fornication, she wrote, the devil used marriage as his weapon. She raged that 'Denied the power to do evil through evil he effected evil through good.'

Heloise took the risk of telling Abelard, now a monk, dedicated to God as she was, about her experience at the Mass, the essential sacred moment of Christianity, when she knelt at the altar before Christ to receive His Body and His Blood yet 'lewd visions of those pleasures take such a hold on my unhappy soul that my thoughts were on their wantonness with you instead of on prayers to Christ'.

Heloise saw Abelard's letter as a God-given opportunity to state her love, her case and her loyalty. Although it hurt her to admit it, it seemed that he could not have known that his *Historia* would end up in her hands and therefore, she reasoned, her first letter would have shocked and alarmed him. He could be forgiven.

Nevertheless he had replied to that letter. Why, she thought, had she not written to him before? It would not have been fitting in the scheme of things for someone as low in the hierarchy as she was to initiate a correspondence. But surely the power of her feeling should have found a way through that. What was the tradition of the Church compared with her need? Must a Bride of Christ be mute?

But eventually she had written to him. And he had replied immediately. She could no longer complain of the lack of his presence in her life, even though the answer he had sent her had been so disappointing. It was a beginning.

Now she was determined to pursue it. The last words of Abelard's letter could in one way be read as final: 'Live, fare you well, yourself and your sisters with you. Live but I pray, in Christ, be mindful of me.'

But what did he mean by 'mindful'? Nothing was too small to use for her purposes. Did he want her to remember him? Did he want her to continue to love him? Both conclusions were possible. Those words of his 'Be mindful of me' went against the rest of his letter but they were the key words, Heloise thought. They revealed the man at last beneath the penitent's mask and the sinner's pose. 'Be mindful of me.' He who wasted no words had given her hope.

Chapter Forty-six

Abelard was excited by her reply. The content dismayed him but the fact they were together again, through these letters, brought him the warmth he had thought lost for ever. Aware of her insistence on protocol, he began, 'To the Bride of Christ, from His Servant'.

She had detailed her miseries, he wrote, and in four counts. After summarising them, he answered all four. Her disagreement over what she called the mistaken nature of his greeting in putting herself before him he rebutted abruptly – when she became a Bride of Christ, a Bride of his Lord, she inevitably became his superior, his lady.

Abelard built on this with a digression involving the Ethiopian wife of Moses. She loved her privileged position, he wrote, and deserved it because 'I am black but lovely . . . therefore the king has loved me and brought me into his chamber.' Abelard, as he had done in their early days, poured out his knowledge to her.

He took on another point in which she complained of being made miserable and fearful at the news of the perils he was facing. He reminded her that she had requested that he write to her often 'with news of the perils in which you are storm-tossed'. So, it was at her request that he had written of the danger he was in. Furthermore, what sort of friend did not want to know the worst as well as the best?

He wrote that being in such danger made him fear for his soul because of his past sins. Yet he would gladly be released from the life he was leading even though the eternal future was uncertain. He produced examples of those who loved deeply, understanding that the death of the loved one was preferable to condemning them to a life of unrelieved misery. Surely if she loved him she must see that death would be preferable to the life he now endured at Saint-Gildas.

But most of all he wanted to be sure that Heloise renounced her obsessive dependence on their past. He put down his pen. He had to pause as he sought to find a way to convince her. He had to save her from the past.

Abelard confessed to himself another reason for this pause. He sat at the table willing himself into a vacant mood in his cell in Saint-Gildas. His mind flooded with scenes of them together; pictures of their past encounters broke against his mind, like the waves battering against the rocks nearby. Images and visions he had tried to excise or at least restrain, and at such cost, over many years now returned and rushed in. They were there – in her bed in the house of Fulbert, naked, entangled, struggling to satisfy a fathomless loving need. The strain had increased, made more exciting by the imperative of silence. Abelard felt a longing for days and nights impossible to replicate. He had to save himself from their past.

The only way to suppress it had been work. Work could drive out everything but itself. From boyhood his mind had been consumed with questions and answers of philosophy. As he had aged, his capacity for concentration had intensified so that, save for the period of what he tried to regard as sinful insanity with Heloise, his mind was wholly dedicated to the problems it set him to solve, from his waking up to his lying down to sleep. Now, with an effort of will that felt like a physical act, he returned to his letter.

What he was about to do was his duty to Heloise. However cruel.

Yet this was to be the expression of his absolute love.

He had to save her. He had to wean her from their history. He would take the axe of logic to these apparently irresolvable and rooted accusations of hers.

'I come at last to your old perpetual complaint,' he wrote, 'and if you really want to please me as you say you do, then you must rid yourself of it. If not you will cut yourself off from me entirely. You do great good: why should you weep?'

Abelard then tried to make her accept what she had and see that what had happened to him, the castration, and to her, the immolation in the convent, were both evidence of God's mercy and justice.

Above all, he urged her, see what He has done for our souls. With a single wound to one body He had saved two. He declared that their beautiful coupling was a 'wallowing in the mire'; they were 'obscene'; he had forced her to do things with 'threats and blows'. It was entirely just that the location of lust, his sex, should have been destroyed.

He confessed all weaknesses, among which he included his desire to keep her for himself alone. It was for that reason, not for the love of God, that he had forced her to take on the habit of a nun. That will help her to hate me, he thought, as he leaned back to survey the catalogue of his crimes. Her cocoon of belief in their perfect passion must be broken.

Finally, in words of command, which he penned so slowly that he felt an equal surge of energy trying to force him to stop, he ordered her to abandon him for her true spouse: Jesus Christ. Christ was her true husband. 'He was crucified for you. Read about the women who cared for Him. Be one of them. Above all, He alone can take us to another country. He redeemed you with His Own Blood.'

Abelard drove in the nail as deeply as he could. 'It was He who truly loved you, not I,' he wrote. 'My love . . . should be called lust.'

The confirmation of her long-held tormenting fear could not have been clearer. Her fears would be justified. She would read that he had not loved her. Lust.

Abelard had aimed for the heart.

This, he believed, with his logic and his care for her, would kill her passion for him. It was a passion that he had concluded was suffocating her. His love had been mere lust, he said. There it was – plain for her to read. He knew what he was doing to her and what he was sacrificing of himself. In killing what was dragging her down he had killed that which most elevated both of them. But there was no other way to save her. The blade had to slice out the disease.

There was, finally, a plea to God that Heloise and himself be reunited. God had joined them on earth in marriage, then parted them for a time. Now, in his last sentence of prayer, he pleaded with God to let them 'unite for ever to Thyself in Heaven . . .'

It was done.

Chapter Forty-seven

'My love should be called lust.'

Heloise put her fingers across her half-open mouth in case the cry on her tongue should escape her discipline and the cry be heard all around the convent.

His words sank inside her, like a block of ice that seemed, infinitely slowly, to transfer the chill to her heart. She buckled under the pain of it: the pain from a word and the fact that it had come from him. She took deep breaths and stood up but the pain in her side intensified. She crossed her arms to cradle and ease it but it would not be moved. Turning to take a few steps, she experienced a sweep of dizziness. She held out her hand, rested it on the table beside the letter and waited for the ache to pass.

So it had all been lust. It rang around her mind and would not be silenced. And all the glories of their love had been deceits, actions not to be cherished for ever more but excised and thrown into the pit.

But what of her feelings? Where were they recognised? She had written that everything she had done had been done for him. That seemed to be of no account. What they had done together was now presented as a gross sin, the consequences of which she must suffer until her death.

If she believed him, then she had been blind. Why had

she not thought as he had? When they were so close together and breathed the same air and were one in body and mind, was that also part of the deceit? Surely that could not be true. She would not let it be true.

Weakened by the spasm of grief, she sat down and forced herself to reread the letter.

What had been his intention?

She began to realise that behind the wounding blows to their past, behind the attempt to kill it off, there was another meaning in this letter – an unwritten but deep intention.

She saw that he wanted to release her not from himself but from herself. She read again and it became clear. He wanted to save her. That was his message. And for that he had lied. He loved her too much to see her suffer. Logic had taken him to the brutal solution, which she now saw as proof of his deep feelings for her.

Hence his words at the end. He would bring them together as he had said in the prayer he had asked that she offer up; 'Now, Lord, what Thou has mercifully begun, most mercifully end, and those whom Thou has parted for a time on earth, unite for ever to Thyself in Heaven.'

This was his intention. Heaven would be their reward.

God, according to Abelard, had seen the danger they were in and led them through it by way of his wound back towards Himself. He had favoured them, rescued them, graced them.

She could see it now. Abelard could not endure her ingratitude. She had to expel it. The prize was to be united in Heaven. She had to put that in the front of her mind for the rest of her earthly life. They would still correspond. And, at last, she would be what she had longed to be – his friend, his *amica*.

Eventually she knelt and, with a guilty sense of new awkwardness, prayed as she thought she should to Jesus Christ to save Abelard and herself, together.

After the prayer she experienced an envelopment of harmony, in mind and in body. At last they were together, would be eternally. That was the message she took from his letter. She wept as the prayers, so long repressed, finally struggled free. Love without end.

'Thanks be to God,' she said, and a tide of peace covered and slowly began to erase the years of pain.

Julia put down the pages without a word.

'What fascinates me,' he said, 'is how she transformed herself.'

'I wish she hadn't.' She spoke very softly.

'You would rather she'd died than survived, wouldn't you? You want a real old-fashioned martyr whom you can call a heroine.'

Julia shook her head. 'No, Dad. I just wanted her not to give in.'

'If you want to think of it as a battle, then I think she won.'

'No! He told her to cut herself off from her feelings. He told her it had been nothing but lust on his part. He crushed her, Dad. It wasn't a fair battle. He was back to being the great philosopher and she had to be the pupil.'

'Careful. She loved the philosopher. He did not ask to be loved as a philosopher. From the beginning she had wanted to be his *amica*. And she got that. Why don't you accept that he did what he did in that letter to liberate her from a past that, as she said, was killing her with its conflicting memories? He set her free. He was cruel to be kind.'

'I thought you might say something like that. What does it really mean?'

'It means,' he said, in a neutral tone, 'exactly what it says. The surgeon's scalpel hurts the flesh but cuts out the disease.'

'It doesn't always work.'

'It did this time. She told Abelard it did. But I think that in the longer term she made it work for her in exactly the way she had always wanted. She was now his beloved friend, as you'll see, and that brought her what she truly wanted.'

'Was she cleverer than him?'

'Some think so. In some ways. But Abelard's mind was unique and truly radical.'

'She didn't give up without telling him exactly what she thought of him, though, did she? I read the beginning of Letter Six while I was waiting for you.' She picked up the book. 'In the first sentence she tells him of her "unbearable grief". Then she says she'll control herself in writing but she'll never do so in speech. Because speech comes from the heart – she's great, isn't she? And listen – because of that "having no power to command it we are forced to obey".'

Arthur countered emphatically: 'But immediately after that she writes that just as one nail can hammer out another, so new thoughts can drive out the old. And there and then she excises the past and takes control. She falls back on the correct argument that as he is the founder of the Paraclete and their master, she and his other daughters in Christ have a right to demand his "parental interest". She takes that association straight back to him and forces him to respond. By doing this he will become what she now wants most of all, perhaps even more than a friend: a constant "presence" in her life. She will be his through letters. She said that was all she'd hoped for at the beginning of their affair. Later the seduction took over their lives. But it was friendship she wanted, the equality of feelings. So she has finally got him back. And on her terms.'

'So she won?'

275

'Julia!'

'Sometimes things are simple, Dad. To me, anyway. She persuaded him to do what she wanted and become her friend.'

'Yes. A solution for both of them.'

'But it's not over yet, is it?'

'Not yet. The best is to come.'

Chapter Forty-eight

After that letter she knew he would reply to her whenever she wrote, whatever the subject. They were united at last. Her demands on him became the mercy in her life and the redemption in his. His replies, she thought, were the evidence of his undiminished love for her, the love she had craved. I am now, she said to herself, his *amica*, for ever.

Her demands were not light. The first was that Abelard instruct his 'daughters', the community at the Paraclete, on the origin of nuns in the Church. Heloise wanted to know what authority they had and what should be their Rule. She asked him to construct a Rule specifically for women. She wanted this in detail. She wanted it to include the whole Rule of St Benedict, which had to be taken on by women although it was written for men. She wanted a revolution: a charter for women in holy orders, which none of the Holy Fathers had laid down and which she, Heloise, thought essential.

As she wrote this she considered adding to it that the words of Peter Abelard would bring an authority to the matter that no other leading philosopher or Church divine had ever or would ever dare give. But flattery, like complaint, had been dropped. She wanted to establish a practical and philosophical engagement on an equal basis between friends.

Elsewhere she had pointed out that in the dawn days of their passion letters had come from him every day, hot and frequent. Now they would be on another plane and one altogether rarer, expressed in their shared passion for learning. The flesh gave way to letters. They would be instigated by Heloise, not Abelard, but with the same intention: to assure the recipient of a life of profound friendship in the present and to come.

Heloise set out her first request in her finest form. The Rule of St Benedict was written by men for men, and even in its most ordinary instructions it made no sense for women, she wrote. For example, what could she make of the rule that woollen garments must be worn next to the skin? Surely 'the woman's monthly purging of superfluous humours must avoid such things'. She questioned whether an abbess, just as much as an abbot, should offer hospitality at their table to visitors when destabilising quantities of wine would be drunk. She brought the words equally of the pagan Ovid, the Christian Father St Jerome and the apostle St James to bear. Wine between men and women could too easily provoke lechery. The scriptures said that wine was the most harmful form of nourishment. Examples were lined up in a formidable array.

She sprayed him with questions that she must have known would take him a vast amount of time, effort and commitment to answer her as fully as she demanded. But she did not hold back. Should nuns do heavy agricultural work as the men did? Was a single year sufficient to test initiates? She brought in St Jerome once again and Pope St Gregory to reinforce her argument.

Aristotle, Paul to the Thessalonians, St Augustine, Job, St Peter, the Psalms. She exulted in the opportunity to resurrect her seriousness, and reclaim her place alongside Abelard. She was no longer merely the object of scarcely forgivable lust. She concluded her letter to him with a command: 'Speak to us, then, and we shall hear.'

And, even more emphatically, her last word in this first letter in their new equality as friends was simply 'Farewell'.

She had thrown down the gauntlet. Would he take it up and join her in a new life of letters, reforms, ecclesiastical ambition? Would he have the time? Would he want to? Would he dare?

His reply stunned her.

Chapter Forty-nine

'And I think it may stun you,' Arthur said.

They were in Matthew's apartment for 'a simple lunch'. He did not want to go to Au Sauvignon. An inclination to stay close to polish what he saw as a key and difficult part of the book had morphed into an instinct to be at his desk as long as possible. Yet he did not want to disappoint Julia. She would have read Heloise's response and demand to Abelard. He wanted to talk to her in that shared knowledge. He wanted to persuade her that Abelard's response was a supreme example of friendship, and the finest love letter he had ever written or could ever write.

'His reply to her first request is two and a half times longer than his autobiography,' he began.

'Wow! How amazing is that.'

'He sent her a unique survey of the whole history of nuns – their origins, their place in Christ's ministry, women in the Old Testament, women in pagan literature: it is a *tour de force*. It would have been a life's work for most scholars. It is, I think, the most convincing letter of love he ever wrote to her. This gift of scholarship is how he could best reveal his deepest feelings for her. In my view he had been waiting for the opportunity to come along, or perhaps he didn't know he was waiting until it did come along.

'He could have answered her questions briskly or at a modest length or not at all. Instead we have an essay of such reach and research that it could only have been driven by his desire to please and to serve her. To show how much she meant to him, to reassure her in the best way he could that she was rooted in his thoughts and feelings, and at last he could tell her what she meant to him in a way that was consonant with their situation. Through a friendship purged of past faults, they had found their way.

'Through scholarship, through teaching, through his genius. This was his homage to her, the only true way to love left to him. She wanted to be liberated. He would be her liberator.'

'I like that. If it's true.'

'Read it.'

'I will.'

'What is, I believe, most important about this letter is that it was an essay which expressed his devotion to her as only he could. This and other letters aimed to set her free from the curse of lust. And – show-off to the last – he wanted to impress her. To be back in the saddle as the man of all knowledge. And, never forget, those two could be compulsive, egotistical, self-aggrandising hyperbolists.'

'I'll try to remember that.'

'These instructions immediately lead the field. Nothing he puts his mind to – ever! – aimed to be anything but definitive, and here he produces the first defining document on the history and place of nuns. Just for Heloise. Extraordinary. No subject that took his interest was worth anything less than his full effort, and he never failed to make that for Heloise. His reply became one of the founding documents about the ordering and regulation of women in religion in the whole of the Middle Ages.' He leaned across the table. 'Am I praising him too much for you?'

'No,' she said. 'But I'm in a bit of a whirl at this torrent of stuff. Are you sure he did all this for her? He hasn't just dug out a few old lecture notes, has he?'

'Not as far as I can discover, and I've looked through his work for more than three years.'

'Okay.' She raised her glass.

'We're on the last lap.'

'I'm lapping it up. Sorry.'

'He writes about sin entering the soul through the senses and draws a frightening picture of the powers of the devil. He insists that convents of women should always be subject to monasteries of men.'

'Oh, no!'

'He says that the "brothers might take care of the sisters". Isn't that being protective?'

'He just can't get it, can he?'

'Not in 1138 he can't, as you get it now in 2017. But you could concede that he's on the right path?'

'Is he?'

'Yes. But for me the richest part is when he lays down the law on everyday life. Miles away from the intellectual stuff. Heavy work is not for nuns. There must not be too much fasting, which would weaken the nuns, or too little sleep, unless the abbess agrees to it. Costly clothes are out. No fat must be used for flavouring on the sixth day of the week. It must be strictly forbidden to wipe hands or to clean knives on bread reserved for the poor. Isn't that good? This is our common and sublime philosopher!

'It ranges on in a flowing sequence where erudition is entangled with common sense, which must have been radical at the time, where spirituality sits alongside daily comfort and then, suddenly, that passage stops . . .' Arthur shrugged his shoulders.

'Why?'

'I don't know. At times that sort of thing drives you mad, at others you count your blessings for what there is.'

'He knew everything, didn't he, about everything?'

'No. Not much about science or gardens! But what he knew he wanted to know to its roots, then bring to the world his version of it.'

'How did she react?'

'Heloise never stopped making demands and he replied to every one at length. The roll call is like a listing of battle honours. Hers. She sent him forty-two problems, which she asked him to solve. He did. That was not too difficult for him. Then she wanted new hymns for saints who didn't have them and others to replace antique hymns, which she said were corrupt. That can't have been easy. He must have worked night and day, and remember, at the same time he was writing his big philosophical books. He sent them to her. A hundred and thirty-three of those hymns are still available. She asked for short sermons for special occasions. This was an art in which he was not confident, he told her, yet he composed thirty-four original sermons for her. He wrote a commentary on the six days of the Creation for her, and there would surely have been much else that has been lost. He sent her bouquets of what she most wanted – words, ideas, explanations, without fail and without compare.

'During the course of her letters, he quit Saint-Gildas and returned to Paris, forgiven, and once again as a master he was writing what would be his most controversial works. But for Heloise he always made time.'

He paused, moved by what he had said.

Julia observed it and decided she must at last challenge him. She waited.

'You see,' he continued, 'they came through. Despite the questionable seduction, the castration, the persecution, the deceits and the stupidities and the failings, they came through.

'There they are, he the master of the School of Notre-Dame, which was imminently to lead to the seeding of the Paris university that would influence "the world". She was using her skills to develop her progressive views about how women in religion should be ordered and respected. She corresponded with abbots, she was visited by the most distinguished men in the Church, she increased the number of her convents across France. And – vitally, I think – she was held on course by what she had always longed for, friendship, and the love of learning. And he, I believe, was surer of the fate of his soul, through her.'

'Can we talk about you now?'

'Is that why you came to Paris?'

'Yes. Yes, it is.'

Chapter Fifty

'I think I've over-rehearsed this,' she said. 'I've had too many conversations with you in my head.'

'Snap!' He picked up the bottle and poured each of them a top-up.

Julia took a deep breath. She spoke steadily. 'Why is it that Alex and I have never been given any explanation? Both of you muttered away, I presume trying to protect us. I used to think that, but now I think you were trying to protect yourselves. And we're adults. We knew you hadn't been getting on for years but you managed. And suddenly you left. You rented that small flat. Mum stayed in our house with us. What happened?'

Arthur did not reply immediately. Did he have to do this? 'I phoned your mother yesterday,' he said. 'We agreed I should tell you all there is to know . . . It's not . . . But it is what it is and I'm finding this hard.'

He steadied himself. It was no help that Julia had the look of her mother, the same long dark brown hair, the same mouth and eyes and smile. And she had some of her mother's gestures, which was somehow the most disturbing factor of all.

As if sensing that he was appraising her, Julia looked closely at her father as if seeing him after a long absence.

He was tall, quite lean, his grey hair swept back from his forehead, his blue eyes like bright surprises in his rather rumpled, weathered face. Old photographs she had studied showed him as a handsome enough young man, her mother as a particularly good-looking young woman. They always looked good together.

'I was seven years older than your mother when I met her. I'd been teaching abroad and written my first book, but I went back to England when I was offered a junior post in the English department at the university. It was secure. There were people like me, though I'd never been much of a mixer.'

He took a deep breath. He was in too far to stop now.

'Your mother was in her final year. I don't know how to say this other than bluntly but, well, I loved her from the moment I saw her. I'd never felt anything like that before and I've never felt anything like it since. From the start she was the only one: she still is. Always will be.'

Julia saw the tremor in his hand as it reached for the glass. He did not pick it up.

'She was – you know this – so brimful of the joy of life. Yes. Whenever we were in any company I could not take my eyes off her. People noticed it. I tried not to. It could be a little embarrassing.

'Why she was attracted to me I never quite knew and never quite believed. I never thought I was good enough for her . . . I suppose I was steady and – I don't know . . . Perhaps she had never been as devotedly liked – loved – as she was by me.

'We married quite soon after we met, and even on that day I feared I might lose her. But from the start I could see it and feel it, and I could never convince myself that she was in love with me anything like as much as I was with her. But we got on. Or I thought we did.

'Then you and Alex came along and a different life made different demands. I liked all that. She got a part-time job arranging conferences through the university. I remained happily stuck as a lecturer and continued to write. This is the difficult bit, Julia . . .'

He paused. She looked away. She feared he might choke. She took the bottle by the neck and filled his half-full glass. He nodded thanks but left it untouched.

'We started having rows when you were quite young. I never fathomed where they came from – for years I just thought rows were part of married life with children. They come and they'll go. But they didn't go. And I began to realise that she was, well, a little colder, impatient, critical . . . and then she fell in love. He was, he is, a publisher in London.'

'Was that Julian?'

'Yes.' He took up his glass and sipped carefully. 'She told me and I was of course horribly jealous. I could see it in her manner, in her eyes, in her smile . . . She loved Julian as much as I loved her.'

'That must have been terrible . . . awful . . .'

He looked away. 'That sort of pain is . . . Never mind. I could see that she was reluctant to cause a rift. Perhaps Julian was, too. But the lack of sex, constant irritation, baseless criticisms . . . She was not with me any more. But it was not her fault, not at all. When you saw them together, just being together, it explained everything . . .' He paused and Julia feared he might not go on. But he was true to his word.

'Despite that I stayed, as she suggested. You see, I loved her beyond all that. And it seemed easier just to jog along – and she was not unkind. But after some time I could see she was tormented by the situation. I couldn't bear it. The lawyer said that the best way was for me to let her divorce me, and the quickest way was to give her cause, so I pretended to have an affair. I regret that now. The truth is I was too upset to think for myself. I knew that the only thing I could do was to let her go.

'I couldn't bear to see her pain. So I left the house and deliberately left you and Alex with the clear impression that I was deserting your mother for someone else. Now I wish we hadn't arrived at that decision. At the time I thought it best for all of you. At least something you could understand . . . A year or so later she and Julian set up together . . .'

'In *our* house.' Julia cringed at the early memories of that. And why had her father not protected them from it? She and Alex were teenagers but the festering unease between their parents had been better than that brutal occupation by a stranger. She had hated her father for allowing it to happen. Even now she could summon up the hurt and anger.

'Yes,' he said bitterly. 'That was a blow. We'd both been proud of the cottage. Never mind. She was happy. That was all I wanted. She still is, isn't she?'

Julia couldn't bear the look he gave her at those wistful words. And what about his children? she thought. What had *they* wanted? Who had consulted them? And her father even now still wanting her mother to be happy, yet all but imploring Julia to say she might not be and so might return to him. No wonder he had kept away from the house and from the family. Too wounding. And still wanting her mother to be happy! And now near tears. But he had been brave in his fashion both then, she thought, and now, and she must be brave too.

'Yes,' she said gently, 'she is happy. And she never says anything about you that isn't . . . warm.' Julia's reassurance, she thought, made up in a small way for the anger she had felt against him.

Arthur breathed in deeply. 'I'm glad of it,' he said. 'And that's all I can say, I'm afraid.'

Neither trusted themself to speak. Julia saw her father plainly and wanted to find a way to tell him how much this meant to her, how much he meant to her, but nothing seemed better than to endure together this long and bruised silence.

'And so,' he said, forcing briskness, 'when I came across Abelard and Heloise, I thought in some related way, in some small way, I saw my story, the story of your mother and myself. I decided to try to write about them.

'Heloise's unbreakable love for Abelard . . .' He hesitated. 'Well, that is my love for your mother, which has never lessened and never been challenged. As for Abelard, of course I'm not even remotely in the same league, but his determination to take the difficult route, as I saw it, was a heroic example. I found it inspiring.' He grimaced slightly. 'The proud lecturer, the unsurpassed intellectual in twelfth-century Paris, and myself! Rather ridiculous, really. Still, a cat may look at a queen.'

'When . . . when Alex and I talked about it, we thought you were the one to blame.'

'That's quite natural. That's what I wanted. And I was to blame. I wasn't right, not enough for her, so why shouldn't she find a fuller life with someone else?'

'All that was happening and we were kept in ignorance. Didn't you think of what it might do to us?'

'Your mother and I talked, but we always reached the same conclusion.'

'After all this time . . .' Julia sucked her bottom lip into her mouth. 'It's so strange. I have a new history. I'm somebody different than I was an hour ago.'

'We should never have married. But we are where we are. And where would you be without us? That's the blessing it brought.'

His tone attempted to be positive but it was so poignant that Julia almost burst into tears.

'And since then you've always lived alone?'

'My days among the dead are spent,' he said. 'They can be good company. One promise from you, please. Don't criticise your mother. I don't. Don't judge either of us. We had our time. Blame is not the point.'

'How do you . . . bear it?' Julia said tentatively, as if just to raise their separation would be to hurt him.

'Solitude can make you resilient,' he said. 'Abelard learned that. His life, I feel sure, was emptied of human love when they separated – but he wrote on. Work held him together. Heloise was always the companion of his thoughts and his very being, as your mother still is to me. And I, too, have work. So there we are.'

'Thank you.'

'I think,' he said, 'if you don't mind, I'll just step outside for a few minutes and wander around . . . But you are the one to thank, Julia. Why did it take me so long?'

He levered himself up from the chair and left – almost marched stiffly to the door.

Julia tensed her face hard against tears, but it didn't work.

Chapter Fifty-one

This was a time of their deepest happiness together, although they were always apart.

Heloise could imagine Abelard in the Cloisters of Notre-Dame: reports of his brilliance reached her from the increasingly numerous visitors to the ever-growing and impressive settlement of the Paraclete. Every triumph warmed her heart; rumours of the gathering menace of his enemies made her anxious but only for a short time. Peter Abelard would always win. She knew that.

She was wholly safe and content. There he was, in pictures in her mind, lecturing, debating, in his study, teaching his students, unequalled, unstoppable, a fearless mind. And she his beloved friend.

He, too, saw her in daydreams as powerful as the dreams that came in the night. She would be guiding her 'daughters'; she would be in ever freer communication with Denise, and the life of Astralabe would be related to her in loving detail. There would be the requests to which Abelard looked forward: what next would she dream up to test him? What test would he not strive to rise to?

In those years it was as if they circled each other around a fixed centre of love known only to them, unmoving, now unchallengeable.

And all was well. God's grace at the last had been revealed. Abelard prayed for her and soon she found she could pray for him and, both believed, their prayers intermingled as they ascended to Heaven.

Chapter Fifty-two

By the time the news of the debate at Sens reached the Paraclete, the argument was over. What some had hoped to be the most significant battle of minds of the twelfth century had ended in disaster. Abelard, it was rumoured, had only just escaped imprisonment and was now attempting to reach Rome to appeal, his life in peril.

Hardened as she was to waiting, and deep though her reserves of patience, Heloise became feverish at the rumours. Her community was unaccustomed to seeing her yield to physical ailments, and panic spread among the nuns. Their abbess was too hot on the brow, her hands burned, her dry lips murmured snatches of prayer or lines from the Fathers, or sometimes she tried to sing from one of his songs. They kept a vigil. Their intense prayers soared to Heaven every hour of the day and night. They quarrelled quietly over who should hold the cooling cloth to her brow. Only the prioress could attempt to feed her the special weak soup they prepared. Their whispers were like a ceaseless breeze throughout the convent. And they, too, wept for their fallen master, their founder, their father.

+ —+

The full account reached the Paraclete days after the event. It was a chronicle of what would be his last battle.

Peter Abelard and Bernard of Clairvaux had been circling each other for a generation. Ten years younger than Peter and every bit as famous, Bernard had taken the Church ever more deeply into its expanding and fierce mission of militant conservatism. For Bernard, Abelard's employment of human and classical logical argument in religious matters was so far beneath the supremacy of faith that it was heretical, trivial, and should be crushed. To attempt to analyse God or His words was futile. To teach young people to question the scriptures was dangerous. Abelard's teaching manual *Sic et Non* – Yes and No – in which he put forward contradictions in the Bible for students to tease out the truth, particularly inflamed Bernard. How dare Abelard test the sacred scripts? It was an insult to God and the Pope.

Yet Abelard was an unflinching opponent. He seemed to be stable again, once more master at Notre-Dame, once more in a loving friendship with Heloise. He had already expanded the book that he had been forced to throw into the fire at the Council of Soissons in 1121 – the *Theologia*. His new working was a deliberate provocation. It said, 'Burn this one if you dare!' He had recently written one of his most important books – *Scito te Ipsum* – Know Yourself – as well as the *Dialogue Between a Philosopher, a Jew and a Christian*, a *Commentary on St Paul's Epistle to the Romans* and the many essays, hymns and sermons for Heloise. He was in full spate, inspired, perhaps by her writing, with brilliance and still by far the most revered and popular philosopher of his day. And apparently unaware of a fanatical conformism gathering to eradicate his influence.

The *Theologia* had been brought to Bernard's attention and he had taken immediate action. Part of this was diplomatically to seek out Abelard and ask him to moderate his views. Abelard not only took no notice, but brought out an unchanged fourth version of the book.

Abelard's arrogance, fuelled perhaps by his new stability with Heloise, slid into recklessness when he asked his friend Henry, Archbishop of Sens, to arrange a public debate between these two dramatically opposed men of Christian thought. Abelard was, as he had always been, wholly confident of the superiority of his intellect.

Abelard ignored Bernard's political power, his intimate association with the Pope, the scheming and zeal that had brought him such an impressive cast of followers sympathetic to his immovable views. Abelard was equally immovable. But whereas Bernard, in his righteous certainty, was heavily prepared and organised for their debate, twenty years on from the burning of the earlier version of his book at Soissons, Abelard dismissed all such preparation. He had no grasp of Bernard's networks of influence. To Abelard, this was to be a contest of ideas – nothing less.

So, when he rode into Sens, with his small cohort of supporters, he was sure that he, Abelard, would be once again the Knight Supreme of Logic, the wordsman unconquerable, the hero of the future. The town was *en fête*. King Louis VII and his court were there to view the prized collection of relics, as were bishops, abbots, dignitaries, courtiers, lawyers, and the entourages of the aristocracy from all over France. All of them would remain for the drama of the debate. Bernard of Clairvaux against Peter Abelard!

Bernard had laid his plans very carefully. He had letters

of support from the Pope and his cardinals; he had falsely linked Abelard with lesser and more violent critics of the Church. He went to the town days ahead of the appointed encounter and whipped up the mob against this heretic philosopher. His speech had been checked again and again by sympathetic scholars.

Abelard sailed in confidently with nothing but his genius.

It was a catastrophe.

The news that struck down Heloise was that Abelard had been condemned by Bernard as a heretic. He and his followers were to be excommunicated. His books were to be burned and Abelard himself incarcerated in a monastery under the sentence of perpetual silence. Heloise was outraged.

Abelard a heretic? Abelard excommunicated? Abelard sentenced to perpetual silence? How could God permit it? How could the Church allow it? Their most noble and revered philosopher. And how could Abelard bear it?

Over the days more fragments came to her from visitors to the Paraclete. She was animated only when they arrived and she could rally her forces to piece the event together.

Bernard had taken the initiative and denied Abelard the promised debate. Abelard's objections were overruled. It would be an inquisition. Abelard knew that he was at an immediate disadvantage. There would be no discussion, no arguments. No dissection of the finer points of truth. No logic, only the blunt instruments of received dogma.

With the overwhelming support of the well-worked crowd, Bernard turned the whole event against Abelard. A list of Abelard's alleged heresies was read out and it was demanded that he denounce or deny every one. No room was given for debate. The fractious audience treated it as a bear-baiting. Abelard looked out at a mob. It was clear to him that, from the royal party to the well-bribed local merchants, this trial was nothing to do with seeking truth in theology. He would be proved guilty without being allowed to offer a word in his defence.

It was beneath him to take part.

He said nothing. His silence was excoriated by the mob. He had come to debate and argue in public – a traditional and noble form of enquiry. This had been abandoned and replaced by a sham. He would not honour it by taking part. Despite the baying, the taunting, the threats, and despite the disturbing tremors in his mind, he would not give in to this barbaric intellectual assassination. Not with a single word. His silence made his inquisitors increasingly vicious.

Bernard's accusations were too falsely based, biased and absurd for Abelard to counter. In the drunken, riotous atmosphere, described later by Abelard's pupil Berengar, the serious exploration of truth had no place.

He fought to keep his mind calm. Who could have calculated that a high Christian debate in the presence of the King of France would be dictated by the inebriated mood of a rabble? Or was God yet again guiding him towards future salvation by testing him to destruction, torturing him and killing his dearest earthly possessions, his books, his freedom, his voice? When she heard of it, Heloise declared his total silence to be the action of a martyr for logic.

Or was it, Heloise thought later, that seizure of mind she had seen when he ordered her to take the veil and watched her so fixedly, as if in a trance, until she had done so? Was it what his mother had described, the sudden fear of going out of his mind, of imminent lack of control? That, Heloise believed, was probably the truest explanation. Something in him that he could not master had transfixed him, something

297

deeper even than his rational thoughts. Bernard's nineteen condemnations were unchallenged and roaringly approved.

Abelard and his followers, who had come for victory and stayed in fear, were shepherded to Cluny to await judgment. Abelard's books were committed to the flames in celebration. Abelard's destructive logic was declared dead as the ashes. Bernard saw his enemy through the flames and smiled as Abelard was led away.

He found refuge in the Abbey of Cluny. He wanted to go to Rome and challenge the Pope, who had supported Bernard and also publicly burned Abelard's books, but Cluny was as far as Abelard's strength took him.

As soon as she learned this, Heloise wrote to her friend Peter the Venerable, the Abbot of Cluny.

Chapter Fifty-three

There was nowhere in Christendom where Abelard could have been safer and no one more certain to protect him.

Cluny Abbey was an architectural phenomenon of the age, bigger than anything else in France, or in Rome, England, Spain or any other Christian country. Peter the Venerable, a Benedictine, ruled with flair and generosity of spirit wholly foreign to Bernard and his Cistercians. No one would dare seize Abelard from his care.

But he was not a man to be seen to be too powerful. Soon after Abelard's entry into Cluny, he escorted him to a neutral ground some miles away where Bernard was waiting. Under the canopy of Peter's persuasiveness, a reconciliation of sorts was formally agreed. This enabled Bernard to return to his followers as the merciful victor now that his enemy was broken and perpetually banished. It enabled Peter the Venerable to write to the Pope and obtain permission for Peter Abelard to remain untroubled in Cluny as a monk for the rest of his life. And it seemed to give Abelard rest.

Peter the Venerable had always been an outspoken admirer of Heloise and Abelard. His letters to her from the first appearance of her Latin translations were flattering and affectionate to the point almost of love letters. His praise for Abelard – 'our Aristotle, the Plato of the West' – never faltered.

In his last months Abelard became an ascetic. The ebullience of his weight, heft and character had all gone, a spare man dressed as plainly as a monk could dress. He was an example to everyone, Peter the Venerable wrote, for his piety, and still revered for his learning.

He moved about like one seeking to find the right place to die. Prayers were said for him on all occasions. The pride of the community that Abelard was now one of them was made the greater by its members being in a position to observe how such a man prepared for death.

He wrote one last letter to Heloise. It was his Confession of Faith.

They had given him a cell behind the High Altar. Here, after intense prayer, he knew that his life was fast ebbing. He took up paper and pen, as so often before, so many thousand times before, and in the solitude of the cell and in the concentration of his mind, he sought out and found the Heloise he had loved, in many ways but unfailingly. His eyes brimmed with tears as he prepared to write. He could envisage her receiving his letter, reading it and reading it again, as he would have done. His final prayer would be to meet her again. God be merciful.

And then, with his customary speed and his irrepressible scholarly flourish, he wrote:

> Heloise, my sister, once dear to me in the world, now dearest to me in Christ. Logic has made me hated by the world . . . I do not wish to be an Aristotle if it cuts me off from Christ . . . they proclaim the brilliance of my intellect but detract from the purity of my Christian faith . . .

He reminded Heloise that his conscience was founded on a rock and she must banish all her anxieties about him.

He then briefly declared his belief in the Father, the Son

and the Holy Spirit. He told her he believed that he would live again: 'the storms may rage but I am unshaken . . .' This phrase, he knew, would be her greatest consolation. These would be the last words he would write.

'So he died without seeing her again?'

'Yes.'

Julia could tell that her father was moved. 'What do you know about his death?'

Arthur paused, then said, 'I think that he died the unremarkable death of a faithful monk. No bells tolled. No special ceremony, only the routine prayers that helped souls to Heaven. There are no details of the death of this comet of medieval thought. He led a rare life like few others: a knight in arms for logic, a scholar for hire wherever he could be most effective, irresistible as a lecturer and writer, peerless in argument, and all but broken by a passion that began as sport and became an obsession, provoking his castration and violent public condemnation. But finally he was resurrected into the imperishable and loving friendship with Heloise, which both believed would defeat death.'

He spoke sadly and quietly and Julia asked no more questions.

At Heloise's request, Abbot Peter the Venerable brought his body to the Paraclete. She had a tomb built for him: a double tomb. Heloise asked for a written absolution for Abelard to hang over his tomb and the Abbot complied. She prayed for him at the tomb morning, noon and night for the rest of her life.

By that time the Paraclete and its daughter houses were admired all over France. Peter promised that Cluny would say thirty masses for Heloise after her death. She also asked him to help Astralabe in his career in the Church and he agreed to do so.

Heloise's influence and the number of her convents grew. She outlived her lover by twenty-one years. At her death, bells tolled. There were processions and psalms were sung. It is reported that when they opened the tomb to place her body alongside his, Abelard opened his arms to embrace her.

Over the centuries their bodies were shifted from place to place until they finally came to Paris to the cemetery of Père Lachaise. They rest in a sepulchre near the gate in a soaring tomb, columned on four sides, elegant, unique, much visited over many generations.

Julia went there in the mid-morning of a summer day. After examining the sarcophagus carefully and wandering around it for a time, she phoned her father. 'I'm here,' she said, 'at their tomb. I wanted to come on my own. I hope you don't mind.'

'Of course not. It's quite something, isn't it?'

'Yes – it's wonderful.' She paused. 'They're lying side by side and I think they're holding hands. Carved in stone. Somehow . . .'

He waited. He wanted her comments to be unmediated by his.

'You know that miracle, when she was put in the tomb beside him and he opened his arms . . . It's really stupid, Dad, but I sort of wish it really happened!'

'Yes . . . How do you feel?'

She hesitated, then her father's kindly look came into her mind. 'I feel . . . that something's been resolved,' she said. She looked directly at the tomb. 'I don't know why. I just feel really happy, Dad. Yes . . . Thank you . . . for all of it.'

She wandered up the hill into the heart of the cemetery that had become a town of the dead. The richness of the summer trees gave the feeling of constant life among the streets and alleys, the squares of tombs and graves from war and peace. At the top of the hill, unthreateningly lost, Julia looked down to pick out the monument to Heloise and Abelard. But it had disappeared among so many dead. For a moment, moved by their story and by the finality of the graves, she wished she could pray.

Afterword

My key source was *The Letters of Abelard and Heloise*, translated with an introduction and notes by Betty Radice, and revised by M. T. Clanchy (Penguin, 2003). This was invaluable and I not only drew on it but it enabled me to follow up half-leads and half-hints.

The second major source was *Abelard, a Medieval Life* by M. T. Clanchy (Blackwell, 1999). Professor Clanchy also generously answered a list of questions I sent to him and gave me in effect a tutorial, for which I remain very grateful. I also used *The Lost Love Letters of Heloise and Abelard – Perception of Dialogue in Twelfth-Century France* by Constant J. Mews (Palgrave Macmillan, 2008). Other reading included his *Abelard and Heloise* in the *Great Medieval Thinkers* series (Oxford University Press, 2005).

Daily Living in the Twelfth Century by Urban Tigner Holmes Jnr (University of Wisconsin Press, 2000) was useful, as was Enid McLeod's biography of Heloise (Chatto & Windus, 1971).

I had read Helen Waddell's *Peter Abelard* (Constable & Co., 1933) years ago, but returned to it admiringly. I also read with pleasure *Abelard and Heloise*, the play by Ronald Miller (Samuel French, 1971).

Those in the novel based on the historical record include

Heloise, Abelard, Canon Fulbert, Abelard's mother Lucia, his sister Denise and his son Astralabe, William of Champeaux, Stephen de Garlande, Abbot Suger, Alberic of Rheims, Gilles de Vannes, Roscelin of Compiègne, and Anselm. Invented characters include Marguerite, Marie, Ralph, Jeanne, the Abbess of Argenteuil, Anne, Master Floriot, Julia and her father.

Thanks once again to my friend Julia Matheson, whose help in this book was more than usually valuable, to Gabriel Clare-Hunt for her suggestions, to Vivien Green, my agent, to Carole Welch, my editor at Sceptre, and to Rosie Alison, whose reading of the book was transformative. And in affectionate memory of my friend, the philosopher Professor Sir Peter Strawson.

MELVYN BRAGG

The Maid of Buttermere

'This is the story of an imposter and bigamist, a self-styled
Colonel Hope, who travels to the North, where eventually
he marries "The Maid of Buttermere", a young woman whose
natural beauty inspired the dreams and confirmed the theories of
various early nineteenth century writers . . . It is a fine story . . .
This is historical fiction with a human face'
Peter Ackroyd, *The Times*

'A terrific tale of passion, lust, deception and moral outrage'
Daily Mail

'A detailed, eloquent and affecting panorama of truth
and lies . . . thrusts Bragg into the front rank'
Mail on Sunday

'Bragg writes with picturesque clarity; his prose accommodates
the formality of the period, the splendidly sombre wateriness of the
place and the robust passions of the people who lived there'
Sunday Telegraph

'A vivid and erudite tour de force . . .
romantic fiction for the thinking reader'
Penelope Lively

'Bragg achieves the most difficult of feats, the telling of
the changing perceptions and ideals of a radical age . . .
He is also as powerful as ever in his description of nature'
Sunday Times

'A fine novel, both sad and tragic. His background descriptions
are beautiful . . . while his evocation of the early nineteenth
century, and his handling of the ever-interesting topic
of English snobbery is impeccable'
Irish Times

SCEPTRE

MELVYN BRAGG

Credo

Britain during the Dark Ages is the setting for the fascinating story of Bega, a young Irish princess who became a saint, and her lifelong bond with Padric, prince of the north-western kingdom of Rheged. This dramatic, far-reaching tale brings to life a land of warring kings, Christians and pagans, and tribes divided by language and culture, illuminating a little-known yet critical period in British history.

'An absorbing epic . . . as splendid a ripping yarn as any of the best classics'
Daily Telegraph

'A gripping saga of great passion . . . sustained, impassioned and uplifting'
The Times

'I loved it . . . Bragg's stately, seething, passionate epic is several cuts above modern attempts at historical fiction'
Literary Review

'A gripping, deeply accomplished work'
Evening Standard

'A beguiling entry into a society strange, neglected, important, tragic in many of its triumphs'
Spectator

'Wonderfully evocative, passionate and erudite . . . No summary could do justice to a book of this erudition, romance and scope'
Glasgow Herald

SCEPTRE

MELVYN BRAGG

The Soldier's Return

Winner of the WHSmith Literary Award

When Sam Richardson returns in 1946 from the 'Forgotten War' in
Burma to Wigton in Cumbria, he finds the town little changed. But
the war has changed him, broadening his horizons as well as
leaving him with traumatic memories. In addition, his six-year-old
son now barely remembers him, and his wife has gained a sense of
independence from her wartime jobs. As all three strive to adjust,
the bonds of loyalty and love are stretched to breaking point in this
taut and profoundly moving novel, which captures what millions
experienced in the aftermath of the Second World War.

'The tension between the security of roots and the allure of
wider horizons is captured with an empathy, subtlety and acute
truthfulness that the Lawrence of *Sons and Lovers* would
have appreciated . . . Bragg's finest novel to date'
Peter Kemp, Books of the Year, *The Sunday Times*

'Outstandingly good . . . Must be one of the best English novels
of the last ten years. It rings true; its characters matter . . .
utterly credible, utterly compelling, and very enjoyable.'
Scotsman

'He writes with tremendous empathy . . .
One of the tautest and fiercest of Bragg's fictions'
Independent

'Sympathetic, touching, infinitely believable . . .
a highly accomplished novel'
Literary Review

'Strong, straightforward, explicit, evocative'
Daily Telegraph

'His study of a relationship between man and wife in difficulties
is brilliantly convincing . . . A passionately moving novel'
Financial Times

SCEPTRE

MELVYN BRAGG

Grace and Mary

Reaching from late 19th-century Cumbria to the present, this elegiac novel celebrates two spirited women: Grace, a farm labourer's daughter who fatefully followed her heart, and Mary, the child she was forced to give up. Unsung heroines according to Mary's son who, as his elderly mother's mind begins to fail, lovingly recreates their lives and the vanished country of their pasts, linking three generations in a chain of enduring love, loss and courage.

'A wonderful book, moving, true, surprising'
Claire Tomalin

'The novel's multiple narratives are skilfully teased out from John's attempts to prolong meaningful life for his mother by stimulating her failing memory . . . For each generation, Bragg suggests, a key component of the quest is coming to terms with the past – a feat his quietly intense novel pulls off with joy, sorrow and precision'
Sunday Times

'Tender and moving . . . a gem'
Independent

'Funny and sad and touching . . . With regular echoes of Thomas Hardy, this quiet, unshowy book proves that novels can tell truths that are deeper and truer than the mere fact of memoir.'
Observer

'The pleasures of this elegant novel are many . . . suffused with the idea and reality of the love between parent and child, beautifully realised without a trace of false sentiment.'
Scotsman

'Impossible to read without a lump in the throat and a tear in the eye'
Daily Mail

'A beautiful book, elegant, restrained and full of nuanced meditations on the nature of identity'
Independent on Sunday

SCEPTRE

MELVYN BRAGG

Now is the Time

At the end of May 1381, the young King of England had reason to be fearful: the plague had returned and a draconian poll tax was being widely evaded. Yet Richard, bolstered by his powerful mother, felt secure in his God-given right to reign.

Within two weeks, the unthinkable happened: a vast force of common people invaded London, led by Walter Tyler, a former soldier, and the radical preacher John Ball. They demanded freedom, equality and the complete uprooting of the Church and state. And for three heady days, it looked as if the so-called Peasants' Revolt would succeed.

'A gripping historical novel . . . His moving portraits of Tyler and Ball, their utopian hopes for England betrayed and destroyed just as they themselves are doomed to be, give *Now is the Time* its real backbone and intensity.'
Sunday Times

'Superb'
Andrew Roberts, Books of the Year, *Evening Standard*

'A beautifully written novel, combining modern insight with historical authenticity, and it is spellbinding'
Sunday Express

'Fast and entertaining – the excitement of a city about to blow up like a barrel of gunpowder is more than palpable – and the period brought to life with visceral minutiae'
Observer

'Bragg excels at conjuring the wealth and squalor of late 14th-century London. And he's equally good on events at court . . . it's impossible not to be caught up.'
Daily Mail

'A vivid and surprisingly tender tribute to one of the wildest moments in Plantagenet history.'
The Times

SCEPTRE

MELVYN BRAGG

The Adventure of English
The Biography of a Language

English is the collective work of millions of people throughout the ages. It is democratic, ever-changing and ingenious in its assimilation of other cultures; it runs through the heart of world finance, medicine and the Internet, and it is understood by around two thousand million people across the world.
Yet it was very nearly wiped out in its early years.

In this book Melvyn Bragg shows us the remarkable story of the English language from its beginnings as a minor guttural Germanic dialect to its position today as a global language. *The Adventure of English* tells not only an enthralling story of power, religion and trade but also the story of people, and how their day-to-day lives shaped and continue to change the extraordinary language that is English.

'Told as an adventure story, and rightly so . . .
There is much splendid intellectual firepower in this book . . .
A superb new history of the English Language'
Spectator

'Melvyn Bragg strides confidently through the origins and growth of English . . . concise as well as learned . . .
an impressive and sage view of the big picture.'
New Statesman

'Always readable, often thought-provoking,
and consistently entertaining.'
Independent

'Bragg's approachable account . . . gleams with
little gems. It has power and clarity.'
Sunday Herald

'Informative, entertaining, sensible and good-humoured'
Daily Telegraph

SCEPTRE